Back to Normal Series Book Three:

PROXIMITY

RANDY
MCWILSON

Moving Images
Publications
Cape Girardeau, Missouri

Proximity

Published by Moving Images Publications
Cape Girardeau, Missouri
www.MovingImagesPublications.com

Lightning Photograph by Erica Murphy-Burrell
Automobile Photograph by Julius Alexander II

ISBN-13: 978-0692570555

Dedicated to

The memory of Dr. Scott R. Gibbs

The Four Accords

First Accord: *Walk Without Footprints*

Second Accord: *Filter the Future*

Third Accord: *Prevent Personal Profit*

Fourth Accord: *Avoid Meeting Yourself*

CHAPTER 1

Thursday, March 18, 1948, 9:12 p.m.
Eldorado Club
Las Vegas, Nevada

Chance encounters are most effective after careful planning.

He hovered above his amber glass of whiskey and swirled it right to the brim. In his dulled imagination the ice cubes tumbled below him like frozen dice, hard and cold. The man glanced up, scanning the sparsely occupied tavern for something a bit softer and a good deal warmer.

A mop of graying hair topped a face-planted drunk three bar stools to his immediate right. Beyond that unconscious mess, a couple of all-business types were entangled in a hushed exchange at the furthest end of the counter. The man grabbed another sip from his lowball glass and spun about. An off-duty soldier was hitting a new cigarette way too hard while attempting to make time with a reluctant barmaid trapped near the entrance.

Good luck, pal. But I don't think Lady Luck is with you tonight.

He lowered his whiskey and had just begun to entertain the notion of his own companionship defeat when he caught sight of her at a table not quite twenty feet away. It was a momentary glance, a quick and silent connection…but a connection nonetheless. The man smiled, but her reciprocation—if there even was one—appeared to be far more subtle.

This intrigued him.

And challenged him.

He sensed a sudden rush of hope-filled anticipation and the surge of adrenaline brought on by the prospect of the hunt. The confident man downed the final harsh ounces of his courage-enhancer and rotated about.

Gotcha.

It was impossible to miss this time…she was staring at him. A fraction of a second later the beauty popped her purse open and dug out a small compact. She appeared to be examining her eyebrows and immaculate bangs as her left hand fumbled for her drink. Her eyes darted over at him and then away again.

Alright…that's three, Mrs. Short-skirt.

He meandered across the empty bar and slid into a dark mahogany chair directly opposite hers. The woman seemed not to notice, even though the ice rattled while he set his glass down and the man snagged a cigarette in a wide motion. As the flame from his Zippo lighter roared to life, he broke the ice. "So, is this Las Vegas, or is it Atlantic City?"

The woman froze.

Smoke wisped out of his nostrils as he waited. "Simple question," he repeated.

She closed the compact with a deliberate snap. "Uh, sorry? What was that?"

He leaned onto his elbows. "I said, is this Atlantic City or Las Vegas? It's not a hard question."

Her hazel eyes raced back and forth. "I, I'm sorry…I'm fairly certain that it's *Las Vegas.*" She scrunched her lovely face. "Am I missing something here?"

The man arched back into the heavy chair and took a long pull on his cigarette. "Well, the way I see it…the only explanation for a drop-dead gorgeous gal like you to be in town is for the Miss America Pageant. So this must be Atlantic City. Beautiful women, crowds, lights, cameras, and lots of action."

She blushed.

Bingo, he thought. *Keep working this table, payout dead ahead.*

"Well, I, uh, I'm not sure what to say about all of that," she replied with some hesitation. "I guess…*thank you.* I suppose." The woman surveyed the room. "But by the looks of this place, I don't think there is very much going on in this town. We do have plenty of lights, but no crowds or cameras. Vegas has been almost a ghost town lately, more or less."

He laughed and scooted his chair in a bit closer. "Well my dear…you can thank good old Uncle Sam for all of that." He forgot that his glass was empty and took a frustrating sip in vain.

"Uncle Sam? I don't understand," she said.

"Monday was a rough day for most people when it comes to *finances.*" He raised his lowball and pivoted towards the bar. "*Hey Mack!* Another whiskey and another *whatever-the-hell* the lady is having."

She tapped on the table, obviously struggling to interpret his reference. "Monday. Monday? Finances?"

He was patient.

"Finances. Monday," she whispered. "Wait, *Monday*. Oh, now I get it. Monday was the fifteenth. And the fifteenth was Income Tax Day."

He whirled the remaining lonely cubes of ice in his thick glass as his eyes grew wide. "Beware the Ides of March." The man slammed his glass down and locked playful eyes with her. "Beware, the Tax Man cometh. Or, has cometh. Or whatever."

They both chuckled as the bartender arrived with fresh drinks. Loverboy reached into his breast pocket and produced a sizeable wad of cash. He peeled off a couple of bills with precision and slapped them into the bartender's excited hand. It was clearly a show and the lady with bright red lips was clearly impressed.

"First…*thank you*," she said as she took a tiny sip, "and second, it doesn't look like the Tax Man bothered to stop at your place. If you don't mind me saying."

He took another hit on his cigarette and held it in for a moment. "I'm like the Israelites in Egypt, my dear. In the days of old."

"Oh?"

He exhaled. "I guess you could say the death angel of taxes passes over my house. Every year."

She paused and smiled. "So, what makes you so special? I thought everyone paid their fair share." She hunched forward and lowered her sweet voice. "Are you in the mob or something?"

With a quick motion, he crushed his half-spent smoke on the glass table top and squinted. "Well, you are a spunky one. I like that in beautiful women." He took a long drink and stared her down. "So tell me something, *Mrs.*—?"

"*Sullivan*. Debbie Sullivan."

"So tell me, Mrs. Sullivan…does your lucky husband find this spunky streak of yours as strangely attractive as I do?"

"Husband? What do you mean, *Mr.*—?"

"Ross."

She paused. "Ross. Wait…is that a first name or a last name?"

He paused. "It's the only name you need right now."

"Um, okay. Well, I am not married, Ross or *Mr.* Ross." She took a delicate drink and glanced up at him. "It's *Miss* Sullivan."

A frown broke out across his brow and he touched her left hand with cautious interest. "I'm sorry. I was just admiring your beautiful ring here."

"Oh," she replied. "*That*. Well, it's not a wedding ring or anything like that. No." She leaned in and stroked lightly across the top of his hand with a perfectly manicured nail.

"It was a gift from my mother."

CHAPTER 2

Tuesday, October 23, 1956, 3:41 p.m.
Nelson Manufacturing
Normal, Illinois

Betty Larson was in full retreat but the massive form of an enraged Garrett Frazier closed the gap regardless.

"Wait! *Wait!*" she screamed, her arms outstretched in protest. "Listen to me. Listen, everyone! I am a time traveler, too! I'm from 1980!"

Frazier thrust his meaty grasp at her throat. "Yeah, that's probably what I would've said if I were you! Nice try."

Over the course of the next three seconds, a convoluted mix of competing events collided. Chief McCloud actually drew his gun and rushed out alongside Shep as Ellen and Terrance yelled for Garrett to back off. Leah shrieked in horror the instant Frazier's hand clamped around Betty's neck. He shoved forward just as her heels slammed into a short wooden crate and she plummeted backward like felled timber.

Doc Stonecroft bowed his head and Papineau turned away with eyes closed.

But it wasn't the sight…it was the sound.

Betty's inevitable fall was sickeningly interrupted as the base of her skull crashed into the sharp edge of a waist-high metal worktable. The nauseating thud doubled over an already-distressed Leah Swan with an immediate volley of hot vomit. As Betty's limp body crumpled down to the unforgiving concrete, Leah snagged Tori's arm and both girls fled from the violent spectacle. Grandma Martha and Officer

Billy chased after them. Alexus departed a stunned second later.

A shiny pool of blood expanded out from beneath Betty's unconscious head, forming a crimson halo. Ellen rushed up and shoved the gawking men out of her way. "What have you done? *What the hell have you done to her?!"*

Garrett bristled. "What needed to be done."

McCloud holstered his weapon, pressing his chest up against Garrett. "Listen to me, Frazier! How'd you expect me, *me*—an officer of the law—to respond to this kinda senseless violence?!"

"A thank you would be nice."

Ellen lunged up at him. *"You smug little bastard!"*

McCloud intercepted her fist just in time. "Whoa, Missie. Whoa. C'mon now. Please tend to Miss Larson. There'll be plenty of time to deal with this reckless idiot later."

Ellen yanked her arm away. "Later can't get here soon enough." She dropped back down and examined Betty's injury. Garrett was stoic.

Stonecroft worked his way up to the grisly scene. "Is there any assistance that I may be able to render, Nurse Finegan?"

Ellen didn't even look up. "A few prayers certainly wouldn't hurt."

"Intercession has traditionally been my first round of medical care." His smile was laced with compassion. "I typically continue it in large doses until full recovery. Is the injury…*life-threatening?"*

"It's hard to say. We're talking about the possibility of severe intracranial bleeding. She might be brain dead already."

"Oh…my," he whispered and turned away. "Heaven help us."

Ellen located a clean-enough towel and began compressing the brutal wound.

"What can I do to help?" the Chief asked.

She glanced up at him.

"I would probably start writing up a police report to explain away the accident…and maybe an obituary."

CHAPTER 3

Denver couldn't believe his eyes, but after this day's discoveries up at Chicago State Mental Hospital, he would still give them the benefit of the doubt.

Is that Leah? He squinted and tapped the brakes.

Why in the world is she out in the middle of the road flailing her arms?

She signaled for him to pull over into a nearby parking lot. He obeyed, killed the engine and jumped out.

"Leah?! What's wrong? Is someone hurt? Is it Tori?"

She tried to speak as her chest heaved up and down. "No, no, no. It's, it's Shep…and McCloud. And Frazier, and the newspaper lady."

He clutched her shoulders and tried to lock his gaze onto her erratic eyes. "What?! What happened? But whatever happened to them, you will never believe—"

"Be quiet. Listen." She shook her head and gasped for air. "They, they know. They know. They know you weren't sick today. And, and that you had my car. And Shep now knows I lied."

Denver frowned. "Okay, well, that's no reason to go to pieces. I got it covered."

She collapsed into his chest. "They told everyone—*everyone*—that you probably went to meet with the FBI in Chicago! To rat us out."

"What? *The FBI?* That's crazy." He leaned her back gently. "Listen. Hey, listen to me. Don't worry about all that. Remember, I'm a war vet. I plan for these kind of contingencies." He smiled. "I called Hank and set up an alibi.

A *watertight* alibi. This soldier has it covered. Hank's got my back."

"Well, that's great and all, but what about the newspaper lady?"

"Betty Larson?"

"Yes, her. Miss Larson. She knows."

"What do you mean *she knows?*"

"Everything apparently." Leah folded her arms and strolled away. "We were having an emergency meeting at the factory in the back conference room and she just sorta waltzed in. She figured it out. All of it. She knows, Denver. A newspaper editor knows we're from the future!"

He hesitated. "I'm sure the Chief has a plan for this. He'll figure it out. He always does."

She spun around. "He doesn't have to. I think Frazier already—*killed* her."

"*What?! Killed Betty?!* Why would you say that?!"

"Because I saw it! I saw the whole thing. And so did Tori. I don't know what happened, but it was bad." She burst into a fresh round of tears. "I had to get Tori out of there."

"When did all this happen?"

She coughed. "It, uh, it was about thirty minutes ago. I've been waiting for you. I just don't know what to do."

Denver jogged over and wrapped his arms around her. "I am sorry. So sorry. But, hey, listen to me for just a minute. Please?"

She wiped her face and stared over at Tori who was perched like a statue in the back seat of the company car. Denver pivoted around and eased into Leah's face. He raised her chin using a single finger.

"Now there is something I need to tell you. And trust me, it will make you forget all this other nonsense. Trust me."

She coughed again and half-way gagged. "I doubt it, but go ahead."

"Well, my grandpa used to say that *'doubt is the first positive step after denial.'* So, I can work with doubt. Doubt's good."

She rolled her red, wet eyes. "Whatever."

"So, this will be a bit hard to believe. But please hear me out. Can you do that for me?"

Leah nodded.

He took a deep breath and fought back an awkward smile.

"Leah Swan…Phil Nelson is *alive.*"

CHAPTER 4

Friday, March 19, 1948, 5:12 p.m.
El Cortez Hotel and Casino
Las Vegas, Nevada

The last twenty-four hours had validated at least as many days of intensive human intelligence.

Oksana thumbed through her colorful rack of spring apparel. It could have been frustrating. The tiny hotel closet didn't allow much space for variety, but she wasn't bothered.

With Howard Ross now located and ensnared by his own predictable carnal tendencies, she would soon be relocating into a modest apartment. Her alter ego, Debbie Sullivan, would land a low-profile job at a low-profile establishment, and assume a low-profile lifestyle to land a *high-profile* target.

Every step, every move, was by design.

She had weighed and calculated each breathless *yes*, and more importantly each firm *no*. She had refused to sleep with Ross the night before. Even denial of service was a crucial protocol in her meticulous itinerary.

Oksana leaned back out of the closet, having finally selected a brilliant red skirt with tight pleats. She draped it across the bed, just below a cream-colored blouse in need of a partner. The combination was suitably attractive, but the skirt was considerably longer than the seductive cocktail dress from the night before.

For their first official date, this planned increase in modesty was designed for a matching increase in interest. She knew that fish like Howard Ross were best lured by a hot, flashy tease followed up by a slower, more moderate pursuit. It was a simple formula: a little tug trailed by a little more slack. Oksana had even resisted his initial request for dinner on Friday night (she eventually yielded after his fifth pathetic offer).

The lustful sap has no idea he is the mouse and that this cat is calling all of the shots.

And Oksana knew how to call all of the shots.

Because she knew Howard Ross.

She had studied Howard Ross.

In all likelihood, she probably knew him better than his late mother ever had.

Oksana dug around inside her luggage and fished out a white lace bra. She lowered it gently across the blouse and toyed with the smooth edge of the crimson skirt.

Sex, of course, was to be delayed as long as necessary. Intercourse was an enticing carrot to be dangled from a very patient stick. Weeks of psychoanalyzing her prey's history had revealed Ross to be a by-the-book egomaniac, a middle-aged American male driven—above all else—by the thrill of the challenge. Low hanging fruit might satisfy the indolent desires of lesser men, but not him.

The further the delicacy was out of reach, the more it chained Ross to a fate bent on insatiable conquest.

A long blast of a car's horn drew her to the window. The vehicular disruption served as a noisy reminder of the impatient close of a business day, and a Friday at that. A splendidly-attired woman exiting a taxi straight below caught her eye. Moments later, a hotel bellman rushed to unload a trunk full of her luggage.

Oksana relaxed in the windowsill and reflected back to her own arrival to the States over a month before. The third of February had been especially cold and blustery as the recently-recommissioned SS Washington drew into New York Harbor at the conclusion of a five-day jaunt across the

Atlantic. With considerable difficulty, Oksana leaned against the rails along the upper deck just below the first of two massive smokestacks. She watched with growing interest as the spastic coastal winds gave the stevedores a worthy battle while they tied up the immense passenger ship.

One hour later, with two suitcases in tow, she slipped into the throng debarking along a crowded gangplank. It took an additional half-hour just to flag down an unoccupied taxi. With the hot engine still running, the driver hopped out and stowed her luggage in back.

"Where to, ma'am?"

Oksana slid into the backseat and removed her hat. "Would you be so kind as to deliver me and my belongings to the Taft Hotel?"

"The Taft it is. Seventh Avenue."

They had scarcely traveled three blocks when he glanced up into the rearview mirror. "What part of England do you hail from, ma'am?" he inquired. "That is, if you don't mind me asking?"

She blushed and toyed with her hat. "Is my accent that obvious?"

He grinned back. "Lady, I pick up folks from all over the world at the port. I guess I'm a regular *international* cabbie, you could say. I've heard every accent known to man."

"Nottinghamshire," she replied.

"*Nottinghamshire,*" he repeated. "Never been there. Sounds nice. Bet it's real nice."

"Depending upon the time of year, it can be. It's about two-hundred kilometers to the north of London, just east of Sheffield."

"Pretty cold up there right now?"

She studied the downtown landscape through the window. "About like here, more or less."

"So, Nottinghamshire. Isn't that the place where Robin Hood lived?"

She was silent.

He bit his lip and looked away from the rearview mirror. "Sorry, you probably get that a lot. I, uh, I'm Carl. All my friends call me Cabbie Carl. Been doin' this for about eight years now. Ain't getting rich, but it's a decent living. Kinda my own boss."

Oksana nodded. "Nice to make your acquaintance, Master Cabbie Carl. I'm Anna. Anna Townsend."

Twenty minutes later she exited the taxi, shedding both her adopted name and accent even before reaching the marble-lined hotel lobby.

CHAPTER 5

Denver pushed his broken apartment door open without much effort. Puzzled and suspicious, he shoved his keys back into his pocket; his soldier's senses on high alert. Before he could even flick the light switch, the last voice he wanted to hear sounded out of the darkness.

"Quite a day, eh, *Colorado*?"

Denver froze, then hit the lights.

"Why the hell are you in my apartment?" He turned to face a smiling Robert Sheppard reclining far too comfortably over on the couch. "I spend over eight hours a day working for you down at the factory…don't I deserve my own space?"

Shep frowned. "Eight hours? *Eight hours?* Uh, not today you didn't. Not even one hour." He sat up and leaned forward. "So, how ya feeling? Been at the doctor's office all day? Perhaps a doctor in, oh, I don't know…*Chicago?*"

Denver plodded into the kitchen. "You know where I was. I already explained it to everyone."

Shep played with a coaster laying on the coffee table. "Oh, of course, that's right. You were with Hank Boden-*whatever*." He stood up and dropped the coaster. "Remodeling kitchens for little old ladies down in Bloomington."

Denver didn't flinch. "Pretty much describes it. But you forgot the word wealthy. *Wealthy* little old ladies down in Bloomington."

Shep circled closer. "Yeah, I called him. Checks out. Seems harmless enough. But why all the smoke and mirrors? Why didn't you just say so? I mean, no need to lie and then get *others* to lie for you? Right?"

Denver hesitated, his blood-pressure rising. "I know how you guys feel about us being friends with Locals and working with Locals." He thumbed through his mail on the counter. "Hank needed help. I made a judgment call. Sorry if it bothers you or anyone else."

Shep chuckled. "What? Bother me? Nah. Not one damn bit, Colorado. Not one damn bit. Now, you know what should bother you?" He pushed up off the couch and folded his arms.

Denver refused to take the bait.

Shep continued, "If I were you I would be bothered that my list of allies was dwindling by the day. By the *hour*. Let's see, who do you have in your hip-pocket? Let's see, we can cross Chief McCloud off that short list. He's finally on to you. Um, the beautiful Ellen Finegan? Nope, that interest was just a passing fling. Anyone else? Oh, wait! I remember! A naïve and impressionable receptionist. That's *one…*"

"I don't know what you're babbling about, Shep. I don't think about or worry about a supposed list of allies. Sounds like you do, though."

"I'm just calling it like I see it, Colorado."

"So, I suppose there is a…*reason* for your little visit tonight, beyond just the pure pleasure of breaking into my apartment and hassling me? Shouldn't you be doing something constructive, like checking on the condition of Miss Larson or something? Everyone else has, except for you and Garrett I've been told."

Shep strolled towards the open door and pulled something out of his light jacket. "Oh, she's in good hands. But, uh, now that you mention it, I did have a reason for stopping by. I almost forgot. Consider me as just a delivery boy. *Here*."

Denver pivoted around just in time to catch a dark object coursing through the air, end over end.

It was Phil's journal.

The moment Shep vacated the apartment, Denver flipped through the volume of handwritten pages. His feared expectation was dead-on.

Phil's last and incriminating journal entry had been carefully removed.

CHAPTER 6

Shep detected the muffled pitch of his kitchen phone ringing the moment he stepped out of his truck. He fumbled through his keys and scrambled through the side door. The complete darkness that engulfed him almost prevented him from answering in time.

"Hello?" he said, breathless.

"Where have you been!? I tried calling the factory several times today."

Shep pulled the slack in the cord and took up a position in the moonlight pouring through a window. "Well, Dr. Montgomery, it, uh, it's been a rough day. I've been a bit preoccupied." Shep clamped his eyes shut and rested his head against the glass. "It started with overpaying you a thousand bucks this morning and then accelerated all to hell—"

"Shut up, and listen! Someone came by to visit with Gordon Thompson today."

Shep jerked his head back and repositioned the phone. "Excuse me. What did you say?"

"Gordon…Thompson…had…a…visitor."

Shep pinched the bridge of his flaring nose. "So, what happened?"

Montgomery cleared his throat. "I was making midday rounds and when I checked on Mr. Thompson, there was a man with him."

Shep flinched. "A man? Which man? What did he look like?"

"Oh, early middle-aged. Brown hair. Well-built. Probably six feet tall, maybe a little more."

Shep rotated about and reclined against the wall. "What did you do?"

"*Do?* There wasn't much time to *do* anything. I asked him to identify himself and he ran out of the room. Security lost track of him about a block away, towards the park."

Shep was speechless, processing the report.

"One of my nurses had spoken with the man," Montgomery continued. "She told me he was a preacher…supposedly visiting from Ohio."

"A preacher?"

"Yeah. She said his name was…Collins. Pastor Collins."

CHAPTER 7

Friday, March 19, 1948, 7:14 p.m.
Flamingo Hotel and Casino
Las Vegas, Nevada

The fresh influx of weekend tourists from California (eager to defy the laws of probability) slowed Oksana's advance towards the casino entrance. She studied her slender watch.

7:15 p.m.

Ross had their table reserved for 7:30. There wasn't a doubt in her mind that Howard was already inside, and he was probably working on his second round of booze. Oksana gazed up at the magnificent lighting adorning the face of the expansive structure. The Flamingo rose out the desert as an electronic oasis and gateway on the southern end of the strip along US Route 91. The nearest competition for gambler's dollars was a few miles north.

"Excuse me, ma'am? Excuse me."

Oksana snapped her head back down and scanned the immediate area. A young couple in formal attire were smiling at her and the man was dangling a Bolsey 35mm camera in her direction.

"Would you mind snapping a few photographs of us, here, in front of the casino?" he asked. "It's our honeymoon. Our first time in Las Vegas."

She forced a grin as she retrieved it. "Oh, yes. Absolutely. No problem. Glad to."

"Thanks," the newlyweds said nearly in unison. The couple embraced one another as she framed up the once-in-a-lifetime shot.

"On three. One…two…*three.*"

They smiled.

Her finger went down.

The flash fired.

The man released his bride and closed in on Oksana. "Thank you so very much," he gushed. "I really, really appreciate it!"

"It was my pleasure. And congratulations. You two make a beautiful couple. Now, go. Go have some fun."

Cause I won't, she thought. They may have been all pleasure, but tonight she was all business.

The man grabbed the knob and advanced the film. "Thanks again, ma'am. I can't wait to see these pictures developed."

Developing pictures, she thought.

The memories of weeks of intense research rushed back into her consciousness. Oksana imagined that her tender fingers still reeked from the tubs of pungent chemicals required to develop the films smuggled out for her.

Early on, she had avoided all contact with the high-level Soviet mole embedded inside the six million square feet of the Pentagon, and that insulated anonymity was both comforting and productive. The Department of Defense employee (who had moderate-level access to the classified archives) was merely known to her as DANCER.

The arrangement had been put into motion months before Darkstar had exited the austere disciplines of Project SUNSHADE in Magnitogorsk. DANCER had been instrumental in providing the initial photographs of Howard Ross, but once Darkstar hit stateside, her needs for far more detailed written information kept the mole busy.

The procedure for the film delivery involved a simple dead drop on the west side of Griffith Stadium in DC. Darkstar was instructed to check the stash every two days, and always in the morning. DANCER had been notified by a handler that the window for pertinent information expired by mid-to-late February.

Unfortunately for the mole, her own expiration would soon follow, a tragic consequence of the ruthless stratagems of a KGB assassin who specialized in *not* existing.

Darkstar set up surveillance on the dead drop location and spotted the female operative through spitting snow showers on the twenty-second of February. She tracked DANCER back to her home in Kensington and suffocated the young woman in her own living room. Darkstar paused to study a family photo atop their television console. DANCER appeared to be the quintessential wife and mother of two.

The ensuing police investigation negated the role of foul play. Detectives labeled the cause of death as accidental electrocution arising from a frayed vacuum cleaner power cord.

Although the doomed DoD operative failed to produce any films of documents concerning Project SATURN directly (an obstacle that was anticipated), the Communist mole photographed over forty-three pages of Howard Ross' personnel file. As expected, the paper trail of these typewritten snapshots of his four-decade progression through Uncle Sam's various agencies went cold after June of 1947, but were still invaluable in Oksana's quest to know the man.

And eventually to *attract* the man.

Darkstar's modest Washington apartment resembled most other flats in Foggy Bottom with the exception of one bedroom that had been converted into a makeshift darkroom. A stunning variety of gorgeous landscapes hung from strings like wet clothing on laundry lines suspended above vats of fragrant fluids. Stacks of recently developed nature prints were positioned on the kitchen counter or were scattered across the living room beside piles of photography magazines, journals, and the occasional lens or two.

Darkstar's mission-critical pictures and documents were safely stowed away below the ragged green carpet that lined the foyer closet.

It was all a clever cover for the irregular prying eyes of her busybody landlord who appeared to thrive on unannounced inspections during her tiny tenure there. Darkstar's lower-middle class existence as Catherine Pruitt—struggling photographer and part-time waitress—never caused so much as a second glance…

…although he once commented that she was far too pretty to be single at her age.

CHAPTER 8

Wednesday, October 24, 1956, 10:14 a.m.
Normal, Illinois

"What are we even looking for?" an irritated Garrett Frazier demanded after he yanked out and dumped yet another dresser drawer. The cluttered floor of Betty Larson's bedroom had begun to resemble a freshman dorm at an all-boys college.

Shep slammed a closet door one room over. "We are looking for anything that looks out of place. McCloud said to pick it clean."

Garrett seized the opportunity. "So, what—you takin' marching orders from *Andy Griffith* now?"

Robert Sheppard hurled the cushions off the couch. "Just shut the hell up, Frazier. Put your gigantic biceps to work and give your overworked jaw muscles a break."

Garrett emptied his last drawer. "I'll take that as a *yes*."

"If she really is a time Jumper," Shep said, ignoring him, "then McCloud's right. We should find some evidence here."

"That newspaper lady ain't from the future. She was lyin' through her teeth yesterday. She was covering her ass."

Shep waltzed into the bedroom and wiped the sweat from his hot forehead. "You better hope so, Mr. Frazier. Or *yours* is gonna be on the line."

"Whatever."

Shep dropped down and pointed below the bed. "Did you check under here?"

Garrett waved his arm. "Be my guest."

A pile of clothes blocked his approach and Shep shoved it aside. He thrust his arm under the skirt of the bed. A few seconds later he slid a small, cardboard shoebox out into the light of day.

"Hmm. What do we have here?" he asked.

Garrett reclined against the wall. "Oh, I don't know…uh…*shoes?*"

Shep removed the lid. "No…I don't think so."

He retrieved a Sony Walkman tape player along with an audio cassette and examined them for a few moments. He peered back down into the box and picked up a photo. A skinny, curly-headed teenage girl was hugging a cake. Shep drew it closer, studying the orange lettering on the cream-colored icing.

Happy Birthday Betty.

His eyes dropped to the white space below the Polaroid.

Sweet 16. March 7, 1964.

Shep raised it aloft for Garrett.

"You better pray she doesn't die, Frazier. You better start praying right now!"

CHAPTER 9

"You got a minute?" a voice echoed across the foyer.

Leah Swan glanced away from her accounting ledger as Denver locked the door to the factory floor and jogged up to her.

"Finding free time for me is a lot easier than finding free time for you," she said. "Shep could be back any minute, you know."

"About that," Denver said. "I hear that Mr. Sunshine and Mr. Muscles are working out over at Betty's place."

"Real funny."

"I know...*keep my day job.*"

Leah paused. "About that. I hear it might be changing. Your job. Again."

Denver rested his elbows onto the receptionist's desk. "Well, we can certainly thank a reckless Garrett Frazier for that. I just can't seem to stay away from the *Journal.*"

"The Chief was in here today talking about it with Alexus, as well. About an hour ago."

"He was?"

"He was. He had some kind of hush-hush meeting with Doc. From what I've gathered, something big went down at the police station this morning. Really big. After that meeting, he brought Alexus out here into the foyer. I heard most of it. She didn't seem overly thrilled. Seems like it's going to happen, though."

Denver rubbed his face. "Crazy plan if you ask me. Beyond crazy."

"Speaking of crazy plans," she noted, looking around and lowering her voice. "What's yours about getting *Phil?* I couldn't sleep last night just thinking about it…about him being alive and all. It seems so…so wonderful…and *terrible*, all at the same time. I'm a nervous wreck. Besides all that, I can hardly make eye contact with Shep."

Denver dropped his volume as well. "I need you to do something. Can Tori spend the night with Grandma Martha on Friday?"

"Shouldn't be too much trouble to arrange that."

Denver grinned and checked behind him. "Perfect. Then we can leave on Saturday. *Early* on Saturday. You and me. Straight to Chicago. In and out."

"How are you planning to get him out of that hospital?" Her eyes began to gush with tears as she glanced away. "You said…you said he was in bad shape."

He patted the trembling hand of his fragile coworker. "Hey, leave those worries to me. Remember, I used to do rescue missions in Afghanistan all the time. This will be a piece of cake. I promise. Denver Collins can handle a few rowdy nurses. As long as they're not packing."

A solitary hot tear splashed down from her soft chin onto the slick surface of the desk. She grabbed a tissue and mopped it up. "I, uh, I want to believe you. I really do. It just seems—"

"*What?* Impossible? Incredible? Unbelievable?"

"Um, all of the above."

"Don't worry," he assured her. "You'll see."

Leah relaxed and leaned hard against the back of her office chair. "I've been doing a lot of thinking. A lot of thinking."

"About what?"

"About what happens after that."

"After *what?*"

She rubbed her eyes and blinked several times. "What happens after you, or we, bring Phil home? What will that do to the group? The questions—"

"The *answers*," he interrupted.

"Whatever," she replied. "Especially if Nellie's in no shape to explain everything. What if rescuing him actually puts him in more danger? Shep is still the same old Shep. He's not going to let anything or anyone break up his little party. Come on Denver. You know what we're up against here."

"I'm counting on the Chief to—"

"I don't trust the Chief," she blurted, almost out of control. Leah composed herself and leaned forward. "Remember what I told you yesterday? He was ready to throw you under the bus. He *did* throw you under the bus. He was walking lock-step with Shep. What if they're in this together somehow?"

Denver pushed away from the desk but kept his voice low. "Shep's probably a lone wolf on this one. And listen, even if not, they're only two. Out of twelve." He strolled back towards the factory floor. He glanced back over his shoulder and whispered, "Actually, when we bring Mr. Nelson home, only two out of thirteen."

Leah returned to her ledger.

"Somehow that doesn't make me feel any better, Mr. Collins."

October 24, 1956

SECURITY LEVEL: TOP SECRET

FOR: Allen W. Dulles, Director, Central Intelligence
FROM: Chief Howard D. Ross, Project SATURN
SUBJECT: Incident Report

Corporal Jennings and his assessment team have completed their investigation concerning the tragic electrical discharge and subsequent explosive fire that claimed the lives of Dr. Fred Hammon and three technicians earlier this month on Level 3-Cryo.

Their detailed findings (which I have included) conclusively demonstrate that the incident was accidental in nature. Jennings determined there was no evidence of sabotage or foul play.

Repairs to the Cryo Lab are scheduled to be completed on or around 15 December.

END

DCI/PS

CHAPTER 10

For the second time in less than three months Ellen Finegan's spare bedroom had been converted into a makeshift recovery area. Though she didn't enjoy the circumstances surrounding her new duties, Ellen certainly appreciated the exchange of a lab coat for a nurse's gown. Mathematics and physics were challenging and interesting, but too far removed from the more *human* sciences.

Ellen peered down at the motionless form of Betty Larson draped across the bed. She hated to admit it, but the newspaper editor's prognosis rested more in the hands of cold probabilities than in her own skill as a medical practitioner.

Treating external wounds in the mid-1950s was one thing. Caring for severe head trauma was quite another.

"One can only hope that her condition is as peaceful as her sweet countenance would suggest," Doc offered as he sauntered up to Ellen's worried side.

"Oh, hey Doc. Yeah, yeah. She does *look* good." Ellen rotated towards Stonecroft. "*Look* being the operative word. One can never know what goes on behind those closed eyes."

"Well then, let us speak of those things upon which we have greater certainty. What is your assessment, Nurse Finegan?"

Ellen sighed and gave her colleague a small hug. "Well, she certainly has a basilar skull fracture. Typical symptoms, including bleeding around the eyes."

He frowned. "How low on the skull?"

"Fairly low, thank goodness. I would say the risks for visual impairment are low. Occipital ridge is undamaged."

She paused. "Of course, that doesn't rule out a subdural hematoma causing pressure there…or *anywhere*. If internal swelling increases, it could affect autonomic functions. That's been my sleepless concern."

She glanced at her watch through bloodshot eyes and blinked hard. "But, we are nearly thirty hours from the initial injury. I would expect that the worst of the internal bleeding and intracranial pressure would be behind us."

Doc reached up and rubbed Ellen's hand. "Have you introduced any anabolic steroids into her system?"

Ellen's head bobbed and she yawned, "Three rounds. Last one about four hours ago."

"Speaking of rounds, my dear Miss Finegan, I believe you need a few rounds of sleep. *That* diagnosis requires precious little medical training." He faced her. "Martha and I are here. We will keep constant watch upon Ms. Larson's recovery. We will keep you abreast of any alterations in her fragile condition."

He smiled broadly. "Now go. *Sleep*. An exhausted nurse cannot render the level of care necessary in such delicate cases."

Ellen refused to budge.

Stonecroft relocated between her and the patient. "Nurse Finegan, whether you remain in a fixed vertical or horizontal position will in no way affect the outcome of Ms. Larson's progress, I assure you." He grinned. "Don't force me to call Chief McCloud."

"Alright, alright," she agreed with hands held high. "I submit, but only under extreme protest."

Doc grabbed her shoulders and rotated Ellen to face the door. "Off you go now, my dear. I will stand watch until 6:30 this evening. Then Mrs. Tomlin will relieve me."

Ellen lumbered towards the hall and spun back around. "What's happening at 6:30? A big date?" She winked with a wicked grin.

Doc shrugged somewhat. "In a manner of speaking…*yes*."

"Oh really?"

"Indeed. She is a fair blonde, by all accounts. But unfortunately, she is over four decades my junior." It was his turn to wink.

Ellen reclined against the doorway and pointed at him. "Gotcha…let me guess, the new time Jumper the Chief met this morning?"

"Spot on, Miss Finegan. I guess it was a fool's errand to seek to keep a lid on it, as they say. We thought it prudent to interview the young woman before we announced our newest addition." He looked away as the playful smile drained from his face. "Admittedly, our latest arrival has proved somewhat of a conundrum, according to the Chief's report this morning."

"How so?"

"Well, she would be a first, a unique case, if you will. Every Jumper since our beloved Mr. Nelson has been found…*located* by the diligent efforts of our group."

Ellen stared up at the ceiling. "But this one, she located us instead. Interesting. That is very interesting."

Doc rubbed his chin several times.

"I would offer, my dear Miss Finegan, that a pretty face mustn't always be taken at face value."

CHAPTER 11

Friday, March 19, 1948, 8:19 p.m.
Flamingo Hotel and Casino
Las Vegas, Nevada

Oksana had hoped that Ross would've been a tad bit more imaginative and stimulating on their first official date.

Forty-five minutes into it, she was rather disappointed.

His physical form and appearance had instilled hope initially. Ross' strong features, flawless crewcut, and a custom-tailored wardrobe were attractive in principle, but marred by an excessive yet unjustified self-confidence. She found it to be tiresome, but not all that uncommon among men of ways and means.

Over the years, she had been exposed to autocrats across a wide spectrum of roles and responsibilities. None of them lacked power, but nearly all of them lacked the requisite social graces and imagination necessary for lasting influence.

Once their power was gone, they were gone.

She knew Ross would join that extensive, unwritten list of men destined not to be remembered. To a spy, his predictability was comforting. To a woman, it was anything but.

"You've hardly touched your steak, Debbie," he noted between his own rushed bites.

She poked at it with her fork. "Oh, it's great and all, but…well, it looks a little rare. A little too *pink* for me. I'm a *well-done* kinda gal, at least whenever I get steak. Which isn't often."

Ross seized a quick drink of wine. "Oh, no, no, no. It's *prime rib*; it's supposed to look that way. It's prepared slowly, over medium heat." He pointed. "The color doesn't mean it's rare. It's a by-product of the cooking process. Trust me, that steak was cooked for at least three or four times longer than most regular beef. It preserves the flavor and keeps it tender."

She didn't appear convinced but donned a smile anyway. "I'm sorry. I just don't get the chance too often to eat food like this…or in places like this. But listen, it's wonderful, it really is. The live band is a really nice touch. And thanks again for dinner. I know this place can cost a pretty penny, even if the Tax Man doesn't bother to stop at your door."

He snagged the cloth napkin from his lap and mopped his grin. "It's time to broaden your palette, Miss Sullivan. A gal like you needs to live a little, see the world."

She set her own wine glass back down. "After the bills are paid, a waitress' salary doesn't allow for much *world-seeing*, Mr. Ross. And that's including tips."

He rested his elbows on the table and studied her. "And just how much of the world have you seen?"

She took a self-conscious nibble of the prime rib. "Um, about four states. Born and raised in Oklahoma, in Locust Grove…about fifty miles east of Tulsa. Let's see, I've been to Kansas, Colorado, Utah, and now Nevada." She hesitated as she counted off the states on her fingers. "Oh, and once I went to Louisiana, but I was only two or three at the time. I don't remember any of it. I hear it's nice."

He continued to gawk. Only a naïve woman wouldn't have realized he was undressing her with his eyes.

"So, uh, Mr. Ross, how about you? Have you seen the world?"

"I have. At least, the parts worth seeing."

She tilted her pretty head. "Do you mean to tell me there's nothing left that you still want to see?"

He grinned and swirled his Cabernet. "Well, I've recently become aware of a new wonder that intrigues me. And it's not very far from where I'm sitting."

Oksana blushed and wiped her mouth. "So, Mr. Ross, what kind of business are you involved in that allows a man to do so much travelling? Are you in sales? International sales?"

"Sales?" He laughed. "Hell, no. No, I am in the business of *acquiring* things, not letting things go. In my opinion, sales is the wrong direction, sweetheart."

Let's see how honest he is.

Oksana acted quite interested. "What sort of *things* do you acquire, Mr. Ross?"

His hesitation was hard to miss. "Things like *information*."

"Information? No offense, but, uh, that doesn't sound too profitable. I've never met anyone working with information. Is there really money to be made in that line of work?"

Ross leaned onto his elbows and clasped his hands together, rubbing them casually. "It ain't always about the money, honey."

"That's what my bosses keep telling me, usually right about raise time."

"Oh, don't worry, money's not an issue with me. But enough about my business."

She sensed a modicum of tension. *Back off, Mizenov. New course. Change the topic.*

Time for another honesty check.

Oksana sliced into her steak. "Call me crazy, but something tells me you didn't grow up anywhere near my home state of Oklahoma. Or Nevada."

"Your womanly intuition serves you well," he said. A waiter waltzed up and Ross dismissed him without even looking up. "*Rochester*. Upstate New York. You may have heard of our little claim to fame, our famous waterway?"

"Sorry, but I was never too good with geography," she confessed. "I'm not really sure what you're referring to."

She was a marvelous liar.

Oksana had spent the last week of February and the first two weeks of March all over Rochester, scouring the city for every piece of relevant information regarding the life of Howard Ross.

He seemed surprised at her ignorance. "*The Erie Canal?* Flows right through Rochester."

Oksana's mind flashed back to her own water-divided city of Magnitogorsk at the southern end of the Urals.

"Oh, yes," she said. "Well, I have heard of that. The Erie Canal. I didn't know where it was, exactly that is. I knew it was out east somewhere. How long did you live there…in Rochester?"

Ross finished his last morsel of prime rib with a generous dose of horseradish. "From birth to draft."

"I'm sorry, from birth to what?"

Ross chuckled and tossed his napkin onto the table. "From birth to the *draft*. Remember that little thing that interrupted all of our lives, that little nuisance we used to call the Great War? The war to end all wars? I know, it was a little before your time."

This is fascinating.

He is being completely honest about his past. No cover story, no deception. Just…Howard Ross.

Time for Debbie Sullivan to pour it on.

"You were drafted into the First World War? How exciting!"

Ross cupped his hands and ignited his third cigarette of the evening. "Big heroes like me were in high-demand to drive those damn Krauts back to Berlin."

She arched over her plate, brimming with enthusiasm. "Wait a minute…are you telling me you fought in Europe? You saw actual, real-life combat?"

Ross released the smoke through his nostrils. "Trench warfare in France," he replied. "I was a machine gunner. We used Colt-Brownings. I sent more than a few dozen Germans on a one-way trip to meet their maker. I've been told some of them were high-level officers."

Oksana beamed and selected her words with careful precision. "I would love to hear more of these stories."

Because that's all that Ross' words were at this point…just *stories*. Oksana had memorized his extensive military service record.

He hadn't fabricated all of it; he actually had been drafted in the middle of September of 1918. But that's the moment when his civilian life ended, and the point in the account when his horrible lies began. Not only had Howard Ross failed to see active duty in France, he never experienced as much as a single hour of boot camp.

Ross enjoyed a comfortable desk on the quiet eastern seaboard, rather than surviving the brutal conditions down in a muddy foxhole along the western front. He typically slaved away at a typewriter alongside a Marconi wireless, a far cry from the 30-caliber machine gun placement he always boasted.

Signal's intelligence in the US military was in its infancy during the closing months of the Great War. Young, bright prospects were screened for code-breaking aptitude to join the ranks of a fledgling division known obscurely as MI-8.

As a result of his exceptional test scores, Ross was whisked away to a non-descript brick building in midtown Manhattan to inaugurate his multi-decade career in cryptology.

Within a few years of the war's conclusion, MI-8 was officially disbanded and then reconstituted as the Military Intelligence Division under the brilliant oversight of Herbert Yardley. Most of the former analysts were let go, but Ross survived the harsh bureaucratic scalpel. Yardley detected an uncommon drive within the young man from upstate New York (Yardley's formative report on Howard Ross in 1921 referenced his "indomitable passion and flash of genius").

Despite a decade of proven results, Yardley's dream team—affectionately known as the "American Black Chamber"—was dissolved. By April of 1930, their enormous intelligence archives were scavenged and transferred to the Army's newly formed Signal Intelligence Service.

After the departmental dismemberment dust had settled, Yardley was out, yet Howard Ross remained. Unscathed.

His tenure persisted as the turbulent years of the 1930s drew to a climax, and his division within the SIS monitored the alarming developments brewing inside Germany, Japan, and the Soviet Union with justified suspicion. Ross endured as those catastrophic regional forces plunged the world into a tragic repeat performance, albeit on a grander and much deadlier scale.

Howard Ross, in effect, became the singular thread of continuity in American signal's intelligence that would span between and through two world wars.

And he knew it.

Six months after President Roosevelt's reluctant entry into the global conflict, he established the Office of Strategic Services as a curious wartime blend of bureaucratic problems and solutions. Ross accepted a promotion within the OSS and was stationed overseas in Istanbul as a high-level intelligence handler. His open-ended mandate led him to travel freely and discreetly throughout much of the Middle East and

Europe until the Axis powers caved beneath the unsupportable weight of their own expansionist greed.

Germany fell.

Japan fell.

Even the OSS fell.

But Howard Ross prevailed.

As the messy and territorial transition from the OSS to the Strategic Services Unit played out, followed by the murky and short-lived ascension of the Central Intelligence Group, Oksana discovered that Ross' personnel records became oddly fragmented before falling totally silent after the spring of 1947.

It was clear to her that once Project SATURN was born, the man Howard Ross ceased to exist.

Oksana gazed in mild fascination as the untouchable intelligence artifact across the table flagged down their waiter and ordered two servings of Cherries Jubilee. Ross smothered the remnants of his latest cigarette into a lead crystal ashtray.

"Now, don't go complaining about how rare and uncooked the dessert is," he teased. "It's supposed to be red, inside and out. And sweet. Just like your lips. Or, at least, that's how I imagine them to be."

She raised her eyebrows playfully as the live orchestra started a fresh melody. "I guess some things are only learned by experience."

"Is that an offer?" he asked.

"Mr. Ross, the word *offer* sounds too…oh, I don't know. Maybe too businesslike. I'm not too keen on business."

"Completely understandable. So let me rephrase it then. Miss Sullivan, was that an *invitation*?"

She frowned. "Well…now it sounds too formal. How about we just let things develop…naturally?"

"I'm a big fan of nature," he mused. "We've got a few minutes til dessert arrives. Join me for a dance."

Concern clouded her face as she glanced towards a growing cluster of couples moving out onto the hardwood. "Oh, I don't know. This tune is a little fast for me."

He circled around the table and lifted her arm tenderly. "That sounded a lot like a *no*. I'm not used to hearing that word in my world. Just relax. Live a little. Come on."

Oksana rose to her feet with some reluctance and they navigated through the maze of tables and out onto the crowded dance floor. It was awkward at first.

He pulled her in close and whispered, "Let me take the lead."

She rested her trembling head against his strong shoulder.

Never in a million years, Mr. Ross. Never in a million years.

CHAPTER 12

Despite Chief McCloud's attempt to create a casual environment at the police station on Wednesday night, the tension was impossible to dispel. Certainly the last twenty-four hours had justified a heightened level of stress and apprehension in almost every respect.

In many ways, it was a tale of two women. One nearly dead, the other very much alive…both claiming to be from the future.

Denver and Doc Stonecroft were the last to arrive to the solemn and unprecedented meeting. McCloud jumped up and led the attractive woman across the concrete to greet them. Shep, the only other participant, remained in his chair.

The Chief pointed. "Brenda Jo Tilley, I'd like to introduce you to Dr. Glen Stonecroft—"

"Dr. Stonecroft," she offered with a subtle nod and a firm handshake.

"The extreme pleasure is all mine, Miss Tilley. And by all means, my dear, call me Doc." He peered down at her hand. "My, quite the lovely ring. Is that a ruby?"

She pulled her hand back and showcased it briefly. "I think so. It was a gift from my mother."

McCloud wagged a finger at Denver. "And this is Mr. Denver…*Jackson*."

"Mr. Jackson," she acknowledged.

"Call me Denver." He paused. "Yes. Like the city in Colorado."

Brenda Jo put on a weak grin as she grasped his hand. "*Denver*. And I love Colorado. Especially the mountains."

The Chief was beaming proudly, and glanced over at Shep for just an instant. "Well, come now, Miss Tilley. Now that we're all acquainted, let's have a seat. Right this way. Denver, would you mind lockin' the door?"

Denver obeyed as McCloud stepped over to the window and reached for the cord to shut the blinds. The Chief leaned forward and craned his neck, laying the left side of his face against the glass. "It can't be," he mumbled.

"What's the matter, James?" Doc inquired.

McCloud shoved back and bolted for the door, almost plowing over a returning Denver.

"Whoa there, Chief!" he yelled in a side-step.

McCloud seemed oblivious to the near-collision as he threw the door open and raced outside. Everyone traded puzzled glances as Denver snuck up behind him.

"Where's the fire, Chief?"

McCloud flung his head from side to side and folded his thick arms. There was a long pause. "I, uh, I don't know," he offered weakly. "I don't know."

"To be honest, I don't think I've ever seen you move that fast."

The Chief spun about and faced him. "I saw…someone."

Denver scanned the area. "Quite a few people out and about. Any particular someone?"

"You could say that."

"Who?"

McCloud grew wide-eyed and took his time. "*You.*"

"Me?"

"Never mind, I must've been mistaken. Let's get back inside."

"So, is this all of you?" Brenda Jo asked, with disappointment hiding inside each hesitant word. "Just four time travelers? I, uh, I thought there would be more. Am I the only lady?"

The Chief started to speak when Shep coughed and shot him a hard look. "Well, I know you must have many questions," McCloud responded. "But…all in good time, Miss Tilley. All in good time."

Doc leaned forward and placed his thick hands on his knees. "Miss Tilley, I must say, it is quite thrilling to meet with you this fine evening. Would you be so kind as to indulge this educated geriatric with just a tiny portion of your personal history?" He took off his glasses and smiled. "And please, my dear…relax. No one present intends any mischief to come your way, I can assure you."

She rubbed her palms across her thighs and cleared her throat. "Thank you, Dr. Stonecroft…*Doc*…I really do appreciate it. I hope you can understand how…how hard this is for me, and why I'm so nervous."

"Understandable. Completely," he reassured her. "Please continue, when you are ready."

She took a moment to gaze at each of the strangers seated around the room before staring at the floor. "As Chief McCloud told you, I am Brenda Jo Tilley. I'm thirty-one years old. I am from Arkansas, all over northern Arkansas actually. *Go Razorbacks*." She hesitated and her smile faded fast. "Anyway, that is, until about three years ago."

Her chin quivered.

"I, uh, it was May back home. May the eighth. In 1987." Her eyes started to flood and McCloud snagged a few tissues for her.

"Thank you, Chief. Really," she said.

Shep didn't waste time. "What was the date when you arrived here…to the past?"

She dabbed the corners of her reddening eyes. "Like I said, Mr. Sheppard, it was about three years ago. It was in

September. September of 1953. The *fifteenth* if I remember correctly."

"You came to us from the year 1987, you say?" Doc inquired, staring over at Shep.

"Yessir, Doc. In May. It had been a beautiful spring."

Doc rested his chin on his hand and then squinted. "Mr. Jackson? Would you be so kind as to escort Miss Tilley outside for a few moments? It won't be long."

Denver jumped up. "Absolutely. No problem, Doc. Miss Tilley? Right this way."

She rose out of her seat with some trepidation. "What's wrong? Is it something I said?"

"No, no, no, my dear," Doc offered. "Just a tiny matter of protocol and procedure that needs to be deliberated. Trust me, it's us…not *you*. It will only be a momentary delay."

Denver guided her across the room and soon they disappeared out onto the sidewalk.

The Chief nodded as the door closed. He turned around and leaned his back against it. "Doc's right, Shep. You know the rules."

A defiant Robert Sheppard crossed his arms. "What? Are you serious? *No*. I'm not leaving. I don't need anyone's damn permission to be here!"

"Ain't no one above the Second Accord, Sheppard. You know that. They exist to protect all of us. You included."

"Oh, so you didn't care about the Second Accord when you asked me and Frazier to do your dirty work down at Ellen's house this morning, but, tonight it's a different story, huh?!"

Doc slid his spectacles back on. "I'm afraid that Chief McCloud and I are in complete and uniform harmony, Mr. Sheppard. Our female candidate is purportedly twenty years into your future. Simple knowledge of physical items is one thing, but discussion of people and events in your presence would comprise a potentially catastrophic trespass of the Second Ac—"

"Spare me another book-length lecture, Stonecroft," Shep hollered out over his shoulder as he stood and made his way for the back door. He glared over at them before exiting. "I told you earlier, McCloud, and I'm telling you again. It's a helluva mistake including Colorado in any of this. You'll see."

He tugged the door open and was gone.

The Chief hurried across the station and relocked the back door. "That could've gone…*better*."

Stonecroft sighed. "With all due respect, Chief McCloud, we both know that such outbursts are but par for the course when it comes to Mr. Robert Sheppard. As predictable as they are unpleasant."

The Chief chuckled as he navigated back to the front entrance. "That's what I admire 'bout you, Doc. Even when you unload your gripes about someone, it still sounds all flowery and gracious."

"Criticism need not be harsh in order to be appropriate, my friend."

The Chief opened the front door. "I suppose not, Doc." He leaned out. "*Hey!* Mr. Jackson and Miss Tilley. Come on back in. The water's fine."

Doc stood as a matter of courtesy. "Welcome back," he chimed as they filed through. Brenda Jo looked around.

"Mr. Sheppard had to…attend to some urgent business," the Chief explained. "Please, have a seat once again, ma'am."

"Miss Tilley," Doc began as all took to their chairs, "what can you tell me about the world in 1987?"

Her face scrunched up. "Um, I'm not exactly sure what you mean by that, Mr. Stonecroft." Panic formed in her eyes. "You do believe me, don't you? Why would I make any of this up? *Do you honestly think I'm lying?!*"

"Now take it easy there, Brenda Jo," McCloud cautioned in a soothing voice. "This's all just standard procedure. Surely you understand just how important it is for all of us to be on the same page."

She blew her nose. "I'm not a liar!"

"And not a solitary figure in this informal assembly would dare accuse you of such, my dear," Stonecroft promised her. "But, please, what can you tell us of your time?"

Brenda Jo lowered her tissue and wadded it up. "What do you wanna know? What? Something about President Reagan, or, or that terrible nuclear accident over in Russia about a year before I traveled here? Chair-something or other."

"*Chernobyl,*" Doc corrected with his trademark gentleness.

"Yeah, that's it." She looked around. "What else? Home computers, video games? What do you want from me?"

Denver joined in. "What can you remember about the 60s or the 70s?"

"Well, I was only four or five when JFK was assassinated. I remember some of it…not well, though." She paused and concentrated on her lap. "Um, the Vietnam War…Nixon, Watergate. I am not making this stuff up. How could I? It hasn't happened yet…none of it has!"

A cascade of tears raced down her red cheeks. "Listen to me! I've spent the last three years thinking I was either crazy or deluded or maybe something worse. I've considered taking my life at least a hundred times."

Brenda abandoned her chair and paced around the room. "I've had to lie, steal, and run from place to place. And then, then I hear about you guys. Finally some hope. Please don't turn me away!"

The Chief rushed out of his seat. "Now listen, hope's right here. Right, guys? Am I right?"

Doc rose up and drew alongside. "More than hope, my dear. Oh, much more. Not merely the chance for hope, but the chance to go home."

She pivoted around, eyes wide. "Really? Go home, as in *home to 1987?* Home? To Arkansas?"

Doc released a comforting laugh. "Yes…and *yes* again."

She kicked off her shoes and danced around the room, exchanging tears for laughter. "*You're serious?*" she cried out. "I mean, really serious? There's a chance I can go home? See my mom and dad again?"

"If that's what you want," the Chief added.

"I wanna see my folks more than anything!" She came to a spinning stop by Denver. "So, tell me, Mr. Jackson, what's waiting for you back home?"

He fished out his new wallet and retrieved a small photograph. She knelt by him and examined it. "Wow, she is adorable! Is this your daughter?"

"My one and only. My whole world. *Jasmine.*"

"Jasmine? That is so beautiful! Beautiful." A question seemed to cross her face. "But what about a *Mrs.* Jackson? Is she waiting for you?"

Denver rubbed his chin. "Well, now that's, it's…*complicated.*"

Brenda jumped up. "Sorry, none of my business. Forget I asked."

"Speaking of asking," Doc intervened. "If I may…where did you jump to, in 1953?"

She studied him. "*Where?* As I said, I'm from Arkansas…near Jonesboro. Craighead County."

"Yes, yes," he replied. "But where exactly did you jump *to?*"

She froze momentarily but recovered. "Well, I was asleep on my back porch in Jonesboro, near the edge of town. The next thing I knew, I was on a farm. In Jonesboro. 1953." She took a few steps toward the windows. "I realized later that it was the same spot, but it was all rural farmland thirty years earlier."

Doc made eye contact with the Chief. McCloud shrugged as his own smile diminished by noticeable degrees.

"And now, after three years of searching—here you are!" McCloud exclaimed.

"You have no idea how happy I am right now!" she declared. "I feel light as a feather!"

"And rightly so," the Chief noted. "So, if you don't mind me askin', who or what pointed you in our direction?"

She lifted the blinds and peered outside. "Well, this may sound far-fetched."

"Oh, in case you hadn't noticed," McCloud remarked, "our whole existence is kinda far-fetched."

"We thrive on it," Denver added. "Trust me."

"Fair enough," Brenda countered as she turned back around. "But the gentleman that guided me asked to remain *anonymous*. Don't ask me why. He was pretty firm about it."

The Chief reclined against his desk. "That's a strange one," he admitted. "But, uh, you can understand our concern about any—*outsiders*—that're aware of our little group here."

"One hundred percent," she said. "Absolutely. And speaking of your little group here, how many of us are there?"

McCloud paused. "Present company included? Oh, that'd be thirteen."

Her eyes brightened up and she inched closer to the Chief. "*Thirteen?* Really? I hope you don't consider me as unlucky. You know, *unlucky thirteen*."

"Not a chance, darlin'."

"I'll take your word for it," she said. "So, thirteen…all here in Normal?"

McCloud bobbed his head. "More'r less."

"Amazing." She knelt to slip her shoes back on. "Now, please don't tell me I'm the only gal." She glanced up and over at Denver. "This isn't a *boys-only* club is it, Mr. Jackson?"

"Oh, yes…that," Doc interjected. "Well, actually Mr. Jackson is Mr. *Collins*, but we will wait for a more convenient season to clarify that necessary point of confusion. But on to your more pressing question—my dear Miss Tilley," Doc said. "You would now be our sixth member of the fairer sex. Perhaps even the seventh, but the proverbial jury is still out on that regard."

"You gentlemen don't know how many women are among you?"

Denver squinted. "It…it's complicated."

She held her hands up. "Well, sixth, seventh…who cares? I'm here! When do I get to meet everyone and see everything?"

McCloud glanced over at Doc. "Soon, very soon."

She tried to suppress a smile. "I've waited years for this day to come."

CHAPTER 13

Friday, March 26, 1948, 6:20 p.m.
Golden Nugget Restaurant
Las Vegas, Nevada

Howard Ross indulged in the finer things.

And on Fremont Street, no restaurant was finer than the Golden Nugget.

"My boss told me this place was nice," Oksana observed. "Dennis never said it was this nice."

"*Dennis* has excellent taste," Ross said.

She eyed the contents of the handcrafted, leather-bound menu by the light of a crystal chandelier suspended far above them. "And he must have an excellent budget. Wow. I couldn't afford the bread and water here."

Ross hadn't touched his own menu. "I'm pretty sure they have complimentary peanuts over at the bar. If you can swipe a glass, you can probably even get free water in the ladies room." He winked at her cute face as she glanced up in protest.

"I just might do that one day. Don't tempt me, Mr. Ross."

Howard sipped on his black coffee. "Well, Miss Sullivan, I hereby give you full and complete permission to tempt me. At any and all times."

She acted like she didn't hear him. "So, what's good here?"

"Anything that starts with a letter of the alphabet," he answered.

Oksana rested the bottom of her menu on the table and peered at him over the top. "I was hoping for something a little more specific."

"What sounds good to you?"

She scanned the pages. "It might help if I knew what some of these dishes even were."

Howard hung a cigarette on his lower lip and lit it. "Try something new, something fresh. Broaden your horizons. If you don't like it, try something else."

She flipped back to the list of entrees. "Are you serious? That could be one expensive experiment."

"It's only money." He released a column of smoke. "Your happiness is more valuable than the cash it takes to achieve it."

"What do you like here?"

Ross slipped the cigarette out of his mouth and slapped it against a metal ashtray. "I'm fiercely loyal to the same meal whenever I visit the Nugget," he noted. "Ribeye and lobster. Medium well. Caesar salad."

Oksana frowned as she glanced down and rubbed her ring. "My mom was allergic to seafood. She almost died one time after eating shrimp at my cousin's wedding. It was pretty scary. I was little, but I can still remember it clear as a bell."

"I have the opposite damn problem," Ross insisted after another pull on his smoke. "I would probably die if I *didn't* get to eat seafood."

"Well, I've never tried it. Like mother like daughter as they say. In my mind, death always seemed to outweigh any dish. No matter how tasty."

"You're playing it too safe. Boring. Living on the edge is more fun," Ross quipped.

Oksana leaned forward and set her menu down. "Personally, I don't like *edges*…or ledges, or anything that has a sudden and long drop anywhere near it." She shot him a smug smile. "So, *no thank you.* I am perfectly happy eating things that walk on the ground or maybe fly in the air."

"Your loss."

Something caught her eye and she craned her neck to the side. "Or that roll by on a cart, topped by strawberries. Beautiful strawberries. You can keep your death-lobster. I'll take a few orders of what they're having."

Ross matched her stare as the waiter eased to a stop at a booth occupied by a few suits along the nearest wall. "Oh, that. Well, maybe there is hope for you, Miss Sullivan. Good choice. Cheesecake. An oldie but a goodie. It's good here, but you can't beat the way they make it back home."

She nodded towards the booth. "Looks like they're celebrating something."

He glanced over then back at her. "This is Vegas. Probably business. Deals happen every day, all day. Some legal, some...*not quite.*"

She took a slow and thoughtful drink as she studied him.

Business.

And you know quite a bit about business, don't you, Mr. Ross?

Darkstar also appreciated the value of business.

In fact, after weeks of searching, it was a business meeting at this same restaurant that had ultimately betrayed the undisclosed location of the invisible head of a non-existent division within an agency rarely acknowledged as much more than the Company.

For Darkstar, business was good for business.

Especially when that business is espionage.

Russian cryptanalysts in the basement of the Soviet embassy in DC had cracked a series of low-level messages three weeks before in early March. One innocuous memo mentioned an upcoming dinner meeting between a Dennis

Masterson, construction contractor out of Los Angeles, and one Howard Ross. The location: the Golden Nugget.

Darkstar had landed in Las Vegas less than thirty hours later.

Their waiter reappeared and lingered like a silent servant beside her. Ross gestured for Oksana to glance up.

"Oh, yes," she said, almost startled. "I'm sorry. I'll take…the steak and *lobster*." She winked at Howard. "Medium well. With a Caesar salad."

"An excellent choice," the waiter commented with a slight nod.

"It's time to live on the edge," Oksana replied.

CHAPTER 14

Chief McCloud eased the squad car into a parking slot in front of the *Normal Journal* and killed the motor. From the back seat Denver gazed through the passenger window at the all-too familiar newspaper office. This hadn't been the first time the Chief had ushered him into the back seat and then dropped him off here.

I break in once, and now I've worked here twice. Crazy, absolutely crazy.

"This'll sure be a nice change of pace from working down at the factory," McCloud insisted.

"Oh boy, can't wait," Denver moaned.

He was overplaying his dissatisfaction.

Come on, Collins…any day away from Robert Sheppard is a good day.

The Chief hunched over and tapped Alexus Daniels on the shoulder. "Don't listen to him…he's actually very excited to be back."

"Oh, yeah. Very excited. My last experience working here was for thirty days, by judicial decree," Denver mused. "How long's our new punishment, er, I mean, *assignment?*"

"Ellen said Miss Larson could be out for a few days, or weeks, or even a few months," Alexus answered. "I'm worried about all of this. She said she could even die."

"Worrying won't change anything," McCloud added. "And irregardless of how you feel, you two're the best qualified to do this, and you both know it."

"All I did was help James print the newspaper on Thursdays," Denver protested. "Wait. What is today?"

"Thursday," Alexus answered.

"Wow. Well, I can't imagine he's gonna be printing anything today," Denver observed. "Especially with Betty out since Tuesday. She usually proofed everything by late Wednesday, sometimes even on Thursday morning. Besides, most of the time I was out assisting Hank on remodeling jobs. I'm not sure what type of real help I'm gonna be."

The Chief caught Denver's eyes in the rearview mirror. "That's why there's two of you. Lexi here has a few years of journalism classes under her belt, and you…well, you've at least worked with James before."

"What did you tell him?" Denver asked.

"Tell who?"

"*James*. What did you tell him was going on?"

The Chief rotated around as best he could, with his left side pressed against the steering wheel. "I told James that Betty had a death in the family and she had to leave town suddenly. I said Betty had called and asked me to give James the keys and to get the two of you to help him cover things til she returned. "

"What if she *doesn't* return?" Alexus asked, her voice cracking.

McCloud yanked the keys out of the ignition and picked up his officer's cap. "I kinda think we need to keep thinkin' positive thoughts. Being negative and all won't change a dang thing."

"It's called being realistic," Denver mumbled.

"Listen, we've been through way worse'n this," McCloud declared. "And we'll get through this little speedbump, too. C'mon, let's go…you only have to put out one paper a week."

The less-than-enthused trio exited the sedan, and the Chief rotated through the wad of keys at the front door. "So I was thinking, Lexi," he said. "I could call Mayor Vorhees and get you an interview 'bout something or another. Politicians are always looking for exposure. You could even interview me. I can always stir things up, getcha a good quote or two."

The lock refused at first but then gave way. "Ah, success." The Chief pushed it open and bowed slightly. "After you, folks."

Denver allowed Alexus to pass through before him. He glanced over at McCloud. "I'm still having some real reservations about all of this, Chief."

McCloud pulled in behind and shut the door. "Reservations or not, we really need you two to do this. We gotta keep up appearances 'round town."

"Appearances?" Alexus blurted. "I don't think a female black reporter in her early twenties is quite normal for Normal. I doubt it's even safe."

The Chief didn't flinch. "Times are already a-changin', Lexi," he said. "Remember, not quite a year ago Rosa Parks set some things in motion."

Denver spun around. "Really? That whole back of the bus thing, and the protests? That *just* happened?"

"December of last year," Alexus explained. "The Supreme Court is about to shock the nation, too. Doc said it's coming in just a few weeks."

"See there," McCloud agreed, "that's what I'm talking 'bout. Change is coming. It's gotta start somewhere…might as well be here!"

Alexus peered down at the floor and crossed her arms.

"A court's decision may change the law, Chief, but it doesn't necessarily change hearts."

CHAPTER 15

Doc Stonecroft was in the height of his glory.

"Are your accommodations with Mrs. Swan acceptable, Miss Tilley?" he asked.

Brenda Jo nodded. "Oh, yes, Dr. Stonecroft. Leah and Tori have been really wonderful. It's nice to see that Southern hospitality is alive and well this far north."

"And how has life as an involuntary journalist been treating you the last few days, Trailer Collins?"

Denver folded his arms. "Well, I don't know who your sources are, Doc…but they are completely mistaken. I am not, nor should anyone under any circumstances allow me to pretend to be *a writer*."

Doc grinned. "Am I to assume that the reports of your journalistic intentions are greatly exaggerated?"

Denver stared up at the white concrete ceiling. "Why does that statement seem so familiar?"

"Twain," Doc replied.

Brenda Jo's face scrunched up. "Twain? Two? I don't get it."

"Mark," Denver offered.

"Still nothing."

Denver patted her on the shoulder. "It's complicated."

With all the fresh enthusiasm of a first-season park tour guide, Doc led the pair back out of the Jump Portal Chamber. "Mr. Collins, would you be so kind as to reseal the chamber door there behind Miss Tilley?"

Denver wasted no time. "Sure, Doc."

Brenda Jo shook her head and examined a control panel as Denver rejoined them. "I really don't know what's more amazing," she began, "waking up in 1953 or walking down here and seeing all of...*this*. It's hard to imagine that I am standing only a few feet away from an atomic power plant."

Doc chuckled as he beamed. "You can be assured, my newest friend, that the summit of your amazement has yet to be ascended. My colleagues and I are preparing a demonstration of our capabilities that will redefine your very concept of *amazement*. You will see, in a mere matter of days."

Denver strolled towards the reactor room. "Brenda Jo just reminded me of a question I never got around to asking you, Doc."

"Well then, ask away, Trailer Collins."

Denver pressed his forehead against the thick glass window inset in the formidable door. "Where in the world did you guys get all of the nuclear material in that room?"

Doc's head bobbed as he strode towards Denver. "An excellent question and one to be expected," he began. "It is certainly not *common* knowledge, but there were several accidental losses of atomic material in the years following World War II by the US Military. Since we were privy to that information, coupled with the general whereabouts of those incidents, Mr. Nelson was wise to lead a few expeditions to recover that material and then relocate it here."

"Wasn't that a severe violation of the First Accord? And risky?" Denver inquired. "I mean, stealing nuclear materials during the Cold War is a heck of a way to avoid leaving footprints!"

"Another volley of excellent and pertinent questions," Doc said. "But, in our defense, since we were afforded with the incalculable benefit of historical knowledge, we knew that those materials were never recovered. So, Mr. Nelson felt we were merely appropriating items that would never have been found."

Denver wasn't satisfied. "But maybe the reason the nuclear materials were never found is because we took them. I guess it's kind of like the chicken-or-the-egg thing."

Doc polished his glasses. "Such are the mysteries of time and temporal causation," he lamented. "There are no easy answers, I will grant you that."

Brenda Jo frowned. "You two are making this poor Southern gal's head hurt!"

Stonecroft slid his glasses back on and laughed. "Please, Miss Tilley, allow me and my colleagues to bear the burden of puzzled minds and aching heads. You need not trouble yours."

She squinted. "Well, a little late for that! But now I've got another question."

"Questions appear to be the entrée of choice on today's tour menu," Doc responded.

"Well, if and when y'all get that portal contraption working…we can't just walk back into the future looking like that, can we?" She pointed at Denver's clothing and then her own. "Or dressed like this. We would immediately draw some unwanted attention, wouldn't we?"

"A most excellent and astute observation, my dear Miss Tilley. Actually, Mr. Nelson, our founder we spoke of moments ago, wisely anticipated that very concern." Doc strolled over to a free-standing double-door cabinet. "Mr. Collins? Would you please relocate this refrigeration unit to the right about four feet? And carefully, mind you. Watch the power cord."

Denver was puzzled but obeyed. Doc continued. "This, Mr. Collins, is probably even somewhat of a revelation for you. With all that you have endured, and your unfortunate incarceration, I do not recall having the distinct pleasure of giving you the full tour."

The tall unit gave way under Denver's considerable strain and slid sideways, exposing a hidden door inlaid into the wall.

"Well, that's new," Denver blurted out.

"New to you, perhaps," Doc observed, "but all part of the original plan several years ago." Stonecroft took a step closer and rubbed Denver's shirt. "Now, to turns things about…let *me* propose a question for you, Mr. Collins. Where are the garments you were wearing when you arrived to Normal back in early August?"

Denver raised his eyebrows and rocked back on his heels. "Hmm…I figured Chief McCloud sold them at a garage sale for a quarter or something. Maybe burned them. Hadn't really thought much about those clothes. I've been busy…being arrested, then electrocuted, then arrested again, sentenced to prison, then community service. Busy."

"Indeed, indeed," Doc noted with a subtle chuckle. "Well, one of our initial priorities after we discover a fellow Jumper, besides taking a TRS sample, is to collect all their possessions including clothing and so forth, and to store them here."

Stonecroft produced a set of keys and unlocked the door. It swung open without a sound. Doc stepped aside and motioned within. "Lady and gentleman, I present to you…The Vault."

Denver allowed Brenda Jo to pass inside first, as he peered over her shoulder. Doc flipped the light switch. Three clothing racks filled with long, hanging garment bags, and a few dozen boxes occupied the musty space. Everything was organized and everything was labeled.

She leaned forward and inspected the nearest rack. "Well lookie here…*Denver Wayne Collins.*"

Denver came alongside and unzipped the bag. He pulled out a familiar sleeve and resisted the urge to smell it. "I love this old hoodie." A fair amount of nostalgia broke through his voice as he pointed. "It still has the dirt stains where McCloud face-planted me in that field with a tranquilizer dart."

Brenda Jo shot him a confused look.

"It's...*complicated,*" he said as he zipped up the clothes bag.

Doc joined them. "Quite a little collection here. We even have Ms. Larson's office safe in the back corner. Besides clothing, we have watches and jewelry, purses and wallets. All perfectly normal and acceptable back in our respective times, but quite a liability here, as you well remember Mr. Collins."

Denver anticipated Brenda Jo's unspoken question and glanced over at her. She grinned. "So, I guess there's a complicated story there as well?"

"Yeah," he said, keeping his voice low. "It's nothing really. It just involves my wallet, and the FBI, and probably a nationwide manhunt that could lead to our eventual capture and probable torture. But...forget it."

Brenda Jo pushed forward and knelt behind one of the racks. "This box says *Phillip Nelson*— I don't think I've met him yet. Didn't you just say he is the founder?"

"Yes, but rather *was* the founder, Miss Tilley," Doc corrected.

She leaned up. "*Was?*"

"Mr. Nelson—*God rest his soul*—passed away about three years ago. It was a debilitating blow. I suppose we are maintaining his personal effects here for primarily sentimental reasons."

Denver looked away.

If you only knew, Doc.

If you only knew. Just wait a few more days.

You'll be needing those personal effects.

Doc seemed lost in thought. "To dispose of them would almost seem a sacrilege, at least to many of us."

"I agree," Denver interjected. "We should keep them. You never know when you might need stuff like that."

Doc proceeded back across the threshold. "But, in any respect, once we overcome our efficiency issues and the portal has been properly calibrated for each respective Jumper, then one by one, and after much tearful embraces and heartfelt goodbyes, I'm sure, each of us will gather our personal effects and don our former attire."

He encouraged them to exit with a wave. "And then we shall individually step into the glorious light of an instantaneous jump back home. Not all at once, of course. The capacitors will have to be recharged after no more than three jumps." He folded his arms. "Miss Tilley, have you managed to retain the wardrobe that you arrived with in 1953?"

"Sorry," Brenda Jo replied as she sauntered out. "That adorable outfit is long gone, I'm afraid. It wasn't expensive, but it was very me."

"Well," Doc said, "that is not of utmost concern at this juncture."

Brenda Jo strolled across the room and examined the walls, the doors, the stairs for several seconds before spinning around. "Are there any other ways in or out of this *tomb?*"

Doc turned to the side. "Pardon me?"

"Well, sorry to sound morbid," she said. "It's just that I can't imagine living, or working down here. Day after day. I've never liked basements. It's nice and all, just not for me. I can help upstairs in the factory or maybe out front with Leah."

"It is a windowless means to an end, child. One grows accustomed to it."

She wandered about. "Dr. Stonecroft, you said a moment ago that you were preparing to show us something. Something *amazing*."

He smiled and removed his spectacles. "Yes, ma'am. We have been somewhat shorthanded of late down here, with Miss Finegan attending to Ms. Larson's recovery. But very soon, I promise you, we will be unveiling our marvelous breakthrough."

"Will you be showing this to *everyone*? To every single Jumper? All at the same time?" she asked.

Doc took a seat at the conference table and slid his glasses back on after a brief inspection. "That is our noble intention, Miss Tilley. Perhaps as soon as Sunday afternoon or evening."

Her face lit up and she clasped her hands.

"Everyone gathered together in one place…how wonderful."

CHAPTER 16

Saturday, March 27, 1948, 9:44 p.m.
Last Frontier Hotel
Las Vegas, Nevada

The coat check attendant returned to the busy counter after a considerable delay. Howard Ross wore his irritation in plain sight.

"Bout damn time."

"Sorry about the wait, folks," the clerk apologized. "One of the tags had become dislodged. These are the correct garments?"

"They are." Ross snatched his overcoat and Oksana's box coat and made no attempt to hide the fact he was shoving the customary tip back into his own pocket. "Come on, let's go." He cupped her right elbow and guided her through the rustic motif of the casino foyer.

She shot him a look. "Whoa…why the rush? It's Saturday night. I don't have to be anywhere until Monday morning. Do you?" She stopped. "Wait, let me guess…the information business never sleeps?"

He slowed to a crawl and assisted with her lavender jacket. "You have no idea just how right you are, Miss Sullivan."

She slid her right hand through the sleeve and loosely twirled into his arms. "So, tell me. Why did you get so grumpy with that poor fellow back there?" She teased the end of his tie. "He's just doing his job."

"You mean *not* doing his job." They strolled through the large front doors as the cool breeze of the Nevada night greeted them. "There are a number of things I hate," Ross began. "First, I hate Mondays—"

"I agree. I wholeheartedly agree. No more talk of Mondays."

He squinted at her and cleared his throat. "I hate being *interrupted.*"

She drew her fingers across her smiling lips like an imaginary zipper and tossed the invisible key over her shoulder.

"Exactly," he affirmed while donning his dark wool overcoat. "And I hate inefficiency and the delays it usually causes."

She circled behind him to adjust the wayward collar on his jacket. "Lighten up, Howard," she scolded. "It has been a wonderful evening. A gal couldn't ask for a nicer, let's see, what was this? Our…fourth date? Anyway, it was a wonderful dinner, wonderful entertainment—"

"So you did enjoy the show? You never said anything the whole time."

Oksana stepped back around and peered up into his face. "Well, I'll admit—the Stagecoach Beauties showgirls were okay, but it was all a little too risqué if you ask me. Their outfits didn't leave much to the imagination. Looked more like bathing suits to me, if that."

"Really?" he asked. "They were risqué? I didn't notice. I guess I was too caught up in the choreography and the music and all. The décor in the Ramona Room is quite stunning."

Oksana punched his shoulder. "You may be a good dancer and conversationalist, but you are one terrible fibber, Mr. Howard Ross."

He looked hurt. "You know, now that you mention it, I think you're right. There was one point I might've noticed that a few of them had nice legs. I can't be positive though. It all happened so fast."

"A few of them had nice legs?" she blurted out on the edge of laughter. "I think that every other woman in the room ceased existing the moment the *Rockettes* back there started kicking for the sky."

He reached down and toyed with her hand. "And I have no earthly idea what you're talking about. Did you at least enjoy the Boyd Sisters?"

"Wait—I see what you did there. You're trying to change the subject, you dog."

He played along. "I will do my best, Miss Sullivan, to overlook the completely unfair canine comparison." He grinned. "So, did you enjoy them?"

She began strolling towards his sedan, with him in tow. "*Enjoy?* Enjoy is hardly the word. Such talent. All three of them. And what wonderful harmonies. I think they must really be sisters or cousins at the very least. It takes blood to blend together like that."

"As far as singing acts go, they're one of my favorites here on the strip," he said. "They always put on one helluva good show. Always something different. I've seen them probably three or four times."

They arrived at his four-door and she obsessed with her own reflection in the passenger window. Oksana primped her blonde hair and pivoted from side to side. "Do you think their hair color is natural?"

He searched for his keys. "Who?"

"*The Boyd trio*. Do you think all three of them are actually blondes?"

Ross rested against the vehicle and slowly maneuvered his arms around her waist. "That question has never even once crossed my mind, but to be honest…other thoughts have. Especially of late."

"I noticed that the youngest one seemed to have darker roots. She was usually on the far right. She was also the best dancer."

He shifted closer. "You don't say?"

Oksana's eyebrows shot up. "Come to think of it, any one of them could've been wearing a wig. Or maybe all of them." She pushed back and looked into his eyes. "Be honest with me, and don't even think about fibbing. Every gal knows that every man has his own particular taste in women. Do you prefer blondes, Howard?"

The insincere question was purely rhetorical.

Oksana was merely making good conversation. It was all for show.

Three uninterrupted weeks of intensive intelligence gathering in Rochester and New York City were rewarded by a wealth of background information not contained in the documents smuggled out by the Pentagon mole. Ink and paper could typically reveal details such as where, what, and when…but the KGB assassin needed more.

She needed the *who*.

The *why*.

Her mission throughout New York centered on a trio of primary objectives. First, to formulate an accurate psychological profile of her target. Second, to determine his hobbies and interests. Finally, to identify any and all weaknesses that could be exploited at the proper time.

As she implemented a host of creative techniques to interview former teachers, neighbors, employers, and classmates, a consistent image came into continual focus: Howard Ross was a brilliant man motivated primarily by ego and lust.

Oksana couldn't have been more pleased.

Manipulating ego required little effort.

Stoking lust…even less.

She ascertained he had been involved in at least two serious relationships by the time he was drafted into MI-8. Several more once he transplanted to Manhattan, often two at a time.

Most of the girls had been blondes. Additionally, Oksana uncovered substantial evidence that Ross had fathered an illegitimate daughter with his last high school steady, Bethany Ford. The young couple broke it off when he was conscripted into military service in September of 1918.

In May of the following year, little Samantha Ford was born.

Each of the next two decades left Ross with a failed marriage in its wake. His first union—with an attractive MI-8 secretary—struggled along for nearly five years. His last marriage—to a dancer whom he had become consumed with at the Republic Theater on 42nd Street—scarcely survived fourteen months. Her lips, hips, and legs were legendary in the ignoble Minsky Burlesque Empire, and Ross had to have her.

After three weeks, Darkstar was satisfied with her investigation of Ross' psychological profile and sexual proclivities. She returned to Washington to begin the second phase of her mission: discovering the physical location of both Howard Ross and CIA Project SATURN.

"Now, go on…answer my question," she insisted. "Do you prefer blondes?"

Ross rolled his eyes and clasped her tight. "Now what kind of a damn question is that?"

"It shouldn't be a difficult one," Oksana replied. "I really wanna know."

He raised his right hand and stroked her hair with the back of it. "Well, let me ask you a question. Are *you* actually a blonde?"

Oksana immediately discerned the wisdom of his counter-question. She weighed her responses.

"As far as you know," she offered with a wicked smile that transformed into a passionate kiss.

CHAPTER 17

Denver flung his arm out and slowed an impatient Leah Swan down to a sudden standstill. He surveyed the area around the main entrance to Chicago State Mental Hospital and waited while two women passed by.

He lowered his voice. "Now listen carefully. When it comes to infiltration, there are two fundamental rules. First, look like everyone else, and second, move with confident purpose."

Another man brushed passed and Denver nodded in greeting, hesitating until the stranger disappeared through the glass doors. The facility seemed unusually busy for an early Saturday morning. Denver knew he could use that heavy traffic to their advantage later on.

"The quickest way to blow your cover in an enclosed space is to act unfamiliar with the layout. You have to move and interact like it's your own home."

She offered a weak nod with a grave stare.

"Oh," he continued, "and avoid eye contact. At least without making it *look like* you're avoiding eye contact. And speak. But only when spoken to…and try to smile. Act natural, but not *too* natural."

She was clearly growing frustrated and he stared off down the walkway.

"Sorry," he said. "It's complicated. But don't worry. I've got years of experience involving hostage situations." He turned to her with a hopeful smile. "But, then again…those were all in Afghanistan. And I had a squad of hardened soldiers with me. And minute-by-minute intelligence. Night Vision goggles. Flak jackets. Pockets full of C-4."

He hesitated. "Oh yeah, and lots of guns. Big, big guns." Denver spread his hands apart. "Bout this long. Oh, and lots of bullets. FMJ boat tails, hollow points, armor piercing, you name it."

Leah forced a smile. "We don't have any of those things."

Denver began moving. "Nope, no we don't. But then again, this ain't Afghanistan sweetheart. Come on. Stay close. Remember, we're circled, we're married. Let's act like it. But I warn you…just try to keep your hands off me. I know…it's difficult."

She punched his arrogant shoulder.

"There ya go," he responded, "now that's more like an old married couple."

Leah flinched multiple times.

Denver had failed to mention the haunting screams and the echoes of broken humanity that she would be passing through. She dug her nervous nails into his arm on several occasions as they traversed the sterile halls of this emotional gauntlet.

He patted her hand. "Easy girl, not too much farther. We will go up the stairs on the right, honey."

A nurse descending the marble steps met them halfway and caught Denver's eyes. "Good morning," she offered.

"Well, yes it is," he returned. "A good early morning to you as well. Thank you." They kept moving and reached the second floor.

He leaned against Leah and whispered, "Phil's room is the fourth door on the left. We're almost there. You'll see." They arrived and slowed with almost reverential footsteps. He scanned up and down the hallway.

Good. No staff. No cameras.

Leah's brown eyes flared red and tears flooded down both cheeks. Denver grabbed her shoulders lightly.

"Hey, those better be tears of joy," he said. "Now remember what I told you…he's probably going to be *different* than you remember him. Actually, a lot different. I imagine they've been feeding him some hefty psychotropic drugs. Let's pray their effects are reversible."

Leah nodded and made an effort to brush her almond cheeks dry.

He stared into her eyes. "You ready?"

She paused. "Uh, yeah. Yeah. As ready as I can be…I guess. This is just so…surreal."

He whispered with a hint of a chuckle. "Now, just try to imagine what it was like for me four days ago when I first found him. Anyway, here we go."

The doorknob was a bit stiff and the metal door itself quite heavy, but it squeaked open and they hurried inside. Denver made sure to shut it securely behind them. The unnerving sounds outside seemed to be swallowed by the room's eerie silence.

The back of a lone figure in a rusty wheelchair on the far side of the room met their expectant eyes. Leah had to catch her breath and brought both trembling hands up to her face.

They strolled alongside the wheelchair. Leah spoke first.

"Ph—Phil? It's me…Leah. Leah Swan."

The pair came to a quiet stop in front of the faceless, shaggy-headed figure slumped before them. There was no visible response.

Denver crouched and carefully lifted the patient's head. "We're gonna get you out of here, Phil."

Wild eyes popped open and a horrific scream pierced the air from her crazed lips. She clawed desperately at Denver's face.

It wasn't Phil Nelson…in fact, it wasn't even a man.

CHAPTER 18

Thursday, March 11, 1948, 7:14 p.m.
Golden Nugget Restaurant
Las Vegas, Nevada

A decade of intense indoctrination at Operation Sunshade in Magnitogorsk had sought to fashion an assassin devoid of conscience and bereft of feeling.

Success regarding the former was complete, but the latter was somewhat lacking.

As Darkstar meandered among the displays that cluttered the aisles of the casino souvenir shop, she was annoyed at the foreign sensation that rose up within her. Hundreds of men had died at her hands, some brutally, but now the mere thought of seeing this one American made her tense up.

This is ridiculous.

Keep calm, Mizenov.

Gathering visual reconnaissance on Howard Ross and his organization wasn't the only thing that disturbed her. America disturbed her. Las Vegas disturbed her greatly.

The cheap golden trinkets that assaulted her eyes, the flashing lights encircling gaudy marquees elevating men and women as gods, combined with irresponsibly lavish lifestyles sickened Oksana as she had navigated the streets of America's oasis of greed.

Across an ocean—another world away—she had been exposed to photos, songs, and stories about the decadence of the West, but there it remained academic. Theoretical.

Here, she was immersed in it.

Her conflicted mind drifted across time to the struggles that defined her past and shaped her present. She reflected on the deprivation experienced as a rejected orphan on the streets of Lubertsy. She recalled the extreme suffering she had endured in the Russian wilderness during the harsh weeks of Mission Prime. Oksana could never forget the lean and difficult months after the unprovoked and fearful German invasion against her homeland.

And now, she had infiltrated a nation that seemed founded upon callous indifference to any and all of that.

It was difficult to reconcile.

The gift shop at the Golden Nugget provided an excellent vantage point on the main entrance to the restaurant. She had memorized his photos, his build, his type. If Howard Ross waltzed through those doors—even in a crowd or wearing a hat—she would know.

The most difficult aspect of her stake out had been fielding the incessant nagging from the otherwise well-meaning sales personnel. She had been harassed no less than a half-dozen times during the hour that passed while awaiting her prey. In her mind, these events provided empirical proof that unfettered capitalism was an economic disease that needed to be cured…or eliminated.

Darkstar glanced momentarily at her reflection in a mirror located near the clothing section. Her jet black dress was perfectly complemented by her dark handbag and matching dark hair. It was an ideal outfit assembled for night reconnaissance. She checked her watch.

7:22 p.m.

Fifteen seconds later, she was certain her heart skipped a beat.

It's him.

Ross. Howard Ross.

The Project SATURN chief carried himself exactly as her profile had predicted. Tall. Confident. Impatient. Another man in an expensive suit trailed behind and spoke to him. She couldn't make out the conversation.

That must be Masterson. Looks like they have a reservation.

The two men followed a tuxedoed maître d' through the ornate doorway and disappeared within the dining area. Darkstar repositioned in the lobby to acquire a new lookout venue. Her targets were guided to a booth.

Damn. Both of the adjacent booths are occupied.

A survey of the immediate area was unsatisfactory.

One unoccupied table, fifteen feet away. No good.

This is going to be a long wait, time to adjust my cover.

Darkstar sauntered back into the souvenir shop and purchased an assortment of small items including a thick paperback romance novel. The clerk wrapped the mementos and deposited them all into a sizable bag.

Reconnaissance consisted of five percent observation, the remainder in the uncelebrated art of waiting. A full ninety minutes crept by while she appeared to be consumed with her book, seated on one of the luxurious couches accenting the marble-lined lobby.

Masterson had made a single trip to the men's room and another to a bank of phones just beyond the foyer. Ross remained steadfast in his seat, a cloud of smoke his constant companion. His only other contacts were the maître d' and their waitress at irregular intervals. The business meeting appeared to be cordial and without incident.

It ended at 8:57 p.m.

Darkstar tossed the book into her gift bag and tailed the men out onto the sidewalk. She had carefully positioned her own vehicle near the entrance and raced over to it. Once inside, she snagged a pair of binoculars, but they proved unnecessary. After seeing Masterson off, Ross lit a cigarette, and navigated the busy street. He disappeared through the swinging doors of the El Dorado Club.

Darkstar threw on a light, gray coat for a slight outfit alteration, and donned a pair of thin glasses. She stared at the sign above the bar.

What are you up to, Mr. Ross?

Perhaps an after dinner drink or two?

Another meeting? Female companionship?

Darkstar exited her sedan and jogged across Fremont Street. After hesitating on the sidewalk for a minute or so, she kept her head down and pushed through the glass doors and into the bar.

Ross was no trouble to spot, seated about halfway down the hardwood bar, with a cigarette in one hand and likely a glass of whiskey occupying the other. Darkstar slid into a chair at a small table, her back to him. She rested a small makeup mirror against a salt shaker, adjusting it until Ross came into clear view.

There you are.

She ordered a margarita and watched the uneventful show.

In just under an hour, Ross downed no less than five lowballs and at least as many smokes. It appeared he only made contact with the bartender and had a brief conversation with an attractive redhead who relocated to another seat in short order.

Don't worry, Howard, she wasn't your type.

He crushed his cigarette, settled up on his tab, and began moving.

Well, that rejection must've really got to him.

Okay, here we go.

Darkstar allowed him to exit before she rushed up to the doors and peered outside. He was lighting a new cigarette with his back to her and began waving at a taxi. As Ross stepped towards the approaching cab, she pushed out onto the sidewalk and hurried over to her car to tail him.

His taxi headed west on Fremont Street and then made a hard right onto US Route 91. Before long the downtown glitz withered to a subtle glow in her rearview mirror as she followed the cab several miles to the northeast.

Where are we going, Mr. Ross?

The sudden flash of brilliant brake lights against the darkness indicated the taxi was finally changing course. Moments later, the vehicle jogged right at a lonely desert interchange. Darkstar pulled onto the rough shoulder to avoid betraying her pursuit. A small sign came into view on her immediate right.

Las Vegas Air Force Base.

She leaned against the steering wheel.

Project SATURN is at an airfield only a few miles north of Las Vegas?

Two cars raced by her from the south and also exited towards the small base. She seized the opportunity for cover and pulled in behind them, maintaining a comfortable gap while she grabbed her binoculars. Ahead and to her left she could make out the taxicab parked along a dimly lit curb near the main terminal. The lead car drew alongside the cab. The other continued on and disappeared off to the east.

Darkstar simultaneously killed her lights and motor and coasted to a quiet stop under the cover of darkness over a hundred yards to the south. She slipped out of her car and then up to the main building like a fleeting shadow, binoculars in one hand and a pistol firmly planted in the other.

Ross and a second man hurried north along the sidewalk and vanished around a corner to her right. Both the taxi and the lead car sped away and curved west back towards the distant highway. She sprinted down the walkway, but slowed while approaching the corner of the terminal. Darkstar dropped down and craned her neck. Fifty feet beyond the brick bend a chain-link fence with a locked gate barred the way. A military aircraft was perched a hundred feet beyond that on the tarmac.

A helicopter. Nice.

She slid east along the dark wall and pressed up against the cold fence. Ross and the other man—moving at a brisk pace—had almost arrived at the aircraft. Her binoculars shot up.

Looks like a…Bell 47.

Second man…is…the…pilot.

Ross is a passenger. Makes sense.

Tail number…RM121.

She scanned the remainder of the area. A jeep pulling into a large Quonset hangar a few hundred yards to the south seemed to be the only other activity.

No guards. No sentries.

At least, not yet.

That's good.

The chopper's engines started their characteristic whine as the blades wobbled and whirled up to flight speed at an increasing rate.

Where are you going, Mr. Ross?

Can't be too far. That bird's operational range is limited to a few hundred miles.

The Bell 47 lifted off and hovered in place for several unsteady seconds before finally rotating away from her. She could feel the blast of air as it gained altitude and accelerated off into the distance.

North by northwest?
She was perplexed.
LA is southwest.
Los Alamos is southeast.
Reno and Carson City are too far.
Must be a short jump; otherwise, he would just take a plane.
She lowered her binoculars.

Where could he possibly be flying northwest of Las Vegas?

CHAPTER 19

Denver's self-consciousness was mushrooming exponentially.

Leah had vanished into the bathroom several minutes before, and unhealthy fears began plaguing him as he hovered out in the hallway of the mental facility.

But he refused to rush her.

She had fled out of Phil's former cell as an emotional disaster. He couldn't blame her. She had been on this painful rollercoaster for over three years, and this latest twist in the track was perhaps the cruelest to date.

A pair of male orderlies lumbered close by with a large, rolling food cart, ready for distribution. He acknowledged them and then turned away, head down. A woman emerged from the restroom.

It wasn't Leah.

He paced. Thoughts raced.

Where have they moved you, Phil?

His level of concern was a mystery, even to himself. He couldn't deny he had a strong attachment and concern for a man he had never even officially met. He could probably thank Leah Swan's fond memories and the fascinating pages of a small diary for that. But now, Denver realized that the powers-that-be seemed to have conspired against him.

Wait…conspiracy.

A conspiracy? But conspiracies are difficult to maintain…especially if you add more people into the mix.

He glanced up and down the active corridor. The main entrance was not quite a dozen yards away. He observed the nurses, orderlies, and patients milling about.

They can't all be in on the conspiracy.

Probably only a few. A few at the top.

Not the rank-and-file workers.

A simple and inelegant plan coalesced in his mind within mere moments. He scurried down the hall, pushed through the double metal doors, and approached the receptionist's window.

A pair of soft, pale hands reached up and slid the single pane of glass to the side. Denver found himself face to face with a young secretary.

"Can I help you, sir?"

He took a half step forward. "Yes, ma'am. Thank you. I am looking to visit with a distant cousin of mine who is a…*resident* here."

She opened a small ledger. "Patient name?"

"Certainly. It is Thompson. Mr. Gordon Thompson."

She traced along a few pages with her index finger and then scanned through another small stack of papers on the left side of her desk.

"You did say Mr. Gordon Thompson?" she clarified.

Denver placed his hands onto the counter. "Yes. That is correct. My cousin. Gordon Thompson."

She busied herself for a moment before making eye contact. "I am so sorry, sir. But I'm afraid Mr. Thompson passed away earlier this week." She peered down at a note. "On, uh, Thursday afternoon."

Denver couldn't repress his shock. "Passed away? What…*how?*"

She perused the report. "It appears to have been natural causes. Possibly heart failure." She glanced back up. "I am so sorry, I really am. Were you close?"

He stared at the floor. "Not really, but kinda."

"My records indicate he had no known living relatives. Mr. Thompson was cremated yesterday. It's our usual procedure in such cases. He left no personal belongings behind."

This can't be. Heart failure? Cremation?

Denver felt paralyzed. He couldn't begin to imagine how Leah would react to all of this. He straightened up. "I, uh, I need to speak with his doctor. I believe it was a Monty something."

"Dr. Montgomery?" she asked.

"Yes, ma'am, that's it. That's exactly it. Montgomery. Heavy-set gentleman, glasses. A little gray in the hair. Likes to take walks in the park."

The receptionist took a deep breath and the color drained from her face.

Denver almost panicked. *What? What did I say? Are they on to me?* In his paranoia he scanned the foyer, but everything appeared to be business as usual.

"Is the good doctor available?" he repeated.

A single tear flowed down her right cheek. "No. He isn't—" Her lips began quivering and she struggled to finish her thoughts.

"I'm sorry you haven't heard, but Dr. Montgomery was...tragically killed Thursday morning in a car accident."

October 27, 1956

SECURITY LEVEL: TOP SECRET

FOR: Chief Howard D. Ross, Project SATURN
FROM: Allen W. Dulles, Director, Central Intelligence
SUBJECT: Suez Canal U-2 Surveillance

Admiral Radford has convinced Eisenhower that the tensions regarding the Suez Canal will likely escalate into a regional conflict.

The President has authorized a temporary retasking of the bulk of the U-2 fleet for high-altitude reconnaissance over Egypt, Israel, the Sinai Peninsula, and the Eastern Mediterranean.

Defense Secretary Wilson will be coordinating this intelligence effort. Current plans include utilizing Incirlik Air Base in Turkey. I do not anticipate this interruption of primary U-2 activities to extend beyond December 1956.

END

DCI/PS

CHAPTER 20

Denver could be lying.

It was an unbearable thought that made Leah's stomach nearly retch its churning contents. She smeared the stinging tears out of her eyes and gazed around at the off-white tile and pale blue metal of the bathroom stall caging her.

She wasn't entirely sure how long she had been voluntarily holed up in the women's restroom at the mental hospital. Her blouse was tear-soaked, her face was hot, and her heart was beyond broken. And now she was beginning to doubt the only man she had been able to trust in the last three years.

Why would he do this to me?

What would possess a good and decent man to fabricate such a painful scam?

In her estimation, the thought of trusting men seemed to have been buried deep along with the body of Phil Nelson. The short-list of remaining men offered few worthy prospects. Shep's iron-fist approach bred obedience rather than trust. McCloud could have been a candidate, but it was difficult to have much of a trusting relationship with a man that she only conversed with in a factory lobby. Officer Billy was young and harmless enough, but his bashfulness forbade any real connection.

Garrett rarely spoke with her (an odd blessing she was thankful for on a daily basis). Terrance treated her well, and often came up front to share lunch with her and Tori, but Shep regularly crashed their irregular party. Doc and Pappy were adorable, but regardless of the intellectual and language barriers, The Basement might as well have been miles away.

An echoing flush in a stall two doors down snapped her out of her introspection. She could hear the woman open a reluctant metal door, wash her hands, pause, and then exit.

Silence.

Leah appeared to be alone. For now.

She cracked the squeaking door and studied the room.

Just me.

After clearing her raw throat, Leah composed herself and sauntered out and up to a large mirror. She examined her dark hair. It seemed to have survived the emotional assault without much damage. Her mascara was another train wreck altogether. The dark streaks resembled a pair of Rorschach test sheets surrounding a frightful pair of bloodshot eyes.

Great, Swan. Real nice.

You look like you belong in this crazy house.

Seconds later she had both cooled her skin and cleansed the visual offense away with palmfuls of refreshingly cold sink water.

Get it together, Swan. This day isn't even close to being over.

CHAPTER 21

Friday, April 9, 1948, 9:03 p.m.
No. 4, Shade Rock Apartment Complex
Las Vegas, Nevada

She lowered the new candle into the base and scanned the dark tabletop without success. The tiny matchbook—present at the beginning of the meal—was nowhere to be seen.

Ross leaned forward and reached into his breast pocket for his Zippo. "Allow me." Seconds later the wick blazed to life, casting a pair of subtle shadows across opposite paneled walls of her small apartment.

Oksana slipped back into her chair and scooted forward. "What's a girl to do? Too much light, and it's not very romantic, too little light…well, then you can't find the matches." They both laughed.

"It's all right," he comforted. "I don't mind being in the dark…as long as it's with you."

"I'm sorry. It's just that I want everything to be so perfect," she complained. "It's just frustrating at times."

"Well, Miss Sullivan, I'm no expert in candles or in romantic lighting, but I am a man. And as a man, it is my *expert* opinion that *you* are perfect."

Her cheeks flushed as she tried to restrain a smile in vain. "One of the benefits of mood lighting is that it hides a gal's imperfections."

"Oh, I doubt you have *anything* to hide, Miss Sullivan." Ross blotted the corners of his mouth and lowered his napkin. "You know, over the years, I've been introduced to a lot of women. I'll admit, I've chased a lot of women. And with each and every one of them, there was always something—*something*—that I would've liked to have changed." He extended his arm past the glass base of the candelabra and caressed her palm. "But with you…I wouldn't change a thing. Not one damn thing."

Oksana seemed to hang on his every syllable. "Talk like that will get even a nice girl into trouble, Howard."

He squinted his eyes and squeezed her hand.

"I'm counting on it."

CHAPTER 22

The silence between them redefined awkward.

Denver hit his right blinker and eased Leah's sedan out of the hospital parking lot and headed south onto North Oak Park Avenue. Leah hadn't so much as uttered a solitary sound since exiting the women's restroom.

He stole a quick glance over at the shattered remains of hope that was collapsed against the passenger door window. She was less than two feet away but miles beyond reach.

At least she isn't crying.

The consolation of this thought quickly waned as he considered the real possibility that she had perhaps exhausted her supply. He then felt worse.

Dozens of scenarios and explanations flashed through his troubled mind as they navigated from urban to residential to rural landscapes south of the city. Memories of empty caskets and occupied wheelchairs gave him hope that things, once again, were not as they might appear.

Could Phil Nelson actually be dead this time?

But who would've killed him?

They've had three years…why now?

Why this week?

A trio of solid black Ford's passed by him not quite an hour north of Normal.

More of those Mennonites.

Denver sighed. The sight of the somber cars stretching off into the distance reminded him of a funeral procession. He looked over at his distraught passenger. Mercifully, she had passed out against the door. He was thankful she didn't witness the spectacle. Denver slowed somewhat to allow a considerable gap between their car and the dark convoy. His mind was jumbled with deep questions and shallow conspiracies.

Did Montgomery kill Nelson?

And then did someone else take out Montgomery to cover this all up? Did the same person kill them both?

Shep?

McCloud?

Why? Why now?

So much is happening…and all at once.

To Denver, there was no doubt this had been perhaps the most eventful week in the history of Normal's time Jumpers (with the notable exception of the tragedy at Roswell in 1947). In the past five days, he had discovered that Shep was involved in a dark plot with a psychiatrist in Chicago, and that Phil Nelson hadn't ended his life from the business end of a shotgun. On that same Tuesday, Frazier nearly killed a newspaper editor-turned-supposed time Jumper, and by Wednesday morning's light a captivating new addition had arrived to the family.

But now, Denver had to wrestle with the real possibility that a recently resurrected Phil Nelson may have been murdered, along with Dr. Montgomery—all because of his own desire to go snooping around. On a certain level, Denver was aware he wasn't responsible.

But he still *felt* responsible.

It was an impression that was hard to ignore, and harder to shake.

Especially today.

It had begun as a gut-wrenching disaster with one woman, and he knew there was a distinct possibility it could terminate in a massive train wreck with another. McCloud's late-Friday night phone call had notified him that Betty Larson had revived from her Frazier-induced slumber. The

Chief was convening a meeting at Ellen's house for late Saturday afternoon to vet the self-proclaimed journalist from the future.

He tried to imagine the implications if she was telling the truth. He tried hard to ignore the consequences if she wasn't.

Leah tossed and turned in the front seat but her nap remained intact. The sleep-induced silence may have provided a needed break in the immediate confusion, but Denver was no fool. He anticipated there would be long and painful conversations before his own head would hit the pillow that night.

It had required a superhuman effort over the past several weeks to conceal his grave-digging discovery from Leah. Her moral sensibilities trumped his *end-justifies-the-means* approach. Denver surmised that the hope it might have engendered within her would have been forever tainted with the horrors of his cemetery sacrilege.

Considering their present state of affairs, the likelihood that he would reveal Phil's latest death and cremation to Leah hovered at or below zero.

She had buried him once already.

A second funeral was off the table.

CHAPTER 23

Friday, April 9, 1948, 9:37 p.m.
No. 4, Shade Rock Apartment Complex
Las Vegas, Nevada

The relationship progression had been natural.

It began with a glance across a bar.

Which led to an expensive meal.

Then a casino dance floor.

A kiss in a parking lot.

Candlelight dinner.

A couch.

It was beautiful…and all by design.

"What took you so long?" Ross chided as her graceful silhouette tiptoed back across the room and slid alongside him on the sofa. He pressed a cigarette to his lips and inhaled deeply. The warm glow from its burning tip swept upon the gentle curves of her face. "I almost had time to forget what you looked like," he said.

"I knew I wasn't imagining it. You really do have a problem with patience, don't you?"

"Only when I have to wait."

"Well, Howard, I hope *this* will be worth the wait." Oksana transferred a tall, chilled glass of wine into his surprised hands. He swirled it like a pro, inspecting the aroma.

"What's this?"

She closed the remaining gap between them. "A treat that cost me a whole week's tips and nearly that long learning how to pronounce. So enjoy it."

"What?"

"Take a sip," she said. "And *savor it.*"

He did. "A *Cabernet?*" Another taste. "A damn good Cabernet."

"Not just any Cabernet," she announced, "but a *1934* Cabernet Sauvignon. Only one place in Vegas carries it."

He clinked glasses with her. "*Tres bien. Tres bien.* I'm impressed. That rolled off your tongue like a true woman of the world. I think I have been good for you."

She grinned. "I have absolutely no idea what it means, but I do love how it sounds...*sauvignon.*"

"And I love to hear you say it." Ross raised his glass aloft and examined it. "When did you say this was from? 1934?"

"Yep." Oksana kicked off her heels and hiked her long legs up and onto the small couch. The tops of her lace garters adorning her thighs peeked out from beneath her dress.

He noticed.

Oksana laid her head on his chest. "I wasn't even ten years-old when this wine was bottled."

"Interesting," he said. "You know, that was the year after prohibition went away."

She rolled her head back and gazed intently into his upside-down face. "I don't remember much about *prohibition,*" she whispered. "But I think that tonight I might be in the mood to lose my *inhibition.*"

Twenty-five minutes of pent-up passion under the influence of vintage liquor—laced with a potent blend of adenosine monophosphate—provided Darkstar with her first real window of opportunity.

She drew the sheets up to his bare chest, kissed his forehead and crawled out of bed in the darkness. Her experience with men of his build and alcoholic consumption was fairly consistent.

She had a minimum of two hours while he slept soundly.

It was enough.

After donning a pair of thin gloves, she rummaged through his slacks, extracting his keyring along with his thick wallet. Darkstar slipped out of her bedroom and flashed the lights in her living room three times in rapid succession. Less than two minutes later, a courier arrived at her apartment door and in a silent and swift transaction she deposited Ross' keys into his hand.

He scurried away.

Darkstar retrieved a tiny camera from below the bathroom sink and lowered the toilet seat as a makeshift table. Her next order of rushed business was to acquire detailed photographs of the front and back of every item in Ross' wallet. Identification cards, personal photos, cash, and a varied assortment of folded handwritten notes littered its interior.

Before capturing each image, she made careful mental notes of the exact location and fold patterns of all documents, and returned each to its particular home when finished.

Time to get even more personal.

Darkstar grabbed a white card out of her closet and coated the topside with a colorless, odorless chemical from the medicine cabinet. She slipped back into the bedroom and beginning with his left hand, rolled each of his fingers across its wet surface in order. After flapping the card back and forth in the air for several seconds, she jogged into the kitchen, threw a small skillet onto the stove, and lit the nearest gas burner.

One minute later, metal tongs deposited the white card onto the center of the hot skillet and she waited. In time, a perfect series of black fingerprints materialized across its white surface. Darkstar killed the gas, dumped the skillet's contents onto a dishtowel and smiled.

A sound.

She eyed her watch.

Right on schedule.

Five light taps against her front door (seventy minutes after Ross' lapse into unconsciousness) signaled the return of the courier. She cracked it open. The original group of keys and a freshly-cut duplicate set were deposited into her waiting hands. It was her expectation that they would eventually permit entrance to more sensitive areas, but right now the keys provided access to Ross' four-door sedan parked on the street a half-block away.

Darkstar lugged a mid-sized briefcase from her closet down to the vehicle, unlocked the door, and crawled into the floorboard at the base of the dark backseat. Utilizing a razor-sharp blade, she crafted an invisible slit along the back of the cushion and inserted a fist-sized listening device coupled with a transmitter and power source.

She checked her watch again.

Damn.

Time was rapidly transitioning from friend to foe, as she stole her way back up to the apartment and locked herself inside the bathroom. Darkstar yanked the receiver from the briefcase and flicked the device on. It took mere seconds to dial-in the appropriate frequency which confirmed the success of her clandestine automobile handiwork.

Perfect.

With minutes to spare, she stowed the camera, fingerprint card, duplicate keys, and briefcase back into a hidden compartment along the rear of her closet and rushed back towards her bedroom. Once his personal items were restored into his pants, her clothing fell to the floor as she slid into bed and snuggled up beside her prey.

Darkstar studied his motionless form in the moonlight, and was thrilled with the variety of ways Ross had been violated in a single night. It was her on-going honor to take advantage of him.

It feels good to get lucky.

CHAPTER 24

He typically avoided using the word *miracle*.

Denver knew people who overused it, and it bothered him. But today, no other term seemed appropriate.

"I know what the headline should read, Miss Larson," Denver announced, strolling up to her recovery bed alongside a much-relieved Doc Stonecroft. Betty was propped up with enough throw pillows to satisfy a Sultan and Ellen stood guard on her left.

The newspaper editor smiled. "I suppose, Mr. *Collins*, that you've found a way to capture entire events and then cage them up inside of a single quote?"

"I have," he affirmed with a hint of forced arrogance. "*Newspaper Manager Makes Miraculous Mend.*" Denver scanned her brightening eyes for tacit approval.

"Not bad, not bad." Betty ventured another sip of the hot-something Ellen had deposited into her hands. "That's, uh, only one word shy of a perfect alliteration. I'm instantly impressed, indeed."

He took a careful seat at the lower end of her soft bed. "I caught what you did there. That was nice. And perfect. Gimme time, I'll get there. I learned from the best. Oh, and from the *second best*, too."

"So I've heard," Betty commented. "I've been told some really wonderful things about Alexus. I've read all of what she's written. From yesterday's paper, or today's paper. Whatever you want to call it."

"Yeah, about that," Denver said. "I'm sorry we couldn't get it out on Friday as usual. Alexus, James, and I were lucky to get *anything* out…even by today. It's been a rough week, for all of us. The Chief really helped out. He got Alexus all kinds of filler stories around town. I know it's a little heavy on the ads, and light on the fresh stories."

"No apologies needed. It's good. Really. You guys did great. Alexus could use a little polish, but that kind of polish only comes with experience. Give her time."

"Speaking of time, Ms. Larson," Doc interrupted, "I believe we need to conference regarding your *exceptional* claim of late...regarding time." He inched closer and shook her hand. "But first, let me initiate proper formalities. I am Dr. Glen Stonecroft."

"Nice to *formally* meet you, Dr. Stonecroft. Under...safer conditions."

"Indeed, indeed," he replied. "So, may I inquire...do you feel up to it? A short discussion, that is."

Betty scooted back and adjusted a few pillows. "Feel up to it? I would've abandoned this posh prison earlier this morning, but Nazi Nurse here won't let me out of her sight." She winked at Doc.

Ellen appeared unaffected in the slightest. "Need I remind everyone, that our patient here was completely unconscious from Tuesday until late yesterday? That's almost four days of unresponsiveness. I might—*that's might*—let her go to the demonstration tomorrow night. But that's a big *might*."

"Let us withhold all such talk of planned *festivities* until we have had time to properly engage our friend here." Stonecroft peered up at Ellen. "Miss Finegan, could Denver and I have a private word with Ms. Larson? I implore you under the guidance of the Second Accord. Unless you object on medical grounds?"

Ellen massaged Betty on the shoulder and sauntered off. "I have no objections per se, but she better still be in that bed when I get back, or I will show you the truth that lurks behind the famous stereotype about redheads. It is quite accurate."

"You have our word," Doc assured, glancing over at Denver.

"Oh, uh, yeah," Denver called out. "Yeah. Our word. Cause those consequences sounded pretty scary."

Ellen's distant voice drifted through the doorway. "I heard that."

"I really am fine," Betty insisted. "To use my nurse's verbiage…my *laceration* is still tender to the touch. But, it's not bleeding, and I'm fine. A little weak, that's all. A few more hot meals and I'll be ready to resume my duties downtown."

Doc slid a chair up beside her and sat. "An impatient patient," he muttered playfully. "Ms. Larson, I have witnessed—firsthand—the exceptional medical skillset possessed by my colleague. It would be a fool's errand to disregard her educated and warranted opinion. She only seeks the absolute best for you."

"And I appreciate that, Mr. Stonecroft, but as a reporter and an educated woman myself, I think I'm fairly qualified to make my own personal health decisions." She studied Denver's reaction. "I know what an impaired person looks and acts like, and I'm neither."

Doc patted her hand. "Let's table that understandably contentious discussion for a later time, shall we? On to more…*pressing* matters." He checked his watch. "The Chief was prepared to join us, but it appears he is running late. But I see no reason to delay our inquiry."

Betty tensed up and her tone shifted. "You, uh, you want to know if I really am from the future. A *time Jumper* as you guys called it the other day at the factory."

"It is a rather important determination," Doc confessed. "If it is true, then our path from here is a well-marked trail. But, if it isn't—"

"If it isn't, *then what?!*" she yelled. "You gonna turn me over to that muscle-bound monster that tried to strangle me?! That nearly *killed* me?!"

Stonecroft wagged his head and caressed her hand. "The rash and violent actions of Mr. Frazier were both inexcusable and unconscionable, Ms. Larson. He acted without authority and without our consent. It will not happen again."

"Of course it won't!" Betty exclaimed. "Because it's *true.* I am from the future. 1980 to be exact. And I can prove it, I can tell you anything you want to know about the future. Events, presidents, music, anything." Her face wore the hallmarks of desperation as she rapidly glanced between the two men's faces. "Plus, plus—I have a box of my personal effects—"

"You mean a shoebox of items you kept hidden under your bed?" Denver asked.

She squinted. "You, uh, you've been in my house?"

Both men just stared at her.

Betty peered down into her lap for a moment. "So, first you guys break into my office and steal my safe. And then you just go waltzing into my bedroom and take whatever you want when I'm down and helpless?"

Doc was gentle but firm. "We had to know." He hesitated. "Surely you can appreciate our predicament, Ms. Larson. Sometimes legal—"

"Sometimes *legal issues* are just plain trumped by a much, much bigger picture," the Chief interrupted as he hurried into the room and tossed his hat onto a dresser. "Sorry that I'm late to the party, but there's a little fender bender over by the courthouse. Nothing bad, everyone's fine."

He studied the frustrated patient who appeared to be on the edge of tears. "And it looks like you're doing fine as well, Betty. Good to see ya awake and all."

She hadn't altered her tone. "No thanks to your personal thug."

"Oh, don't you worry 'bout that loose cannon," the Chief said. "He so much as looks at you wrong and I'll throw 'em on ice for two weeks. I've warned him."

"He needs to be in prison," Betty said.

Denver had to turn away as the Chief grabbed a chair. *You're probably more right than you know, Betty.*

"Not to defend the reprehensible behavior of Mr. Frazier," Stonecroft added, "but the circumstances surrounding the horrific incident could be construed as somewhat mitigating. But let's put it behind us...for now."

She mumbled. "That's easy for you to say."

Doc nodded. "So, Ms. Larson, would you be so kind as to indulge us concerning the occasion of your arrival to the past?"

"What do you want to know?" she replied. "The date? It was in February of 1952. The fourth. Late in the afternoon." She folded her arms and concentrated on the ceiling for a moment. "It was cold…I remember that. Very cold."

"Where exactly did you Jump to?" Denver asked.

She glanced at him. "Where do you think? *Here*. In Normal. Actually on a farm just north of the University. I walked out of a field and got picked up by an older couple from Bloomington. They were nice enough to take me into their home." She returned her gaze to the ceiling. "I had to tell a bunch of lies. I felt awful about it. They, uh, they got me in touch with a local church charity. I had a place to stay until I could get on my feet again."

Denver squinted and rubbed his chin. "So all that stuff you told me down at the *Journal,* about your past. That was all a lie?"

She pierced clear through him with a hard stare. "I wouldn't be accusing people of lying, Mr. Jackson. Or, wait…is it Mr. *Collins?* Let's see…you said you didn't know the names of the people who stole my things. But you obviously do know. So, what *other* lies have you told me, Denver?"

He had zero defense. "Fair enough."

She continued. "Anyway, I really do have a degree in Journalism, and I have worked all over Missouri for different papers. But after I *jumped* back to Normal, I moved to Chicago to find work at a big newspaper. But I always kept my eye out for any openings down here. When the *Journal* had one, I jumped on it."

Doc peeled off his glasses and polished them using the edge of her bed sheet. "Ms. Larson, do you recall what the conditions were back home? Prior to your Jump?"

"Conditions? What do you mean? The economy? What?"

"Let's begin with something simple. The weather."

"That's an easy one. Wet. The conditions were very wet. That's why I about froze to death after I arrived here. I was soaked." She stared at nothing in the distance, obviously reliving the event. "I was in a parking lot, getting ready to go shopping. I had just left my car and I didn't have an umbrella, so I ran towards the entrance. It was a terrible electrical storm, one for the books."

The Chief locked eyes with Stonecroft, and they nodded to each other.

"Anything else?" the Chief inquired.

"Not much. I can remember that there was a super bright light…I guess it was a lightning flash, then a huge crash. I came to, or woke up, or whatever in a field. Like I said, a few minutes later I was picked up by that couple. It took forty-five minutes in a hot bath before I got my chills to go away. It was miserable."

The Chief straightened up and smiled proudly. "Well, my record still stands. My story continues to beat anyone's. Being cold and wet is one thing, Betty. Being caught in one's birthday suit, now that's quite another!"

She spoke with obvious hesitation as her brow furrowed. "I'm not sure if it's appropriate to admit it, but I have a morbid interest in hearing more about that. But strictly off-the-record, of course." She paused. "Even though *Naked Normal Newcomer Unnerves Nice Neighborhood* could be a headline that moves a lot of papers, Chief."

Denver shook his head. "How do you do that? And so fast?"

"A good reporter never reveals their sources, Mr. Collins. I guess good criminals don't either." She winked.

"Do you remember the date of your departure, Ms. Larson?" Doc asked as he slid his spectacles back on.

"Absolutely. It was the fifteenth of August, 1980, a Friday afternoon. I had just left the office and was going to buy a birthday gift for my niece. Next thing I know, I'm in the wrong state and about twenty-eight years too early for her party."

She glanced at the ceiling again. "In some ways it was a nice change of pace. And I know that sounds crazy. But news had become so depressing. I was getting tired of covering Carter's declining presidency, and the diplomatic disaster surrounding the Iran hostage situation. *Unofficially* the leadership at the newspaper was pro-Carter, but I was a closet Reagan supporter."

Denver stood up to stretch his legs. "Do you want to know who won?"

Neither of the other two men seemed to find that offer very amusing. Denver smirked. "Come on, lighten up. I was kidding. The Second Accord is safe with me."

Betty's eyes raced between all their faces. "Now that's at least the second time today someone has mentioned the *Second Accord*. Anyone care to illuminate me on that one?"

Doc patted her hand again. "All in good time, my dear."

Denver nodded. "There's four of them. They're called the Four Accords. You can thank Phil Nelson for that. And Leah, eventually. Maybe."

Betty appeared totally lost.

Denver sighed. "It's complicated."

Betty focused her confused attention to McCloud. "Tell me, Chief, didn't you ever wonder why I set up that meeting with you on the bridge a few months ago? When I told you about my mysterious, *futuristic* items? Right before your henchmen broke into the *Journal* and swiped them." She leaned forward somewhat. "Didn't you find that conversation a little strange?"

He shrugged. "To be honest, Betty…as time Jumpers, we see and talk 'bout strange things most every day. I never put two and two together."

She sank back against the pillows. "Once I started finding those items, or people started giving them to me, I knew I couldn't be the only one. I knew there had to be others from the future." Betty looked at McCloud. "I suspected you were a time traveler, too, Chief. That meeting was part of my investigation, I was fishing, testing the waters…seeing if I could get a nibble, a reaction. I got a reaction, but it wasn't at all what I was expecting."

McCloud let out a controlled chuckle. "Ain't no way you could've seen that one coming!" He angled himself in the small chair and faced Denver. "Actually, you can thank Mr. Collins here for that bit of larceny, if memory serves."

Denver blushed and protested with his hands. "Whoa, Chief. I just said that night what everyone else was thinking. *Everyone*, including you. And don't forget the whole plan about faking the robberies at Ellen's place and Martha's house. You know whose idea that was. He's the only person in the room right now wearing a uniform."

It looked like Betty was trying hard to suppress a contagious smile. "Wait a minute. Are you all admitting that the police chief of Normal authorized a robbery and was then responsible for the cover up?"

"*Authorized?!*" Denver exploded. "How about he planned it. McCloud is a world-class criminal mastermind."

The Chief nodded. "I've always found that successful crime fighting involves thinkin' like a criminal. To catch one, ya gotta be one. At least sometimes."

"Well, I had my suspicions," Betty said. "To tell you the truth, with all these bedside confessions today, I could easily take the *Journal* from a weekly paper to a daily rag. You guys are giving me new material by the bucket load!"

The Chief bowed slightly. "Glad to be of public service, ma'am."

"Now get me out of here so I can return to work."

Several quiet seconds passed, and then a pale female hand flapping a white handkerchief appeared just inside the doorway. "Is it safe for me to come back into my own room yet?"

Doc responded with a warm invitation. "Well, yes. Of course, you may return, Nurse Finegan. Of course."

A playful Ellen peeked around the corner and folded the cloth. "Have we reached a consent concerning diagnosis, Dr. Stonecroft?" She strolled in and he rose to meet her halfway across the rug.

"Indeed we have, my dear. Your delightfully impetuous patient is suffering from an acute case of temporal displacement. She is a fellow time Jumper. Henceforth she shall be known to you as Trailer Larson."

"*Trailer?*" Ellen mused.

"1980."

Denver leaned against the wall. "That's the year after I was born. Or will be."

Betty's interest was clearly piqued. "You were born in 1979, Mr. Collins?"

"Yep."

"And let me guess…you traveled from the year *2013?*"

The reaction of the small group bordered on looking rehearsed as everyone glanced over at the newspaper editor in shock at much the same time. Denver's eyebrows shot up. "Wow, that's pretty close. Actually, 2014. But how could you possibly know that?"

"Isn't it obvious?" Betty asked. "You're a big tipper."

Every trace of emotion drained from Denver's face. A single word leaked out as not much beyond a whisper. "*Katie.*"

"Word gets out about you big spenders."

Ellen traded glances with the Chief. "Um," she began, "is anyone else as lost as I am right now?"

"Remember what Deep Throat said about Watergate," Betty announced. "*Follow the money.*" She paused for effect. "I did."

Ellen started to speak when Doc interrupted her. "I regret having to invoke the sanctity of the Second Accord for the third time today, but I must insist. Any and all conversations regarding that event in our history must be halted. For Ellen's sake. For all of our sakes."

Betty's right hand shot up to her own mouth in horror. "Oh, I said something wrong, or illegal or something. Didn't I?"

"An oversight which is perfectly understandable and frequently violated within our diverse ranks," Doc replied.

"It happens all the time," Denver explained.

The room fell silent once again.

"So, where do we go from here?" Betty asked. "That is, once I'm released from pillow prison."

McCloud cleared his throat and snagged his hat. "The most important thing is for life to go on as normal as possible in town. Change brings interest and suspicion. We need to getcha back to work."

Ellen paced to the opposite side of her patient's bed. "Forgive me, Miss Larson, but I'm still wondering about the fact that you called Denver a *big tipper* a few moments ago. Must be a story there."

Betty's face broke out in an embarrassed grin and she pointed across the room. "Ask him. He started it."

Denver squirmed. "Uh, refresh me on that one, Miss Larson. Was it something that happened while I worked with you down at the paper? The first time, that is."

"Not at the *Journal,*" she corrected. "Down at Amanda's Diner. Way back in early August."

Doc's concerned face brightened up. "Are you referring to the five-dollar bill that was concealed within your safe, Ms. Larson?"

"Very good, Dr. Stonecroft. You should be an investigative journalist. I could always use a good mind like yours downtown."

"The conclusion was fairly straightforward," Doc explained. "The year on the currency in question was 2013. Unless there are gaps within our understanding, Mr. Collins is the only Jumper capable of providing an item of that late date."

Ellen bent over and picked up a pillow that had tumbled to the floor. "So, Miss Larson, how did you get Denver's money from the diner? Through normal change, or was it something else?"

Betty's expression fell grim. "It was something else. Oh my, we may have a problem."

"Whatsa matter, Betty?" the Chief asked.

She collected her thoughts. "I bought that money from a waitress. Katie Long."

"*Bought money?*" Ellen repeated.

"Oh, yes…it's a long story. But not the most important one," a tense Betty replied. "Listen, Katie knows Denver's real name, and that there is something *different* about him. But just about him. She doesn't know anything else. At least, that I know of."

"How is that possible?" Ellen inquired.

"It's my fault," Betty acknowledged. "When I was trying to find out more information, I hired Katie to pay a little visit to Denver down at a bar in Bloomington. I asked her to use Collins instead of Jackson." Betty stared down into her lap and then over at a very uncomfortable Denver. "She said that you responded to Collins without a second thought."

At first everyone stared a hole through him, but then each of them looked away from Denver. The Chief broke the silence. "Well, listen, it ain't the end of the world. Heck, the FBI knows his real name and we're all still fine. They even got his picture! I ain't worried in the slightest about a little ole waitress in Normal."

"That makes one of us," Ellen mumbled.

"We can't change the past," McCloud bellowed. "But now that Betty's onboard, she can clean this up." He nodded towards her. "Surely a reporter can come up with a good story! We just need to keep things quiet and do our level-best to try'n not stir the water."

"I wholeheartedly agree," Doc said. "The issue with the waitress is unfortunate but of little potential consequence.

Until we surmount our efficiency issues and the Jump Portal is in full operation, it behooves us to maintain the status quo."

"Plus," the Chief continued, "it could be strategic as heck to have a Jumper in charge of the local paper. It keeps your ear to the ground, Betty. *Our* ear to the ground."

It was Betty's turn to be shocked. "Can we please forget about ears and the ground and just back up, folks? Did Doc just say something about someone building a *time travel* machine?"

"We're very close," Ellen shared, brimming with excitement. "We've planned a demonstration of our huge breakthrough for tomorrow night. If you're up to it, you should get to see it and meet all the other Jumpers."

McCloud folded his arms. "You know, Betty, somethin' just hit me. Any stories or tips that pop up that could expose us, well, you can ignore 'em, kill 'em, or bury 'em on page fifty. You know."

"Wait, let me sort through all of this," Betty said as she felt the bandage on the back of her head. "So, there is a group of time travelers in Normal, Illinois, who are on the verge of constructing a time travel machine. And the chief of police—who is also from the future—is responsible for masterminding three robberies, a massive local cover up, and is currently seeking to abridge the freedom of the only press in town?"

McCloud slapped his hat on and shuffled his feet.

"That sure sounded a whole lot worse the way you said it, but, uh…*yeah*."

CHAPTER 25

Without triggering a single sound to arouse suspicion, she locked the door to her bedroom in Leah's house, drew the curtains together and sat on her bed.

Alone.

It was a consequence of a profession thrust upon her, yet one that found within her a complicit victim. KGB assassins operated in isolation, known by precious few, and trusting even fewer. It espoused an existence that abhorred all physical attachments, while simultaneously embracing a fervent bond to cold, intangible ideals.

Darkstar sensed the unfamiliar rise of tension within. Her last brush with this unwelcome visitor had been consciously forced from her memory many years before. These sensations had been stirred the evening she first reconned Howard Ross in Vegas in 1948.

History seemed destined for a powerful recurrence in Normal. But the debilitating feelings were ill-timed.

Old World emotions couldn't be allowed to interfere with a deadly mission in the New. Before day's end, over a decade of training and years of pursuit would converge in a lethal climax.

Darkstar folded at the waist and laid hold of a bulky piece of hard-shell luggage stowed beneath the bed. She lugged the heavily-scuffed case out into the open and slid down beside it onto the rug. With a swift motion, she retrieved a tiny key skillfully concealed near the hinges and popped the lone padlock.

The lid eased open in silence, revealing a haphazard jumble of folded slacks, blouses, and undergarments. Oksana inserted her fingers along the messy perimeter and tugged upward. The clothing raised out of the suitcase collectively, supported within a shallow but convincing tray. She reached into the newly exposed cavity and withdrew a pair of flat black M1911 semi-automatic pistols, four seven-round magazines, and an NR-40 combat knife. She loaded the firearms and then deposited the mixed cache of weapons into the bottom of her purse.

Darkstar took a peek at her watch while returning the luggage to the secure location below her bed.

She had just over twenty minutes until the big show down at Nelson Manufacturing.

CHAPTER 26

McCloud nodded over at Stonecroft as Officer Billy guided Grandma Martha along the final few steps down into the festival-like atmosphere filling The Basement. "And these are the last two. Looks like we're all here now, Doc. Let's get this show on the road! We've been waitin' years for this!"

The clamor of fourteen excited people packed into a concrete bunker overpowered all of Doc's attempts at communication. Shep noticed and came to his rescue. "Hey! *Everybody!*" he shouted. "Listen up!"

They did.

Shep waved his arm. "It's all yours, Stonecroft. Keep it sweet and keep it short. If you can."

"Thank you, Mr. Sheppard. I can assure all of this fine assembly that it will indeed be sweet. Very sweet." He basked in the ensemble of smiling faces staring back at him. "And based upon the consistent results of the scores of tests we have undertaken, what you are about to witness will be short. Very short, indeed." He clapped his hands together and grinned. "But it will be worth it."

Ellen pointed at a box in the center of the table. "Just as a precaution, everyone will need to wear a pair of safety goggles for the demonstration. Everyone grab one. You'll be thanking me later."

Denver grabbed a few extra and distributed them to Leah and Tori.

"What do we say, Tori, when someone does something nice for us?" Leah asked.

The teenager rotated towards him. "Thank you." Pause. "Mr. Collins."

He patted her on the back. "You are very welcome, Tori."

Leah looked over at him. "Baby steps."

Denver agreed. "Baby steps."

Ellen addressed the crowd again as Dr. Papineau busied himself at the master control panel. "We know that the Jump Portal Chamber wasn't designed for a large audience, but the sooner we could all start moving in that direction the sooner we can get started."

Shep utilized his considerable strength and opened the chamber door a good bit wider.

"Thank you, Mr. Sheppard," Ellen commented. "Now, we should be able to fit at least seven or eight of you into the Portal Chamber along the metal walkway. The rest will have to watch through the door here."

The small sea of bodies flowed forward, yet Denver detected that Brenda Jo was deliberately shifting towards the rear of the group.

Now that's odd, he thought.

CHAPTER 27

Friday, April 16, 1948, 11:12 p.m.
Las Vegas Air Force Base
Las Vegas, Nevada

RM121.

The consistent tail number was a dead giveaway.

There was little doubt it was the same helicopter that continually ferried Howard Ross off to desert destinations unknown. Always north by northwest. And now it was resting unguarded, in a warm pool of incandescent light not quite thirty yards beyond the chain-link fence.

Darkstar lowered her field glasses and rummaged around in her satchel for the duplicate set of Ross' keys.

There they are.

I've got a feeling that one of you guys opens this gate.

After scanning the quiet area a final time, she rushed over to the gate, bag in tow. Seconds later the lock yielded to a surprisingly small key and she slipped within. A considerable swath of deep shadows beneath a wide overhang to her right provided immediate sanctuary.

With swift precision Darkstar outfitted her M1895 revolver with a suppressor and took aim at the light pole closest to the chopper. On her third attempt, the bulb went dark with minimal fanfare. She was disgusted with her delayed success.

I'm glad General Fyodorov wasn't here to see that.

The combination of a moonless, overcast sky with an out-of-commission tarmac light yielded optimal conditions for her mission; a mission that had to be postponed for well over a month. The discovery of Ross' frequent—*often daily*—

jaunts to the north by helicopter necessitated the acquisition of highly sophisticated tracking equipment. Darkstar's primary handler smuggled a portable HF/DF receiver with a corresponding transmitter through recently developed channels in Los Angeles. Oksana had personally retrieved the gear from a remote drop site in the foothills east of Pasadena two days prior.

She reclined with her back against the building and surveyed the lack of activity across the Vegas airfield. With her pistol, an assortment of tools, the transmitter, and dark packing material, she scurried across the tarmac and afforded herself a prone position beneath the smooth belly of the two-seater.

Over the passage of the next six minutes, Darkstar removed an endcap from the aircraft's tubular frame, activated the transmitter, and stowed it deep inside the pipe. Once the endcap was reattached, she reconned the area and prepared to scramble back to her shadowy sanctuary.

A sound.

A low rumble.

She plastered herself low to the ground and glanced north. A single set of headlights approached in haste.

A jeep. I've got about forty-five seconds.

CHAPTER 28

Denver couldn't deny the obvious.

Brenda Jo was making a deliberate effort to take up a position by the only exit out of The Basement.

She seemed so happy about tonight's meeting.

I wonder what's wrong.

He drifted around the back of the table and snuck over to her. "Hey, stranger."

Brenda Jo seemed shocked and looked up. "Oh, hello, Mr. Collins."

"It's Denver, remember?"

"Sorry. Denver."

"Are you nervous?"

"Nervous?" she replied. "Oh, no. More like excited. My stomach's all butterflies."

He squinted. "Then why are you retreating towards the stairs?" He pointed forward. "The show is that way. I figured you'd be right up front."

She seemed at a loss for words. "Well, uh, Ellen said we needed to put on goggles and such. I imagined there must be some kinda danger involved. After all, Doc said this whole place is nuclear. So, yeah…maybe I am a tad bit nervous."

Denver chuckled. "Listen, Miss Tilley, if that power room goes *boom,* then it doesn't matter if you're back here, or upstairs, or wherever. It's game over." He grinned. "I've had just a taste of what it can do. Trust me. I know."

"You keep hinting at all these great stories," she lamented. "One of these days you're gonna have to actually *tell me* some of them." She motioned towards the portal. "But if what they're about to show us is real, then you better hurry up. We may not be here long. At least I certainly hope we won't."

"Do you like milkshakes?"

Her eyes flitted back and forth. "Um, where did that come from?"

"Just answer the question."

She appeared offended. "Hello? Who do you think you're talking to? I'm a female. From Arkansas. Need I say more? Yes, Mr. Collins…we love milkshakes."

"It's a date then."

"Uh, date? Did I miss something, cause—"

"Corner of Main and West Virginia."

"Excuse me?"

"Corner of Main and West Virginia. *Steak 'n Shake.*"

She adjusted her goggles. "Maybe it's perfectly acceptable in 2014, but back in 1987, it's not polite to keep a girl confused."

He gazed into the Portal Chamber, pokerfaced. "Best milkshakes in town. Join me for a drink and I'll tell you some of those stories."

"Sounds deliciously tempting."

"So it's a date?"

"A *tentative* date," she replied.

Denver nodded and walked forward. "Well, I'll let you scaredy-cats monitor the back row. But this cool cat's going to get a better seat. Later."

"I wouldn't count on it," Darkstar whispered as she reached into her heavy purse.

CHAPTER 29

Friday, April 16, 1948, 11:23 p.m.
Las Vegas Air Force Base
Las Vegas, Nevada

Darkstar flipped over onto her back and cradled the backside of her ankles on the lower portion of the helicopter's tail framing. She reached up and jammed her fingers into the small gaps surrounding the skid supports. As the jeep closed in on her, she strained to mold her body to the undercarriage like a dark human leech. Her muscles vibrated under the strain.

The squeal of brakes and a reduced engine-RPM indicated the jeep was slowing. It stopped.

A door opening.

Probably a pair of boots hitting the ground.

One man.

Footsteps.

Not getting closer…good.

Darkstar inched her head around to optimize her pitiful view as the smell of burnt oil and hot motor wafted across the asphalt. She could barely make out a single soldier wandering at the base of the failed light pole. He flipped on a strong flashlight and trained it far above him. Seconds later he reached for his radio.

"Base, this is Security."

His receiver crackled. "*Go ahead, Security.*"

The soldier knelt to examine the shards of glass on the ground. "We've got a busted bulb near Gate Two. The pole by the chopper. The 47."

Darkstar's upper arms began to ache.

There was a slight pause. *"Roger on that burned out tarmac bulb."*

The soldier shook his head. "Not burned out, Base…*busted*. Shattered. Glass's all over the place. Not sure what could've done it."

Another hesitation. *"Copy that, Security. We'll turn it over to maintenance. Base out."*

The soldier rose and ambled back towards his jeep.

She took deep breaths and resisted the overwhelming temptation to simply collapse to the ground. Her arms and shoulders continued throbbing and burning under the stress of her predicament. She was fairly certain her right hand was bleeding as well, but the warm trickle dripping from her wrist and trailing down to her elbow could've been long beads of sweat.

From her position glued below the chopper she could only see the soldier from the waist down. He stopped short of the jeep and began walking directly behind the helicopter. She pivoted her head to the opposite side.

A horrible thought raced through her mind.

Damn! The gate.

I didn't lock the gate behind me.

Stupid, Mizenov.

Stupid.

As she contemplated various scenarios, she realized her mistake might have just cost this young man his life. There were four rounds left in her gun. At this distance, she only needed one. He flicked his light on and played the beam all around the gate area. The soldier took a few more steps before his radio squelched to life.

"Base to Security."

He halted. "Go ahead, Base."

"You got any jumper cables in your jeep?"

The soldier spun around. "That's affirmative. What's going on?"

A pause. *"Security, please assist Captain Roland outside Gate Four with a vehicle."*

The soldier jogged over to his vehicle and hopped in. "Roger that, Base. Tell the Captain I'll be there in two minutes. Security, out."

With a grinding of heavy gears and the protest of tires angled too sharply, the jeep whirled about and accelerated north.

Darkstar released her grip and plummeted to the rough tarmac below. Her gnarled fingers seemed frozen in painful shock, refusing to even wiggle for what felt like an eternity. As the agonizing minutes passed by, her shoulders shuddered less and less, but the burning sensation appeared to flourish. She deduced that the primary culprit was the sudden rush of fresh blood surging back into the strained tissue.

Regardless of the cause, the misery was debilitating.

Come on, Mizenov. Gotta get out of here.

Get moving.

In an act of sheer willpower, she rolled out from beneath the metal beast and ventured back through the gate and out into the darkness.

Howard Ross could run, but now he had lost the ability to hide.

CHAPTER 30

It was show time.

Ellen relocated over by the power level control bar and locked her eyes on Doc as if on a master conductor.

"Please engage power and take us to ten percent of full power, Miss Finegan."

"Increasing to ten percent," she echoed.

"Dr. Papineau," Stonecroft called out as a dull hum reverberated throughout the two rooms, "would you be so kind as to activate the magnets?"

The French physicist tripped three different toggle switches. "*Aimants engages!*"

The intensity of the surge in power vibrated the concrete and started rattling anything and everything made of glass. Several people grabbed their goggles to stop them from tickling their scalp. Ellen smiled and pointed. "Watch for the blue electric smoke, folks," she hollered.

Everyone leaned in. She wasn't wrong. An illuminated mist traveled erratically across each of the three sides of the huge portal. Denver had been all over the world; he had seen a wide variety of bizarre phenomena, but this was impressive.

Incredible.

It does look like blue electric smoke.

"Take us to that magical milestone of twenty-five percent of full power, Miss Finegan," Doc ordered.

Ellen inched the power bar yet higher. The flickering light show and resultant roar were both wonderful and frightening. Leah grabbed Tori (whose eyes were already shut) and covered the child's ears. Martha raised her right hand and shielded her squinting face. Billy and Garrett drifted closer, drawn as moths to the flame.

Ellen hollered out. "I've brought the magic, Dr. Stonecroft."

Doc cupped his hands around his mouth. *"Dr. Papineau!* It is time for synchronization!"

Emile leaned forward and twirled three large dials in sequential order, left to right.

After glancing down at his watch, Doc cupped his mouth a final time. "Ladies and gentlemen, behold the wonder of temporal displacement!"

Denver cocked his head at an angle, irritated by the pulsing waves of sonic energy assailing his ears. He caught a glimpse of Betty Larson reclining against the table. She appeared to be in pain, but Betty looked up right as the magic happened.

The portal pulsated and a bizarre optical spectacle ensued as all three magnets matched exact velocities. A swirling mist interspersed with tiny electrical arcs pulled towards the center of the device.

Then…it happened.

A flash.

A shockwave of pure sound.

Two of the women shrieked…then, silence.

Silence, but with a view. Such a view.

The demonstration lasted just shy of six seconds. Everyone pushed forward, even a distant and reclusive Brenda Jo. The city scene that materialized before them was nominal. The sky was overcast. But the time period was undeniably future.

Denver was awestruck.

That's gotta be the early to mid-1970s. Gotta be.

Freaking amazing.

Betty Larson pushed off the table and forced her way through the enraptured crowd. Several of the faces in the two rooms were becoming wet with fresh tears. "Oh my!" Betty yelled. "It's home. Home!"

Doc's smile threatened to crack his own face in two. "It's not *home* to all of us, Ms. Larson, but it is *hope* for all of us!"

And then it collapsed.

Ellen killed the power immediately and Papineau was careful to disengage the magnets a few seconds later. As the thick hum of raw power began to dwindle, the group began stirring and staring at one another. Several danced, everyone hugged.

Brenda Jo snuggled up to a well-pleased Dr. Stonecroft. "That was unbelievable! Amazing! Inspiring! Doc, you are so wonderful! I could just hug and kiss you forever!"

His round face flushed. "Well, my dear Miss Tilley, I am flattered. But to be fair, most of your praise and adoration should be directed at my colleague." He gestured towards Emile. "None of this would even be remotely possible without his considerable background in theoretical physics."

She leaned back. "Well, whatever…I still think you're amazing."

Doc grinned. "Well, if and when we are able to overcome our substantial efficiency issues, it will be Dr. Papineau and his irreplaceable expertise that will send us all home. I have often said, that when it comes to our research…I am the mouth, Miss Finegan is the heart, but Emile is the brain."

Ellen's head shot up. "Hey! I thought I was the pretty face?!"

They all chuckled. "To be fair, Miss Finegan," Doc offered, "you are the most fair. By far. By far, my dear."

Brenda Jo snatched Doc's arm and after weaving him through the crowd, they sauntered towards the Portal Chamber. "I have a question," she said.

"As do I, my child. Multitudes of them."

"Listen," she said, pointing. "Does that thing only work in one direction?"

"What, my dear? The portal?"

"Yes."

He studied her. "I imagine that you are inquiring about the possibility that another party could jump here through our wormhole? Hijack it, so to speak."

"No, no," she said. "I mean, does it only go forward? Forward in time. Or could you jump back to an earlier time?"

"Oh, goodness gracious me, I'm sorry, my dear. I'm a little dense at times," he said. "Now I understand your perfectly acceptable question."

"Well, could you?"

He traced his finger horizontally through the air. "Your confusion, Miss Tilley, arises from the hypothesis that you envision time as merely a *line*. That view would dictate that we are at a certain point in time along that line. Everything before that point is the past, and everything after that is the future."

Her eyes flitted back and forth. "So, um, is there *another way* to think about time? I thought that's the way it was, or is, or whatever."

His eyes grew wide. "Oh, my dear, there are myriad theories about that mysterious entity we arrogantly label as *time*. There is even a particular school of thought that denies that time even exists, at least as a distinct property of reality." He hesitated. "Think about a pool."

"A pool?" she asked. "You mean like a *swimming* pool?"

"That will do," he agreed. "What our models and research here have shown is that time is not at all like a line, rather it more resembles a pool of water. Consider it as the sea."

"Okay," she nodded, eyes closed, "I am picturing your sea of time."

"Good. Good. Now imagine hundreds, thousands of ships afloat on that ocean, and innumerable aquatic creatures, majestic and miniscule. An entire ocean just teeming with life and activity."

Her expression brightened. "Wait—I think I just saw a whale!"

"Very well. Now, just as those mighty manmade vessels and schools of fish are moving freely about, both beyond and below its surface, this is a metaphor of time. The same water that bears up the boats is the same water that surrounds all marine life. Time, like water, is the medium that surrounds us, and holds us. Not a line, but a *sea* of possibilities."

Brenda Jo seemed lost in wonder as she pried her eyes back open. "Okay. Okay. Got it…I think. So, um, how does that answer my question about going back in time?"

Doc patted her hand. "We are often tempted to employ phrases such as *back in time* or *forward in time*. I have become increasingly convinced that all such conventions are oversimplifications at best, and thoroughly misguided at worst." He chuckled. "Time, my dear, is just that…*time*."

She furrowed her brow and squinted. "So, the answer is…*yes?*"

"Once we have properly calibrated the Tesla portal, and have overcome our efficiency barriers, then we should have the capacity to transfer anyone to any point in the sea of time."

He took a few steps towards the portal with his hand on his chin. "They may mean a great deal to us, but the temporal realm is blissfully unaware of concepts such as backward or forward, Miss Tilley. Our narrow-minded concepts need to be brought into agreement with the data. Sadly, many of them are not."

She wandered down the metal mesh walkway toward the impressive triangular contraption. She caressed the radiating fins on its left side before glancing back.

"You're telling me that it is just as easy to send someone to, let's say, 1937, as it is 2037?"

Doc adjusted his spectacles and shrugged.

"Not to merely a certain year, my dear…but to a certain day, at a certain hour, during a certain minute, and even arriving precisely at a certain second."

CHAPTER 31

Friday, April 23, 1948, 10:03 p.m.
South Central, Nevada

The brilliant disc crept back into sight, accenting the colorless desert in varying tones of gray.

A full moon.

Stay with me, I'm going to need you before long.

Darkstar had invested six days and as many nights endeavoring to isolate the cryptic destination of Ross' Bell 47 helicopter. The frustrating investigation had added over seven hundred and twenty miles to her odometer with precious little to show for it.

The lack of paved roads to the north and west of Las Vegas hampered her efforts to monitor usable readings from the HF/DF receiver hidden in the trunk of her car. The state of the art tracking system–powered by a second car battery—grew increasingly erratic as she had ventured towards Tonopah.

This westward deficiency forced her reluctant hand in adopting a less-optimal strategy elsewhere. The topographic irregularities along US 93 to the north afforded partial success, with her clearest reception arising thirty-five miles west of the insignificant ghost town of Crystal Springs. Through careful signals analysis aligned with basic triangulation she had identified a *more-probable-than-not* area of interest a few miles south of the base of Bald Mountain.

The investigation turned off-road, and Darkstar purchased and modified a rugged motorcycle to complete the final leg of her desperate search.

She turned onto a heavily-rutted dirt path jutting south from State Route 25 and killed the engine. The heat radiating off either side of the bike's motor offered welcome relief to ten fingers that had endured two hours of temperatures in the low thirties aggravated by handlebar-level, road-speed wind chills. Darkstar dug into her saddle bag and fished out a flashlight. A quick scan of her map indicated at least forty miles of rough (or non-existent) trails leading south to the mystery location.

She packed the guide in her coat pocket and trained her flashlight at the base of a pile of desert rocks off to her left. The two gas cans she had hidden there the day before were still intact, and she replenished the thirsty tank on her military-grade bike.

The infiltration had been meticulously orchestrated. With any luck, she anticipated reaching the search area in just under two hours. This provided a comfortable window for initial reconnaissance before the unwelcome exposure courtesy of a 6:00 a.m. sunrise. Her incursion was timed to coincide with a full moon so that she could navigate without a headlamp for the last leg of the journey.

The muffler had been modified with generous helpings of glass wool and perforated metal to minimize engine noise, and she had even coated the entire chopper with flat black paint to eliminate any threat of unwanted reflections.

As the repetitious, uneven and bone-chilling miles clicked by, Darkstar pondered what might await her.

If Project SATURN is headquartered out here, it's a brilliant location. Inconvenient, but brilliant...I'll give them that.

Dry, desolate desert.

Far away from civilization, airports, air traffic. Away from Washington.

Not too far from Roswell. If that even matters.

Does that matter, Mr. Ross?

What does matter, Howard?

Her list of questions was considerably longer than the supply of answers. But it was of little concern. She had Ross.

Her motorbike topped a low ridge, and Darkstar brought the vehicle to a standstill. By her crude calculations, she was less than five miles out from the area of interest, so she extinguished the headlight. The pale radiance of the moon appeared more than adequate to complete the mission.

The terrain, which had been level for the last ten miles, began a noticeable descent in a gentle curve to the southeast. She eased off on the gas and allowed gravity to perform its irresistible work. Within minutes she shut the motor off altogether and coasted.

What's this?

In the distance…a bright pinprick.

A light.

Several lights.

A thousand yards out from the bright anomaly she studied the immediate vicinity to locate an obvious landmark. A cream-colored, rocky outcrop on her left caught her eye.

That will do nicely.

Darkstar hopped out of her seat and walked the bike under the ledge. She snatched a gun, a camera, and her binoculars before running down the loose soil of the slope. There was little doubt that the number and diversity of the lights was growing as she rapidly covered the distance.

What's that sound?

It began as an indistinguishable, muffled rumble.

It matured into the unmistakable roar of large engines.

Heavy equipment? Aircraft?

Four hundred yards out she dropped to the sandy soil and raised her field glasses. Her first guess had been accurate.

Heavy equipment. Bulldozers, dump trucks, backhoes.

Dozens of workers scurried about. Large floodlights rimmed the scene. She continued to scan the area as her heart rate climbed.

Looks like hangars, barracks, offices.

Tremendous manmade mountains of rock and sand littered a much wider perimeter. There seemed to be only one probable explanation.

Underground construction?

Beyond all that, a familiar vehicle.

Ross' helicopter. And a plane. Looks like a C-47.

And trucks. Several trucks.

At last…Project SATURN.

She lowered the binoculars and prepared to advance on the operation. Darkstar was satisfied.

The science of location always preceded the art of infiltration.

CHAPTER 32

Leadership usually discouraged such gatherings, but Martha insisted that Betty Larson's sudden recovery (coupled with Brenda Jo's arrival) deserved a traditional southern Sunday supper, even if it wasn't a Sunday. Grandma Tomlin's stately charm and enviable wisdom were difficult to ignore and well-nigh impossible to overrule at times. The handpicked guest list included all of the female Jumpers and a select group of males including Denver, Doc, and the Chief.

Martha's formal dining room, accented in various shades of blue, housed an elongated colonial dining table. As the evening meal began to wind down, Denver admired the exquisite lathe work on the nearest leg.

"It's solid mahogany, Mr. Collins," Martha called out above the chatter of casual conversation. "Hand built by Amish craftsmen settled in Pennsylvania. It was a gift from Mr. Nelson. Christmas. 1952."

He glanced up without raising his head. "It's very nice. My grandmother, on my mother's side, she had quite a collection of Amish furniture."

Martha nodded. "I imagine that she and I would have gotten along marvelously."

"I have no doubt, ma'am. I have no doubt."

Brenda Jo wiped her mouth. "Mrs. Tomlin, as a girl from the South, I am well-aware of every dessert recipe known to man. But your chocolate bread pudding...it is absolutely divine." She squinted. "What is your secret?"

Ellen and Leah erupted with uncontrollable chuckles, but were squelched in short order by Martha's hard and fast gaze. Mrs. Tomlin sat up and deposited her pale hands on the table, composing herself. "First, thank you, my dear. That particular delight is a cherished recipe that has been handed down in my family for over six generations."

Ellen and Leah raised their napkins in a desperate bid to conceal their giggling. Brenda Jo took another bite, savoring it. "I detect a harshness, yet a smooth sweetness I've never tasted in a bread pudding. Is it the type of chocolate?"

Ellen couldn't seem to restrain herself. "Oh, it's not the chocolate!"

Brenda elevated her dessert bowl and inhaled deeply. "The aroma is almost…intoxicating!"

"You're definitely getting warmer," Ellen blurted out with an infectious smile. Leah turned and busied herself with Tori in an obvious bid at self-distraction.

Betty Larson snuck a sample from her own bowl. "Oh," she said. "*Oh.*"

"Could someone let me in on this little inside joke?" Brenda Jo implored.

"Not with the Chief around," Ellen responded between small bites.

Martha rose suddenly. "Here, now, what a miserable hostess I have been. Let me deal with these dishes."

Brenda remained puzzled and peeked over at McCloud. "The Chief? What does it matter if the Chief is around?"

Ellen pushed her chair back and helped to clear the table. "Well, now…why don't you tell her, Martha?"

"It is a secret and cherished family recipe, Miss Finegan," Martha almost scolded.

"Oh, it's a family *recipe* all right," Ellen jabbed. "If you don't tell her, I will."

"You wouldn't," Martha chided indignantly.

"I would."

Martha's furious activity came to a screeching halt and she lowered her stack of plates back down to the table with controlled subtlety. Ellen was anything but subtle in her explanation. "What Grandma Martha here has tried to hide is that her secret culinary weapon is…*whiskey*."

The room fell silent with the exception of a few gasps punctuating the tension. Denver stared up at Mrs. Tomlin; her frustrated expression was priceless.

"Miss Finegan is incorrect, Miss Tilley," Martha retorted. "Quite incorrect."

"Okay, well then," Ellen said playfully, "by all means…please enlighten us with the truth."

Martha paused. "The recipe requires *bourbon*."

"Oh, come now, Martha," Ellen protested, "they're the same thing. Bourbon is just a more socially acceptable name for whiskey."

Doc Stonecroft peeled off his glasses and shook them towards Ellen. "My dear Miss Finegan…your alcoholic assertion is not entirely accurate. All bourbon is indeed whiskey, but not all whiskey can be properly designated as bourbon. Bourbon requires the use of corn…traditional whiskey does not. And that is merely one of the differences."

Brenda Jo leaned to her left and whispered to Denver. "So, why does it matter if the Chief knows there is bourbon in the bread pudding? Is he allergic to it?"

Denver pulled her in closer, keeping his own voice low. "Well, uh, Normal has a city ordinance against alcohol. It's what they call a dry town. The Chief is supposed to, you know, enforce that law, too."

Her eyes grew wide. "Oh. Gotcha. Gotcha."

"Aren't you gonna break out the handcuffs, Chief?" Ellen teased. "You should probably raid her fridge and basement right now! Probably loaded with contraband."

Martha returned to the stack of dishes before her and ignored the taunt.

McCloud arched back. "No. No…there won't be any rumrunners hauled down to the station tonight. Ain't no way I would lock up someone that could cook so well as to make heaven itself jealous. Ain't no way!" He leaned forward and slid the offending bowl of chocolate bread pudding toward himself. "But, in the interest of public safety, I'll have to commandeer the remainder of this here dessert. Before anyone else tries to consume the evidence."

Everyone laughed and Martha slapped him across the back. McCloud shrugged with an almost-innocent smile. "Just doin' my civic duty as a duly appointed officer of the law, ma'am."

"Sounds like a great story for the paper, Betty," Ellen offered as she spread her hands out in the air. "*Extra! Extra! Read all about it!* Normal Police Chief busted with bread pudding booze buddies!"

"Whoa! Whoa, there!" Betty protested. "Awful alliterations are the exclusive domain of *my* profession, Miss Finegan. It's one of our few true joys in life…please don't take it away from us!"

Ellen waved her hand in feigned submission and continued to clear the table. Betty dropped her napkin on the table and stood.

"But, while we are on the subject of newspapers and headlines and such…I would like to make a somewhat *public* announcement." The room's attention shifted to her en masse. "I would like to publicly acknowledge the *above-and-beyond* the call of duty efforts of Miss Alexus Daniels and Mr. Denver Wayne Collins-Jackson down at the *Journal* in my absence."

She grabbed her glass and raised it. "They kept the floundering ship afloat whilst the captain was away. And I want to thank them both."

Several other glasses went up, and Leah struggled to help Tori raise hers to join in on the fun.

Alexus took a drink and nodded. "It was a pleasure, Miss Larson. And…I would like to continue working at the paper, if I may. If you need me, that is."

Betty stared over at the Chief. "Well, that is not my call, sweetheart," she said. "But I would love to have you. I've scanned over your articles. They're great. Really. What do you think, Chief?"

McCloud lowered his cup as the weight of a roomful of silent attention fell upon him. "I'll discuss it with the powers that be. But remember, folks, the less attention we draw, the better. We need to ease into things. Kinda like when I moved into the position as police chief. I basically took the job at the end of March in '52, but it wasn't until a month or so later that I had the official title. We kept the fanfare down. Changes bring attention, specially in a small town."

"You mean *black skin* brings attention, don't you Chief?" Denver asked.

"Changes," McCloud reiterated. "*Changes* bring attention."

Silence.

"Well, now that Betty has started a round of toasts," Denver said as he raised his glass. "I would like to offer one in acknowledgement of your terrific home-cooked meal, Mrs. Tomlin."

Martha blushed and waved her hand as everyone joined in on the fun. "Cooking is one of life's purest and simplest pleasures," she noted. "The good book says that it is better to give than to receive. I'm delighted that you have enjoyed it."

"Enjoy's not quite a strong enough word," Ellen offered.

"I'll second that," Leah said.

"I think we need to do this again…and real soon," the Chief blurted out. "Tell me, Mrs. Martha, when's the last time you cooked crappie?"

She wiped her mouth. "Oh my—that particular delicacy has not crossed through my kitchen since William delivered several pounds to me late last summer."

"I remember that," Ellen nearly shouted. "It was to die for. Southern fried. Poor Billy barely got to eat any of his own catch!"

Martha leaned in. "Why do you ask, James?"

"I heard a rumor," the Chief began. "A lil bird told me that Denver might be headin' up to Lake Bloomington. Crappie are bitin' right 'bout now."

"I didn't know you were an angler, Mr. Collins," Ellen said.

"That's because I'm *not,*" Denver admitted with a light-hearted grin. "But, Hank wants to go and drown some worms, and I love the outdoors, so I'll see what I can do."

"What kind of alcohol goes well with fried fish, Martha?" Ellen asked.

"That's easy," McCloud responded. "Beer. Cold, and I mean *ice cold,* beer."

Ellen jumped and departed for the kitchen. "I'll check the fridge," she teased.

Brenda Jo cleared her throat and spoke up. "Well, talking about alcohol and all…I for one am glad it's a dry town, as Mr. Collins called it." She peered across the table at Doc. "Grandpa Tilley was an alcoholic. My dad told me stories about…about how grandpa would get liquored up every night and then do…*terrible* things to his family. Grandma finally left him over it. Nobody who really knew my grandpa ever challenged her decision. Alcohol turned a good man into a monster."

"Heavens, child," Martha said, "that's awful. My favorite uncle on my father's side passed away due to liver disease. We all knew that it was alcohol. Daddy refused to address it."

"I can tell each and every one of you," McCloud said as Ellen returned, "from miserable first-hand experience, that alcohol is a destroyer of families, and careers, and lives."

Doc blinked a few times and dropped his head. Leah chimed in. "I, uh, I lost a cousin to alcohol. But, he didn't drink it, at least as far as I knew. But someone else did the drinking. My cousin was riding his bike home from work one evening. A drunken driver swerved and hit him. Crushed him." She hesitated, her voice trembling. "He…he was twenty-three."

Doc fetched his napkin and wiped his cheeks.

"What about the driver?" Brenda Jo inquired.

Leah concentrated on the glass of tea in her hand. "A few scratches. Not even a year in jail. I think he got out early for good behavior or something. My cousin's mom—my aunt—she had a nervous breakdown. Never was right after that. Ever."

"I write about it every day," Betty mourned. "The innocent pay, and the guilty walk free among us."

Doc Stonecroft exploded into tears and shoved away from the table. "I…I…must beg your leave." He tried to look over at Martha and fumbled through his words. "Thank…thank you for your kind hospitality…Martha. I must…must depart."

Leah sprung up from her chair as she and Ellen rushed to his side. He seemed determine to leave.

"Hey, hey there, Doc," Ellen comforted. "Whoa. What's wrong? What's going on?"

Leah furnished him with a fresh napkin and rubbed his soft back with wide and gentle strokes. "Talk to us, Doc. Don't shut us out. Whatever it is…it can't be that bad."

The weeping mathematician brought himself to a standstill and leaned against an oak china hutch. His stubby fingers shook as he ripped off his tear-soaked spectacles. "To…be *disagreeable* is not within my nature, my dear Miss Swan, but…with all due respect, you are wrong. It *is* that bad." He buried his face in the napkin as his chest heaved in a second wave of sorrow.

Martha slid a nearby chair away from the dining room table and cautiously guided him down into it. "Professor…professor, please. Please sit here. Do it for me. It would be unconscionable to allow you to leave in such a state." She motioned towards Ellen and whispered. "A fresh glass of ice water."

Ellen nodded. "I'm already on it."

Martha caught Leah's eye. "Mrs. Swan, let's give Dr. Stonecroft some space. Please."

Leah slid her arm down and retreated somewhat. "Oh, yes. Absolutely. Just trying to help."

"As we all are, dear. Thank you."

Ellen reappeared and settled the chilled cup into his waiting hands. He smiled as he seized the tiniest of sips. "Bless you, my dear."

Ellen winked. "Well, I'm a nurse, and every nurse worth her salt knows that cold water is often a miracle medicine."

With the drink still held aloft, he stared while the light danced across the shifting cubes. "It does refresh the body, but I'm afraid it cannot touch the heart, Miss Finegan. Or erase the past." More tears cascaded down his enflamed cheeks.

Martha scooted her own high-back chair closer and patted his hand. "Well, you know we love you, professor.

And if there is ever anything...*anything* that we can do for you, we count it an honor and a privilege to do so." She daubed his face with a dry napkin.

He bit his lip. "The playwright once penned that *'to weep is to make less the depth of grief.'*"

"*Shakespeare?* Only you would draw upon Shakespeare at such times," Martha observed, grinning.

His head bobbed with a matching forced smile. "It pains me to wax disagreeable once again, but...I have weighed the poet's words in the balance...and found them wanting. The grief has yet to be lessened."

Ellen slipped into her own chair and locked eyes with him. "Now hear me out, Dr. Glen Stonecroft. We have worked, side by side, for years, and I have only caught glimpses of this private pain of yours. I don't know what's wrong, but I do know two things. First, it's getting worse, and second, it involves your younger self. Am I right?"

He looked down into his hands.

"I am right, aren't I?" she insisted.

Martha motioned towards her. "I'm sure your intentions are honorable, Miss Finegan, but Professor Stone—"

"Professor Stonecroft," Ellen interjected, "is being slowly destroyed by the agonizing memories of days gone by. I studied psychology, Mrs. Tomlin, and I can confidently assure you that the only remedy in such cases is the courage to face these demons openly, honestly. Talk about them. Regrets are silent killers...far more dangerous than heart disease, or cancer."

Martha folded her arms. "Perhaps we should —"

"*Carolyn,*" Doc declared.

His single utterance caught everyone off-guard.

Nobody moved. It was doubtful that anyone breathed.

"Her name was Carolyn. Carolyn Anne Boulden."

CHAPTER 33

He was employed as the second-in-command of the most covert division of the most covert agency in the free world, yet Neal Schaeffer didn't enjoy espionage, per se.

He was an analyst by trade—an analyst now thrust into the clandestine realm of field work by necessity rather than choice. Between an office desk back at Dreamland plastered with scenarios and statistics and the daily physical grind of fake identities and human intel, he would have declared the decision a no-contest.

But today Agent Neal Schaeffer was Inspector Dean Schaeffer, and his desk 1,750 miles to the west would have to wait.

"Sorry to keep you waiting, Mr. Schaeffer," a smartly-dressed, lanky gentleman offered with a handshake as he rushed into the small receiving area just behind the counter. "I'm Oliver Lancaster, director here at Chicago State Hospital."

Neal slid his briefcase to the side and returned the gesture. "No inconvenience at all, Director Lancaster. Certainly far less aggravating than my delayed flight from Washington yesterday." He paused. "Terrible fog, terrible."

Lancaster shook his head. "Trust me, we have quite a bit of experience with fickle weather. You deal with the effects of the Potomac, well, we have Lake Michigan to contend with, and she borders on the unpredictable most days."

"Indeed," Neal agreed. "I trust that you received notice concerning the nature of my visit from the under-secretary?"

"Of course," Lancaster replied. "Two days ago. We are happy to comply with any and all requests from the Public Health Service during your audit, Mr. Schaeffer."

Neal retrieved his briefcase. "Good, good. And please…call me Dean. No need to make this formal inquiry any more formal than necessary."

Director Lancaster led him down a narrow hall. "I have arranged a temporary office for you right here on the first floor. My staff has been notified to provide you with any and all records you require."

He pulled out a wad of keys and opened a door on the left. "If you need access to any physical locations on the grounds, please notify the front desk. They will provide you an escort with a set of keys."

Neal slipped into the modest office. "You are most kind. Thank you."

Lancaster lifted his sleeve and checked his watch. "I would have been delighted to take you to lunch today, but I must beg your leave. I have to attend an eleven-thirty memorial service for one of our psychologists."

Neal frowned as he laid his briefcase down. "Ah, of course. It was a Dr. Montgomery, wasn't it? Car accident?"

"Unfortunately, you are correct on both accounts, Mr. Schaeffer. A huge loss. He had been with us for over twenty years. So sad. A lot of my senior staff will be there as well. Please forgive any delays it may cause today."

Neal tossed his dark suit coat onto a chair and loosened his tie. "It's a bit of adding insult to injury, isn't it?"

Lancaster took a step inside. "I'm sorry, come again?"

"Well, it has to be difficult handling two tragedies in less than one week, Director."

"*Two* tragedies?"

Neal navigated his way around and dropped into his new desk chair. "Sorry, I was referring to the bloated body that washed up on the west shore of Lake Michigan earlier this week."

The director bit his lip. "Oh, yes. Of course. Mr. Taylor. Andrew Taylor."

"He was an orderly here at Chicago State Hospital for what, three years? Four?"

"Four."

"What do you think, Director Lancaster—accidental death, murder, suicide?"

"Well, Inspector, I…I will have to defer to qualified law enforcement for that determination."

Neal stared up at the ceiling fan. "A broken neck can be self-inflicted, often associated with falling. But in a body of water? In Lake Michigan? Seems suspicious. Especially since the body lacked traditional impact trauma."

Lancaster folded his arms and studied him. "I must admit that you are very *thorough,* Mr. Schaeffer."

"The devil's in the details," Neal quipped with a confident grin.

"So I guess that makes me the Devil."

CHAPTER 34

Doc concentrated on the center of the table, now surrounded by human statues.

"She was nineteen. Her friends and family fondly called her *Cookie*." He began to dry his glasses. "I was never able to ascertain the source for such an odd and adorable nickname." He paused. "But…it must've been important. Somehow essential. Her parents had it engraved on her headstone. *Cookie* it said. Cookie."

A few people traded somber glances.

"It was on a Tuesday. A Tuesday night. Late. November twentieth, 1956. She was coming home from college for Thanksgiving recess. She…she was a student of accounting. At Youngstown."

Doc examined his spectacles.

"November twentieth. That's my birthday, you know. My birthday. My *twenty-first* birthday. The big two-one, as they say, with all the attendant rites of passage thereunto. Sixteen days from today, in fact."

Tori bolted up out of her seat with an announcement. "I'm tired."

Leah blushed and took her by the shoulders. "Oh, of course, Tori, I'm sorry. Why don't you lie down on the couch in Ms. Martha's living room? Would that be okay?"

Tori walked off. "Okay."

Martha followed after her.

Stonecroft's confession didn't miss a beat. "I cannot recall, for the life of me, the name of that tavern. There was certainly no lack of local watering holes. They practically dotted the landscape along that southern stretch of Franklin

County." He further polished his glasses, rotating them in the warm light of the chandelier.

"I imbibed...once and again. My youthful recklessness was only exceeded by my naïve foolishness. I greatly *underestimated* the effects of the alcohol, and I greatly *overestimated* my ability to navigate a motorized vehicle in the immediate hours following. A Chevrolet…and one on loan from a friend."

Doc exchanged his spectacles for his cup, twirling it in the hot puddle formed by his own incessant stream of tears. The ice clinked and tumbled from side to side. "Some numbers are engraved, as it were, on your mind. Mile marker number 243 on US 62. At a quarter past ten o'clock. At least…that's what the report from the local authorities indicated."

Martha returned and slipped inaudibly into her seat. A reassuring nod over at Leah was all that needed to be said between the two women.

"I suppose I drifted into the far lane," Doc rehearsed, his voice sinking deep and raspy. "I…remember…a brilliant flash of light. Carolyn swerved in her Chevrolet. It was white. Her tires etched dark arcs upon the pavement." He took a moment to dry his face again. "It…was…at the base of an oak tree where those cursed streaks ended, and…her young life ended as well."

Martha's wrinkled hands descended gently upon his. "Oh, professor, I am so sorry. So terribly, terribly sorry. Forgive us for our insensitive trespass into this most private of matters."

His sorrowing head swung low in her direction. "For nearly three-score years I have carried this burden of shame. And now, Providence has seen fit to bring me back in time…could it be to cleanse these guilty hands stained with innocent blood?"

Ellen cleared her throat. "You know that we all love you, Doc. And any of us would do anything—*anything*—for you. At any time. But what's done is done. We can't even entertain the notion of changing the past. Or this past. Or whatever. The Fourth Accord is there to protect all of us."

He peered deep into his shallow cup. "I am assured of two equal and opposing positions, Miss Finegan. First and foremost, that your admonitions are indeed correct. And second, that one cannot ignore the opportunities which transcend mere coincidence."

"Perhaps the intervention of the elder may yet reverse the indiscretion of the younger."

CHAPTER 35

Forty-eight hours and three hundred seventy-six patient files later, Neal Schaeffer stumbled upon the intriguing promise of pure gold.

He grabbed the phone and dialed a short extension.

"Yes, hello. This is Inspector Schaeffer…down the hall. I need all files and pertinent records related to a particular patient."

He adjusted the phone on his weary shoulder.

"I am looking for all information regarding a patient…"

"…a *Mr. Gordon Thompson.*"

CHAPTER 36

"If everyone'll cut the chitchat and grab a seat," Chief McCloud shouted above the noisy din, "then we can get started."

With the exception of Billy O'Connell, all of the men were present in the main factory conference room. Representation among the ladies was limited to just Ellen and Brenda Jo. The clusters of conversation broke apart and everyone eventually sat down, with the solitary exception of Garrett Frazier who chose to lean against the wall by the door.

"There's a free chair over there, Garrett," the Chief gestured.

"I'm fine," came the instant and defiant reply.

"Suit yourself. I'm gonna turn this over to Doc and let him give us the update and all. It's all yours, Doc." McCloud sat as the aged researcher rose to his feet.

"Thank you, my friend. As everyone is still basking in the glow of our recent demonstration, my colleagues and I wanted to address what is lacking in our research and to elicit a plan to rectify that need. It is not my desire to burden you with a detailed account of—"

"Look Doc," Shep interjected as he sank back into his chair with folded arms. "I think all of us are pretty damn sure that what we saw was the *good news*...so just treat us all like adults and cut to the chase. What's the *bad news?*"

Stonecroft paused, measuring his response. "Browning once penned that '*All we have willed or hoped or dreamed of good shall exist.*' Our recent demonstration was indeed good news, but it was surely not the final word on the matter. It has provided visible and empirical proof that the prospect of intentional time travel no longer lingers within the domain of merely *theoretical* physics."

Doc surveyed the sea of faces. "The Victorian poet was right. All we have willed and hoped and dreamt of will come to pass. Intentional time travel using a Tesla portal is now merely a matter of time."

Shep sighed. "Do I need to draw a diagram so that your enlarged brain can grasp the meaning of *cut to the chase?* Is the concept of brevity not mathematical enough for you, Glen?"

"Let him talk, man!" Terrance called out.

"Let him talk?! Talking is his biggest problem," Shep retorted.

"No," Denver added. "Right now, your mouth is the problem."

Shep half-rose out of his chair and glared across the table. "Right now, I'm staring our number one problem dead in the eye, Colorado."

"You boys can take this...*playground fight* outside, but only *after* we finish this meeting," Ellen shouted. "So just shut the hell up and let Doc explain our real problem for Pete's sake."

The tension remained but the bickering subsided. Doc cleared his throat. "Our dilemma is two-fold. First, the amount of energy necessary to transmit or receive photons of light through a temporal rift is miniscule when compared to the task of transporting, let's say, a two-hundred pound human being."

Ellen spoke up. "Don't worry, everyone. We can generate enough power to do that. But the problem is *time.* We need to find a way to transfer that huge surge of energy in a very short window of time. Similar to lightning, and everyone remembers how important lightning is."

Doc nodded. "Thank you for that crucial clarification, Miss Finegan. Our first problem involves the efficient transfer of energy. The metals we are currently employing contain far too much resistance. We need efficiencies that are at least three orders of magnitude greater than our present results."

"Three orders of magnitude? Is that a big difference?" Brenda Jo asked, somewhat timidly.

Ellen's eyebrows shot up. "Oh yeah. Big difference. Big, big difference. It's about a thousand times different, Miss Tilley."

"What's the other problem?" McCloud inquired.

"Our other area of concern," Doc offered, "is our stability. At present, we can create a temporal rift…a *wormhole* if you will. But what we cannot create is a *stable* rift. And we need a very stable rift to transport an entire human being."

"So, we are facing two very different and significant problems," Denver said.

Stonecroft's face brightened with excitement. "Yes, indeed, two different obstacles, Mr. Collins, but two obstacles with one rather elegant solution. And thankfully a solution that Dr. Papineau is uniquely qualified to employ. We are so fortunate to have someone of his caliber."

The Chief piped up. "*One solution?* I like the sound o' that! "

Ellen smiled. "Don't let the idea of only *one solution* fool you, Chief. It won't be easy. We need about ten pounds of a superconductor."

Dr. Papineau began nodding with noticeable interest. "*Oui. Supraconducteur!*"

"Superconductor?" Brenda Jo repeated.

"Yes, Miss Tilley, a superconductor," Doc answered. "And not just any superconductor. More specifically a high-temperature superconductor. Our current necessity is to obtain a material that can achieve sustained superconductivity at or above the balmy temperature of liquid nitrogen."

"And how warm is that?" Denver asked.

Doc squinted and folded his arms. "Somewhere in the vicinity of seventy-seven Kelvin."

"*English* please."

"Oh, yes, Mr. Collins. On the traditional Fahrenheit scale, that would approximate to roughly three hundred and twenty degrees *below* zero. Depending on a few other factors, pressure being primary of course."

"Oh, yes, of course," Denver remarked as he winked over at Brenda Jo.

Garrett finally took a seat. "It's 1956. Are you telling me the technology exists now—*right now*—to go all the way down to somewhere over three hundred degrees below zero?"

Doc took a few careful steps towards him. "The short answer is *yes,* Mr. Frazier. Liquid nitrogen is readily available, and has been for years. But, that is not the problem. The problem is acquiring the requisite superconductive material."

"Does it exist yet?" Denver asked. "Please tell me that it exists."

"You can put your uneasiness to rest, Mr. Collins. At least two varieties of cuprate materials have been developed at this time which exhibit superconductivity at those elevated temperatures. And with Dr. Papineau's guidance, we should be able to fashion our elegant solution from either one of them, in a matter of weeks."

"*Weeks?*" Brenda Jo repeated.

"Weeks," Doc assured.

"Well, then," Terrance said with growing excitement, "gimme the keys to the company car and a blank check and I'll head to the hardware store. What's the holdup, man? What're we waiting for?"

Ellen grinned. "You won't find the kind of metals we need at the local hardware store, Tee. Or any store for that matter. Anywhere. It isn't for sale. If it was, we would have already ordered it."

"Everything and *everyone* has a price," Shep countered with a smirk.

Doc picked his way back to his chair and unfolded a large map. "Actually, Mr. Sheppard, price is not the issue. It is location. *Location* is the issue."

"Well, where the heck is it? *Fort Knox?*" McCloud asked with a subtle chuckle.

"One could only wish it was that easy, Chief McCloud. No, we don't need bars of gold bullion housed in a fortress to our southeast in Kentucky. Not by a longshot. We need to set our sights on a different metal, and a different direction. To the west. To the desert."

"Which desert?" Terrance inquired.

Stonecroft dropped a stubby finger down to the map. Everyone leaned in.

"Nevada?" Brenda Jo asked.

Denver leaned back. "Wait. Nevada? Where in Nevada?"

"Not quite one hundred miles north by northwest of Las Vegas," Doc answered. "Groom Lake to be exact."

"Groom Lake?" the Chief repeated. "What's that, a marriage retreat place?"

Denver pushed away from the table and started pacing. "Sorry, Chief, it isn't your typical honeymoon hotspot. There isn't even any water at Groom Lake." He hung his head down. "Wow. Of all places, Doc. You're positive they have it there?"

"Quite sure," Doc replied.

"Whaddya mean *no water*?" McCloud asked. "A lake with no water? How is that a lake?"

"I'm totally confused," Brenda Jo admitted.

"It is a facility that has acquired many different designations over the years," Doc explained. "The most common perhaps being Area 51."

Shep shrugged. "Never heard of it."

"Me neither," Ellen added.

"Wait! I have," McCloud said.

"And with good reason," Doc continued. "The general public will not even learn of its existence until sometime in the decade of the 1980s."

A concerned expression grew across McCloud's round face. "Um, Doc…seems like we're starting to trample all over the Second Accord here quite a bit. Dontcha think we should kinda—"

"With all due respect to both your concerns and the Second Accord, it is my sincere belief that the desperate nature of our condition mandates a bit of *indiscretion* if you will." Doc rubbed his pained face. "What I am proposing will require an immense and intricate plan for any hope of success. I doubt that simple knowledge concerning the existence of a classified military base will significantly harm our futures."

"Wait? Classified? You mean like a secret, a top secret military base?" Brenda Jo asked.

Denver looked over at her. "Yeah, but it's only the most secret of all top secret military bases in the entire world. No biggie."

Garrett jumped up. "Even if it was just your regular, run-of-the-mill military base, it would still take some real firepower to get in and get out. And probably fake IDs. And base maps."

Brenda Jo looked over at him.

Garrett was far from finished. "This kinda mission is a helluva lot more complicated than busting into a small-potatoes newspaper office and cracking a safe in the middle of a sleepy Sunday night."

"I'm guessing there's a complicated story there," Brenda whispered.

"There is," Denver whispered back.

"Will you tell me later?"

"It's a *long* story. Maybe over a milkshake at the—"

Brenda Jo laughed. "At the corner of Main and West Virginia."

"You got it. It's our officially-unofficial Jumper celebration hotspot."

Ellen ran her fingers through her auburn hair. "Even if we could plan it all out, who would go?"

The room grew silent for several seconds.

"We don't have to go," Shep announced. "We've got enough money to hire the job done."

"Work with organized crime?" McCloud asked.

"Who cares if they're organized?" Garrett demanded.

Ellen wasn't buying it. "No. That's a horrible plan. On so many different levels."

"Oh, I'm sorry," Shep said. "Were you right in the middle of sharing a brilliant plan?"

"Denver and I have military training, you know," Terrance offered. "We could go. Two man team."

"You gotta be kidding me, Tee!" Shep exploded. "*Denver?!* Let's see, of all the people in this room, which one of us cannot even keep track of his own damn wallet and is also currently the subject of a Federal manhunt? A few weeks of boot camp and an overseas desert vacation on his resume doesn't qualify him for this." Shep arched back and shook his head. "He couldn't even get away from a damn farmer with a crowbar!"

Denver drew in a deep breath and began counting, silently, slowly.

"The man has advanced training," Terrance countered. "Special Forces training. That includes interrogation and torture resistance. I think Denver's watertight, man. Our best chance."

Denver held his peace.

It wasn't easy.

"It's suicide," Shep declared.

"It's impossible," Garrett said.

Doc's brutally honest assessment caught everyone's attention.

"It's our *only* hope."

November 6, 1956

SECURITY LEVEL: TOP SECRET

FOR: Allen W. Dulles, Director, Central Intelligence
FROM: Chief Howard D. Ross, Project SATURN
SUBJECT: U-2 Surveillance

I am respectfully requesting a reconsideration of your decision regarding U-2 surveillance flights over the Continental USA.

I am confident that our current track record of maintaining classified information is unparalleled within the intelligence community. The risks are minimal, the rewards are inestimable.

The current reconnaissance initiative over the Suez has only required 70%-80% of our fleet.

Please advise

END

DCI/PS

CHAPTER 37

Brenda Jo hadn't been any trouble at all. She was a tad more talkative and quite a bit more inquisitive than Leah could've wished for, but she more than pulled her own weight. Normal's newest female arrival was the first boarder that the group had asked Leah to take on since Tori had relocated from Martha Tomlin's place.

Brenda Jo's outgoing personality provided nothing less than a complete culture shift within the modest home. Added to that, Leah actually found it refreshing to meet a Jumper who didn't need to endure weeks of her monotonous Temporal Orientation Classes. Brenda Jo's fluency with 1950's Americana had convinced leadership to forego the typical educational regimen (though she was asked to memorize the Four Accords).

Leah shielded her eyes from the rising sun as she struggled to read the dining room clock from across the table.

7:45. Hmm. Maybe she overslept.

"Tori, honey?" Leah called out after wiping the orange juice off her lips. "Would you please stand up and go down the hallway and wake up Miss Tilley for me? I think she is still in bed."

Tori rose immediately and took a step. "Okay."

Leah grinned. "You can leave your fork at the table, Tori."

"Okay." Tori dropped the utensil onto her plate and disappeared down the hall.

Leah listened with great interest and a subtle swell of pride. Tori had grown significantly in her ability to process and perform multistep processes. This latest challenge was at least three steps.

The young teen trotted back into the room and slid into her chair. She took a sizable bite of her toast.

"Did you wake her up, Tori?" Leah prodded.

Tori took a second bite. "No."

Leah lowered her own fork full of scrambled eggs. "No?" She paused. "Did you *try* to wake her up?"

"No."

"Didn't I ask you to wake her up?"

"Yes."

Leah rested her elbows on the table and leaned forward. "Why didn't you do as I asked, Tori?"

Tori pulled a glass of milk away from her face. "She wasn't there."

"Oh, I see. Well, she was probably in the bathroom, then."

"No."

"No?"

Tori shook her head. "No. I looked."

Tori must be mistaken, Leah thought as she pushed away from the table and dropped her napkin. "I'll be right back." She jogged down the hall and pried opened Brenda Jo's door carefully.

Tori hadn't deceived her. The room was unoccupied. Leah peered over at the open closet. Brenda's small collection of clothes was missing. She stepped inside and investigated a few dresser drawers.

Nothing.

Empty.

Leah's pulse quickened as she darted towards the living room. She threw back the curtains and scanned the driveway.

What? Where is my car?

Tori's voice almost made her jump. "What's wrong?"

Leah allowed the curtains to fall back into place and hesitated. "Oh, I'm…I'm not sure, Tori." She strolled back across the dining room to check her purse on the counter. Five seconds of thorough examination proved what her heart had feared.

My keys. She took my keys.

CHAPTER 38

"Gone? What do you mean *gone*?"

"Do ya want me to draw you a picture, Sheppard?" Chief McCloud taunted as he met him halfway across the production floor. "G-O-N-E, gone. As in Brenda Jo Tilley is not here anymore."

Shep inspected a small section of aluminum framing and peeked down at his watch. "It's not even nine yet. Maybe she went to the diner for breakfast or something."

McCloud rolled his eyes. "*Breakfast?* Honestly, how many folks you know pack up all their clothes and steal their friend's car just to go out for a little mornin' snack!?"

"Stole whose car?"

"Well, let's see…who else does Brenda Jo live with, Shep?"

"Leah's car is missing?"

"Bingo. Along with all her keys…including her *factory* keys. Miss Tilley cleared out her own closet and dresser. Everything. Gone. I got Billy up and we checked everywhere. And I do mean everywhere. I'm tellin' you, she ain't in this town anymore."

Shep pivoted away from the Chief and hung his head. "I told you. I told all of you that night at the station that you should've let me stay!" He glared over at McCloud. "But, oh no! No, no, no," he mocked. "We can't risk breaking one little damn accord. Oh, hell no! Can't be doing that. Why that would be too dangerous!"

"That dog ain't gonna hunt, Sheppard! You had a week to raise any red flags. I sure don't recall you havin' any problems with her. I guarantee you've talked to her more'n I have!"

Shep spun about and hurled a piece of metal past the Chief. "Well, let's see. Who was in the station the night of her interview? Hmm...you, and Doc, and, oh yeah—*Colorado.*" He marched up to him. "Open your damn eyes, McCloud! This ain't the first time Leah's car has been taken." He lowered his voice but not his ferocity. "Remember when *he* took it? He went to Chicago. *Chicago.* You know what I'm talking about. And then, just out of nowhere, little Miss Arkansas shows up the very next day?!"

McCloud was silent.

Shep wagged his head. "*Hello?!* Those two got something cooking, and you got your head so far up someone's ass you can't see what's right in front of your face!"

"*You think I got a problem?!*" the Chief exploded. "Speakin' of problems, Robert Sheppard, I think it's high time you took a short look in a long mirror, cause you got enough problems with—"

"Problems? Do my aging ears detect someone discussing problems?" Doc Stonecroft echoed out from the far side of the factory. "Because I would wager that the severity of your problem does not match the intensity of our current condition downstairs, I can assure you. In my estimation, it is even a crisis."

Shep pivoted and dismissed him. "We're busy, Doc. And I don't hear any alarms. So, whatever it is, just head back down to your little nuclear playground and handle it. You're a big boy."

Doc continued towards them, undeterred. "My height and weight is irrelevant to this particular type of crisis, Mr. Sheppard."

McCloud pushed passed Shep. "Ignore him, Doc. Now, what's the matter?"

"I guess it is rather serendipitous that you, an officer of the law, are present, Chief," Doc noted as he came to a full stop. "So, that being the case, I suppose that I would like to officially report a burglary. A theft at the very least. A most unusual theft."

That got Shep's attention. "Excuse me?"

"Yes. A burglary, Mr. Sheppard. Someone has broken into The Vault. I checked all the boxes against our records. Several personal items including driver's licenses and money have vanished. Most of the garments appear to be intact. But curiously, everything pertaining to Mr. Nelson is missing. And some paperwork that wasn't stored in The Vault."

"*The Vault?*" McCloud repeated in surprise. "In The Basement? But how could anyone get down there?" He looked around. "And why in the world would someone take any of *those* items?"

Shep rubbed his forehead. "Well, it doesn't take an experienced cop to figure out who the hell the perpetrator was."

"You are already certain concerning our criminal's identity, Mr. Sheppard?" Doc asked.

"Yep. And you two just welcomed her with naïve and open arms," he said. "Unbelievable."

Doc glanced over the Chief.

"Miss Brenda Jo Tilley," McCloud offered quietly. "Apparently she took off sometime in the night. Stole Leah's car. And now it looks like she packed her suitcase with more'n just her clothes."

"Wait," Shep said. "You said *paperwork*. What kind of paperwork?"

Doc removed his glasses and polished them. "Nothing current. It will not harm our present research. As far as I can tell, it appears to be Emile's schematics detailing his early attempts at constructing a Tesla portal."

"To put it into layman's terms, gentlemen…they were the plans for the now ill-fated Roswell device."

CHAPTER 39

Friday, April 16, 1948, 9:34 p.m.
Las Vegas, Nevada

It was secluded.

Oksana would have expected no less.

"It's nice. Nice and quiet," she observed while Ross veered off the unlit street. His house was a modest single story that seemed to grow out of a small rise at the end of a crushed clay driveway.

"Just the way I like it," he said as he lowered his window and flicked away his second cigarette since they left the restaurant. "I have wonderful neighbors."

She swung her head around and scanned in every direction. "But, Howard…you have no neighbors."

He raised his eyebrows and threw the car into park. "You catch on quick."

Quick? Oksana thought.

Everything is happening at my speed and at my timing, Mr. Ross.

It had taken Oksana only a handful of weeks to weasel her way into his life, and now into his home. And if all went as planned, into his bed within the hour.

She had long suspected that Ross maintained a secondary, local residence in Vegas. As a division chief of a non-existent agency within the CIA, she had ruled out the likelihood that it would be any type of apartment or flat. Combining that inference with his sexual proclivities, an isolated dwelling at the outskirts of town not only made sense, it was the only thing that made sense.

Ross had scarcely passed through the front door when Oksana tackled him against the dark wall of the foyer. She pressed both her warm body and her warmer lips against his. Ross was a surprised, predictable, and willing victim.

He came up for air. "I never get tired of your sweet lips," he whispered.

She squinted and backed away. "There's more where that came from, Army boy." Oksana strolled into his living room with all the tempting grace of a runway model. "But first, you better get me drunk."

He pushed off the wall and hit the lights. "Right this way."

As he passed by she slid a hand down into her purse and retrieved a tiny tablet.

"The kitchen's not far," he said.

And neither is deep sleep, Howard.

Two glasses of wine and a king-sized bed later, she was right.

Oksana rolled across his satin sheets and borrowed a robe out of his spacious closet. For the first time in their relationship, time wasn't her enemy. She passed through weak shafts of moonlight while embarking on a self-guided tour throughout the bachelor's residence. There was no pressure to hurry, no rush for photography, no equipment to conceal.

Now that Ross had tipped his hand revealing his occasional home, she had been afforded a liberating new luxury.

Oksana could return to sift through his belongings and install electronic monitoring devices whenever convenient.

And she did…many times. For years.

CHAPTER 40

"Please, please have a seat, Nurse Unger," Neal Schaeffer urged as he circled behind her and closed the door to his temporary office. "My name is Inspector Schaeffer."

She eyed him warily as she complied.

"Now," he continued with just a hint of a chuckle, "I am well aware that the rumor mill works overtime in every hospital I audit, Mrs. Unger." He sat down and leaned onto his elbows. "But, regardless of what you may or may not have heard, I want to set your mind perfectly at ease."

She grinned. "I'll admit…I am a *little* nervous."

He smiled back. "Completely natural, but completely unnecessary. Look, this is Chicago, Illinois…not Salem, Massachusetts. I am conducting a health services audit, Nurse Unger, not a witch-hunt."

He slid a piece of paper towards her and tapped on it. "This document details your rights and privileges as pertaining to any information you share with me during our conversation today."

She arched forward and perused it.

"Mrs. Unger, I want you to know that absolutely every syllable of every word that you utter will be kept completely confidential from any staff member at this institution. Including *Director Lancaster*." He hesitated until she looked up at him. "You can be totally honest with me. Think of me like a lawyer. But a free one. A friendly one."

"I, uh, I understand. I have nothing to hide."

Neal moved the paper out of the way and grabbed a few file folders. He thumbed through them. "It would obviously take an army of bureaucrats with a whole slew of secretaries to investigate the services and care rendered to each and every patient within an institution the size of Chicago State Hospital."

He glanced over at her. "Not to mention the sizable team of medical experts that would be required to verify and evaluate all treatment plans and pharmacological activities."

She sat up in her chair. "I guess I really never thought about it. That does sound like an impossible amount of work."

He shut a folder and then opened another. "Exactly right, Nurse Unger. Exactly right. That is why we select a handful of typical cases and then audit them thoroughly."

"Makes sense."

He spun the folder around and slid it towards her. "I would like to begin with this patient."

She angled forward and shook her head. "Good old Flash. That was our little nickname. I already miss him."

"You are then familiar with the deceased? A Mr. Gordon Thompson, admitted on or about July eighth, 1953?"

"Uh, yes sir. Very familiar, or at least, as familiar as one could be...given his particular *condition*."

Neal sat back and flipped through a notepad. "Could you describe your interactions with Mr. Thompson?"

The nurse stared at the paperwork. "Well, my interactions were of the normal variety. If his wing was on my rounds, then I performed my usual duties. Medicine, food, bathing, bedding, and such. At least once a day he was taken outside for at least thirty minutes, weather permitting."

"The physician's notes and my interviews with the other nurses and orderlies indicated that Mr. Thompson suffered from...*severe* delusion."

"Yes, sir, that's right."

"Could you describe his particular malady?"

She nodded. "Well, he had a very specific psychosis. He, uh, he thought—or at least others told me that he thought—that he was…from the *future*. A time traveler of sorts…I suppose."

Neal scribbled a few things down. "Just about all of the nurses have shared the same thing. Did the patient ever speak to you concerning these ludicrous ideas?"

"Oh, not much. Once he arrived, his condition appeared to degrade rapidly. I've rarely seen such a steep deterioration."

Neal peered up at her just above his notebook. "How about early on? Any ramblings or phrases?"

She rubbed her chin. "The, uh, the only thing that I can specifically recollect, was probably within the first two or three weeks after he was admitted. After that he just mumbled. Nothing sensible."

"Go on."

"Well, it was a name. A man's name. He kept repeating it over and over."

"Do you remember the name?" he asked with mounting interest.

"After you've heard the same thing repeated hundreds of times, it is sorta permanent in your memory. The name was Phillip Nelson."

Neal almost dropped his pen and fought hard to conceal his excitement. "Do you have any idea of why he was repeating this name? Any idea whatsoever?"

Her head swung side to side as she shrugged. "Nothing that I can think of. I mean, the only other thing that really stands out is that he was always pointing at his chest. Pointing and chanting '*Phillip Nelson*'."

Neal tapped the pen on his chin and squinted. "Do you think this was his delusional identity? Perhaps he was imagining that he was another person?"

"Could be, I guess. I don't know. All I do know is that it was so sad. Very sad. The only consolation is that, at least he is at peace now."

Neal was lost in thought for a few seconds. "Let's change gears. What can you tell me about Mr. Thompson's primary psychiatrist…Dr. Ferrell Montgomery?"

Tears began to form as she took a deep breath. "Sorry," she said, wiping her face several times. "His death is still very…*raw*."

"Take your time; I know this is difficult."

"Can I stand?"

He waved his hand. "Please, be my guest. Whatever you need. Whatever helps."

She rose and paced across the tiny office. "Dr. Montgomery—he was a committed doctor. Very smart. And a very, very intelligent man. He was already on staff when I hired on. In fact, he helped to interview me. Decent man. It's a big loss for us. A terrible loss for his wife, Shirlene. And the boys. They're grown…but still. You know."

He waited for the emotion to subside. "Now please don't be offended by this question, but did you ever suspect that Dr. Montgomery was involved in any…*illegal* or inappropriate activities?"

She spun around. *"Excuse me?"*

"Let me explain," he offered. "His wife has not held a substantial job in over ten years, and neither of them came from families of means, so to speak."

"What are you getting at? How is any of this—"

He raised his hands. "Calm down, Nurse Unger. Please don't jump to any conclusions. Hear me out." Neal collected his thoughts. "While Dr. Montgomery's salary was far above average, his physical property, including two homes, and three cars, as well as generous bank and savings accounts are…well, difficult to reconcile."

She folded her arms. "Listen, I don't know anything about all of that. I try to stay out of other people's business. We worked together, and that's all. To be honest, I'm not comfortable with the direction of this…*interrogation*."

Neal pushed up out of his chair and rested on the edge of his desk. "I am sorry, Nurse Unger. Trust me, I had no intention of making you feel compromised in any way." He closed the folder. "Part of our audit does involve financial investigations concerning potential abuses of authority or medicine. Surely you must understand the temptation and the ever-present danger."

"I guess I do." She glanced up and pointed a finger at his face. "But you promised this wasn't going to be a witch-hunt. Sure feels like one."

Neal nodded. "Fair enough. I sincerely apologize, ma'am. I can see your point. Clearly."

She folded her arms. "So, I am through here? Can I leave now?"

He squinted. "A final question…if you will indulge me?"

Her expression and voice were saturated with cynicism. "Do I have a choice?"

"Technically…*no*. But I don't want to pressure you. I promise, this will be my last *official* question. It's not about money or Dr. Montgomery."

"One more."

He grinned. "Great!" Neal stretched across the desk and picked up his notebook once again. "Besides the staff, did Mr. Gordon Thompson ever have any visitors? Friends, family, *anyone?*"

She concentrated on the floor as her head wagged. "Visitors? Gordon? No. No. The sad reality is that he was trapped, alone, in his own fake world. I wish I could tell you that his case was rare, but unfortunately, we see them every day."

"No one? *Ever?*"

Unger rolled her eyes. "No one…well, wait. Except once. Just one visitor. It was actually just a few days before he passed away. Let's see, I was working days, so it would have been on…*Tuesday*. The Tuesday before he died."

Neal's eyebrows shot up. "Really? Who was it? Family?"

"No. Not family. It was actually a member of the clergy. From out of town."

"Clergy? Like a priest or a nun?"

She pursed her lips. "No, definitely not a nun. Wrong gender. And not a priest. He was a preacher from…Ohio. Said he knew Gordon's family. I led him up to the room. Now that I think about it, Dr. Montgomery wasn't too happy about it. It's a shame that our unpleasant encounter is, uh, is my last memory of my colleague."

Neal hesitated. "Did you get a name on this preacher?"

She cocked her head. "Hey, wait a minute…you promised! You said that you would only ask me one more question."

Neal shrugged. "Well, technically it's all part of the same one, big question. Come on. We're almost done here." He held up some fingers. "Scout's honor." Neal stared into her skeptical eyes. "A name?"

"He only said his last name, if I am remembering right. It was Collins. Pastor Collins."

Neal nearly shouted and he rushed over to his briefcase. He flipped the latches and dug through several pockets. Neal snagged Denver's driver's license photograph and delivered it to her.

"Is this the man? Is this Pastor Collins? Minus the beard perhaps?"

She nodded freely. "Oh, yes. Absolutely. I never forget a handsome man, even if he is a man of the cloth. Why do you have his picture?"

"Trust me, it's a long story. Did he, Pastor Collins, share any other information? Can you remember any other details? Any at all?"

She grinned. "Now *technically* that is a whole new question. But, don't worry…I'll answer it. Um, he just said he was in town with his family on vacation, and that some of his parishioners back home in Cleveland had asked him to check on Mr. Thompson."

"Cleveland, okay. Anything else?"

"He did promise to pray for us."

"That does seem to be part of a pastor's job description, now doesn't it?" Neal observed.

"If you ask me, Inspector, I think we could all benefit from more time on our knees."

"I'd have to agree with you."

Neal slid Denver's photo back into the briefcase and circled around the desk. He shoved out his right hand. "Nurse Unger, I sincerely appreciate your candid and helpful answers regarding these *sensitive* matters. Again, I apologize if any of my actions or questions were uncomfortable or unsettling in any way."

She returned the handshake. "Oh, I'm a big girl, Inspector. I deal with life and death every day. I will get over it. Plus, it's near the end of my shift. I'm headed home within the hour."

Neal scurried behind her and opened the door. "The end of my shift fast approaches as well. I have only one more witch hunt today." He winked at her. "It is with a Nurse…*Beussink*."

She started to walk out but stopped midway. "Well, now…that just might present a bit of a problem for you, Inspector."

Neal leaned against the door. "Oh? How so?"

"They didn't tell you?"

"Tell me what?" he asked.

"Last I heard, no one has seen Nurse Beussink since before last week. Trust me, I've had to cover for her."

CHAPTER 41

Everything about the moment resembled a postcard photo.

Wisps of steam fog arising from the glassy surface of Lake Bloomington licked playfully across Hank's jon boat, backlit by the golden rays of the late morning sunrise. The warm light caught the remaining oak leaves on the western shore in a blaze of late fall glory.

Denver could have enjoyed the wonder of the moment if he hadn't been so distracted by the chilled parts of his body that were growing numb.

"I can't even feel my butt, Hank."

"Well," Hank snorted, "that's actually a good thing, buddy. See, cause then it won't hurt so bad when I whoop yours in our little fishing contest. I'm gonna win in a landslide victory, just like ole Eisenhower did on Tuesday." He glanced down at Denver. "You voted for Ike, didn't you?"

"Listen Hank, when it comes to politics, I treat it more as a spectator sport. I don't get too involved."

"Well, fishin' ain't a spectator sport, my friend. So get busy."

Denver strafed his palms across his thighs rapidly. "I thought fishing was a summertime sport, except, of course, for *ice fishing*. Which we can't be far from." He blew into his hands and his breath transformed to smoke in the frigid air. "Are you sure it's legal to fish when you can actually see your own breath?"

Hank stretched his arm back and cast out his line. "I swear—you city folk wouldn't last two days in the real world. Gimme a break. A hundred years ago, if you didn't hunt or fish, you didn't eat. Plain and simple."

"A hundred years ago they didn't have Walmart," Denver countered.

"Walmart?" Hank asked. "What the devil's that? Building supply?"

Denver couldn't believe his slip up. *Getting sloppy. Stupid, stupid mistake.*

The cold must be getting to your brain, Collins.

"Oh, it's a store chain you guys don't have around here," Denver replied. "Yet."

"You guys had 'em back home?"

Denver acted like he was digging around in the tackle box. "What? Oh, yeah. Back in New York. In Brooklyn."

After a short fight and a quick reel, Hank lifted a flopping, hand-sized crappie into the boat. "And that's five." He swung the fish into Denver's face and waited. "You said Brooklyn. So forgive this country boy, but that's like a city within a city, right?"

Denver donned a pair of filthy gloves and yanked the hook from the gasping fish's mouth. "Yep. And there are neighborhoods that are almost like a city within the city within the city."

"Sounds confusing as blue blazes. Or to use your lingo...*complicated*."

"Oh, it's not that bad. When you grow up in it, it all makes sense. You just don't know any different."

Hank loaded another minnow onto the barbed hook. "Were you born there? In Brooklyn?" He rose up and threw out his line.

Denver nodded. "I lived there for over twenty years. The stork dropped me off at Victory Memorial in Dyker Heights. We moved to Midwood when I was in the second grade, right in the middle of the second grade. But I survived."

"No offense, pal. I'm sure they're nice and all, but I've never heard of any of those places."

Denver grabbed a pole. "Well, no offense, pal, but I never heard of Normal, Illinois, either. At least, not until very recently."

Hank started to respond, but apparently thought better of it. He flicked the tip of his pole a few times and kept the line taut. Denver did a fair job of imitating him but tried to hide that fact while fishing the opposite side.

"The secret to finding crappie in the fall," Hank announced over his shoulder, "is to look for bait fish." The local expert paused to take a deep breath. "Crappie usually stay pretty shallow, no more'n six or eight feet deep. And they love bait fish."

Denver never bothered to turn around. "Fascinating stuff, Hank. Really."

"Now, in the warmer months, you should stick closer to the shore. And Lake Bloomington has plenty of shoreline." He gestured off to the west, and Denver tried to ignore him. "I think there's over fifteen beautiful miles of it. Old stumps, root wads, fallen trees, that's the closest thing to heaven for most fish."

"Stumps. Root wads. Heaven. Got it."

Hank hoisted his line and inspected the lifeless minnow. "Didn't your mom and dad ever teach you the facts of life, Denver?"

"You mean the birds and the bees?"

"No," Hank retorted. "The other facts of life, like fishing, and cooking, and all."

"Oh, I can't even imagine Terry…*Jackson* picking up a fishing pole, let alone baiting a hook."

Wow. That was a close one.

"Who?"

Denver finally turned around. "My dad. The only fishing he does is luring a poor sucker into the lot with a shiny hood or flashy wheels and then hooking him. He has sold cars as long as I can remember."

"Well, there ya go, buddy. See, fishing is a fundamental life skill, even in Brooklyn." He sat down on the cold aluminum to load fresh bait and it rocked the boat. "What's your mom's name?"

"Valerie. Of course, no one calls her that. It's always been Val. Dad calls her *Valkyrie* whenever he wants to get her all riled up. He has a lot of fun with that."

Hank wobbled the jon boat as he stood up. "Speaking of fun, how are things down at the *Journal*? Is everything okay with Miss Larson? I've heard a few rumors."

"Well, the rumor mill is probably right for once. She had a death in the family. That's why I was helping James, like I did before, and a few other odd jobs." Denver recast his line.

"What about the other gal?" Hank asked. "The new girl."

Denver looked over. "There was a…*temporary* gal brought in to help with the writing. She's pretty good."

"Black girl?"

Denver weighed his response carefully. "Yeah. What of it?"

Hank glanced back over his shoulder. "Well, Denver…Hank Bodenschatz can't remember ever seeing or hearing about a black reporter in these parts."

Three seconds later Hank abandoned his pole and dove into the water, and with good reason.

Denver Wayne Collins had just collapsed into Lake Bloomington, face first.

CHAPTER 42

Officer Billy had no sooner pushed through the front doors of the police station when Chief McCloud barked out an order from the cluttered comfort of his desk.

"Shut it and lock it, Billy."

The deputy looked puzzled, but complied. "You got it, Chief. Everything alright?"

"Grab a seat. Thanks for gettin' here so quickly."

Officer O'Connell removed his cap and slid a chair across the dusty concrete. "No problem." He plopped down.

McCloud finalized some paperwork. "Everything okay around my town?"

"Quiet as quiet can be, boss. Well, had to warn the Wilson kid to keep it under the speed limit. Again."

The Chief chuckled and set his pen down. "What's new, huh?"

"Yeah."

McCloud grew quiet and just stared at his deputy until Billy broke under the strain.

"Something wrong, Chief? I mean, besides all the regular concerns?"

McCloud rose out of his seat and relocated it next to his second-in-command. He lowered himself back down and leaned forward. "I need a favor, Officer O'Connell."

"Just name it, boss."

"But this one needs to stay just 'tween you and me."

Billy started to respond, but McCloud cut him off.

"Strictly—*off the books*."

"I, uh, I understand. Whatcha need?"

McCloud squinted and refused to blink. "We did not have this conversation. Certain people can't ever know 'bout this. Especially people like…Robert Sheppard."

Billy arched back and exhaled. "Oh, yeah. Okay. Sure, boss. Not a word."

"I need ya to keep'n eye on someone. See what they do…after hours. Weekends. And then report back to me. Me only."

"Alright. Is it…Shep?"

The Chief shook his head. "No Billy. Not Shep. I need ya to keep track of Dr. Papineau."

"Pappy? You're kidding. Why Pappy?"

McCloud stood once again and moseyed towards the window. "Let's just say he's done a few things that've got the hairs up on the back of my neck. One thing very recently."

Billy pivoted around and rested against the hard back of his chair. "Really? I just can't picture him doing anything…well, dangerous and all."

The Chief halted and stared a hole through the floor.

"Something's going on, Billy…and I aim to find out what it is."

CHAPTER 43

The socket set was not on the table.

And it wasn't under the table.

"Did you look under the table?" Terrance called out as Denver scrambled in and amongst the equipment.

"Yes, I looked *under* the table," Denver replied. "Twice. And over it. And beside it. You were the last one to have it, Tee."

Terrance continued examining the underside of the framing machine. "Hey, I keep up with my tools, man. Don't be blaming me."

Denver bent down and smiled. "Oh, you do, huh?"

"Yep. My daddy taught me right. He was a mechanic, you know."

"Well, tell your *daddy*, that his son's socket set is below his son's right leg, right where his son put it."

Terrance glanced down to the concrete as a boyish grin spread across his grease-smeared face. "Very funny. So…when did you put that there?"

"*Me* put that there? No, no...that one's on you, pal."

Terrance rolled to the side and looked up. "You know what I think? I think that little dip you took at the lake last week messed you up in the head, man. You don't even remember putting those sockets there."

Denver knelt down. "Hank blew that thing all out of proportion. I was merely taking a little swim in the *lukecold* waters of Lake Bloomington."

"Must be a New York thing, cause in these parts we call it *drowning*, not swimming." Terrance grabbed a rag and wiped his sweaty face. Seconds later both the dirt and his smile were gone. "So, it was another one of your...*episodes*, huh?"

Denver bit his lip. "Yeah. Yeah, it was. Not as severe as the last one. But pretty horrible all the same."

"Seems like Hank is bad for your health. He's been nearby about every time, hasn't he?"

"Come on, Tee...Bode's harmless."

"Didn't you tell me that Leah thinks it might be some kinda leftover trauma from your military service overseas?"

"That's her opinion," Denver replied. "She might be right."

Terrance sat up and wiped his hands. "This's just a longshot, but did you have a friend or a fellow soldier named *Hank* in the service? Or *Bodenschatz?* Maybe his name, or something about him is instigating these little episodes of yours?"

Denver paused. "I think there was a Hank back in Basic, but not in Afghanistan. At least I can't recall one. A few Henrys who went by Henry. But no Hanks."

Terrance angled his head to the side and furrowed his brow. "Uh oh, better act like we're busy or something." He raised his voice. "Cause here comes the boss."

Denver rotated around. Leah was closing fast with a box in her arms. "That's right, boys," she said. "Live in fear. Work in fear."

"Those must be the parts I ordered for the floor jack," Terrance said, pulling himself up to his feet. "Came in quicker than I thought."

She spun the box around and reexamined the label. "No. I don't think so. Not unless your name is now *Denver Jackson*. And not unless you are expecting something from the state of Nevada."

"Las Vegas?" McCloud asked.

"That is the point of origin noted on the parcel," Doc observed after adjusting his glasses.

Shep seized the package and shook it. "I don't like this. Something isn't right."

"Only one way to find out," Ellen said. "We need to open it."

"Or destroy it," Shep muttered.

"We need to *open it*," McCloud affirmed.

"I think Mr. Collins should have the honor," Doc said. "Mr. Collins?"

Denver stepped away from the Jump Portal door and strolled over to the table. "If it turns out to be a box full of cash, just remember who it's addressed to."

A few tense smiles broke out in The Basement.

"It's from Las Vegas," Ellen noted, her voice rife with sarcasm. "Money doesn't usually flow out from there. It only flows in. If you know what I mean."

Shep shook his head. "Not when I'm at the poker tables."

Ellen rolled her beautiful eyes.

Denver's fingers peeled the tape away from the top. "Here goes nothing." He grabbed the flaps and spread them apart. Everyone craned to see. "A few layers of newspapers, folks. But, uh, no money yet."

Doc nodded. "Packing material, no doubt."

"Yep." Denver set them aside. Using both hands, he raised up a beige, folded shirt. Hidden underneath was a matching pair of pants. "And some…*work clothes*?"

"Probably a uniform," McCloud suggested.

Denver continued to dig. "Maybe. Here's some paperwork. Looks like instructions, and some dates. A metal key. And an ID badge? Says *Joel Jackson.* And…it looks like…a map, or two."

He was right.

Doc took possession of them and spread the sheets out across the table. "They appear to be a pair of hand drawn maps. Above ground. And *under*ground diagrams."

Shep squinted. "Underground?"

"Maps of *what?*" McCloud asked. "Where?"

Doc's hand began to tremble as he gestured towards the corner of one of the pages. "Look."

Terrance did and shook his head. He slapped Denver on the shoulder. "I'm gonna go and change the oil on my Ford and check the brakes. Looks like you and I will be taking a long road trip, my man."

Ellen navigated around beside him and hunkered over the maps. Her eyes brightened.

"Area 51."

CHAPTER 44

Exhaustion.

Project SATURN Agent Neal Schaeffer was certainly no stranger to impossible workloads and inhuman work shifts, but his investigation at Chicago State Mental Hospital may have shattered all personal records. He had slept only a handful of hours in the last several days, interviewed dozens of witnesses, and perused many thousands of doctor's reports and health records.

Prior to his recruitment by Ross, Neal had been known as a dedicated player—almost a zealot—at the Secret Service, but rarely had he logged more than eighteen hours in a single work day (The only notable exceptions were the turbulent times associated with President Truman's irregular trips. Schaeffer's stress level and work load at the Protective Research Section during such occasions were enormous).

Neal rubbed his hot face and arched back against his noisy office chair. Between yawns, he continually reminded himself that one day...*one day*...it would be worth it all. It was all for the public good. Neal was a public servant and the son and grandson of public servants. It was all he had ever known, instilled from his childhood back in Norfolk.

Many of his friends and family had died defending freedom. He imagined he could at least donate his waking hours in honor of their sacrifice. But that dedication had yet to prove a perfect remedy to clear his conscience from the scourge of self-inflicted guilt.

Especially when it came to Leslie Coffelt.

Most of Coffelt's friends—Neal included—knew him as Les. Leslie had joined the White House Police Force as a private near the end of the Second World War after a medical discharge from the Army. His Secret Service duties had overlapped the boundaries of the Protective Research Section, and those intersections spawned a vibrant friendship with Neal Schaeffer.

But that professional relationship was severed permanently in a hail of gunfire that erupted in the early afternoon on the first of November 1950. Coffelt was mortally wounded while defending the president's temporary residence at the Blair House, but not before his own pistol dispatched the life of a Puerto Rican nationalist seeking to assassinate Truman.

Novembers had been tough for Neal ever since.

And it was November.

Even though he had accepted Ross' offer and joined Project SATURN just after Christmas in 1949, Neal had always been stricken with guilt concerning his friend's demise. In all honesty, even if he had still been with the Secret Service, the likelihood was high that he would not have been anywhere near the Blair House. In all probability, he wouldn't have been able to assist Les, let alone save him.

At least, that's what his friends had assured him.

But likelihoods and probabilities are miserable comforters, especially when standing next to a grieving widow beside a silent grave.

Of a fallen husband.

A hero.

A friend.

Neal's only consolation in the horrific nightmare was that he had been instrumental in developing the threat response plans that had probably saved President Truman's life on that Wednesday afternoon.

That realization helped…a little.

A light knock on his temporary office door shook Schaeffer out of his November regrets. He sat up. "Uh, yes. It's open. It's open."

One of the female office clerks strolled in. "Sorry to bother you, Inspector Schaeffer, but I thought that you might want to see this." She stepped around a chair and handed him a folded piece of paper.

"What is this in relation to?"

"It had been misfiled," she replied. "I just found it. It appears to be information concerning Mr. Gordon Thompson's admittance. It looks like it is from July of 1953. There is a signature. It appears to be a Denver Collums, or Collins, or something like that."

He scanned the document with a fresh surge of adrenaline. "Yes. Yes, I see that. It is."

"You had asked about his family, about where he came from." She leaned over and pointed. "There is a phone number right here. Maybe it's for this Collums individual. I think that area code's out west somewhere. Maybe he'll know something."

Neal followed her finger.

It was a phone number.

"Uh, yes, thank you. Thank you. You have been very helpful." He looked up. "Please, let me know if you find any other misfiled files."

"Yes, Inspector." She spun about and left the room.

Neal scrambled for the phone and dialed.

"Yes, Clara. This is Schaeffer. I need some information. What region of the country uses the area code 5-7-5?" He paused. "New Mexico? Okay. How about the exchange code…2-3-0?"

There was a longer delay. "You're kidding. Really? Would this have been the same back in, let's say, 1953? Yes, I can hold."

Neal leaned back and let the revelation process for a few moments. He checked his watch. It was just before nine in the morning. His shoes could be hitting the tarmac at Walker Air Force Base in less than nine hours. Better than that, he could sleep for most of it.

Neal's well-trained mind crowded with potential explanations. *Clever plan,* he thought. *If you have to put him away, put him as far away from the action as possible. Clever. We're spinning our wheels in Chicago, when we need to be down in—*

"What's that?" he asked. "Oh, it was the same. You are sure? *Absolutely* positive? I need this to be dead on, Clara. No margin for error on this one. Okay, well, thank you. I'll call back with the rest of the number later, for an exact address. This line is not secure. Thanks again, Clara."

He lowered the handset, still lost in thought.

Roswell.

CHAPTER 45

Hank tapped the brakes and guided his dusty pickup truck off the asphalt. His work vehicle rattled and shook as he navigated the country lane riddled with potholes. To have labeled it as a gravel road would have been too generous. It was far more road than gravel. A quarter-mile further down a small clearing opened up on the left, and he spotted a dark sedan parked in the center.

There he is. And I'm late.

Hank pulled over and killed the motor as a choking cloud of dust enveloped his truck from behind. He threw the door open.

"You're late," a voice called out through the dirty haze.

"Well, I had to stop for gas." Hank ambled over to the other vehicle. "And wouldn't you know it, one of my good, *repeat* customers was there as well. She went on and on about a China hutch she wants me to refinish. She's a talker. But she's a *loaded* talker. So, yeah, sorry 'bout that, Pappy."

Dr. Papineau rested against his car and wiped the dust from his glasses. "Our plans we have to adjust."

Hank lifted his ball cap and repositioned it. "Okay. What gives?"

"Mr. Collins is leaving town."

"When?"

"*Saturday.*"

"This Saturday? Day after tomorrow Saturday?"

"That is correct."

Hank paused and folded his arms. "Ouch. Where's my buddy goin'?"

Papineau lowered his voice. "Nevada. He will be traveling with Mr. Gaines. They will be breaking into a government base there."

"Denver? Really?"

A grave expression washed across Papineau's face. "It is a high probability that he may not...*survive*."

"Oh. Wow."

"Now you understand."

"Uh, yeah. That could be a big, big problem."

Papineau shoved his hands into his coat pockets and began pacing.

"If he dies or is captured, Mr. Bodenschatz...then we have nothing. Nothing."

CHAPTER 46

Ellen Finegan rubbed the tops of her arms vigorously as she waited on his porch. The light breeze transformed the brisk mid-November night air into something far colder. Her breath rose up and clouded her face like frozen smoke.

Come on, McCloud. Answer your door.

Answer your door.

Your squad car is here, so I know that you are.

Nothing.

She rapped on the wood for the third time. A light sprang to life somewhere deep inside. Five seconds later his door cracked open.

"Bout time," she complained. "I'm turning into an icicle out here."

The Chief opened it all the way as she pushed through. "Sorry, Ellen. I was back in my bedroom studyin' the effects of sleep on the body of an exhausted police chief."

She strolled into his living room and sank down into his small couch. "You were sleeping? It's barely ten o'clock."

McCloud dropped down into a comfortable chair on the opposite side of a glass coffee table. "The clock says *ten*, but my tired body says *two*. Maybe *three*. It's been one heckuva week."

Ellen angled forward. "We need to talk."

"Okay," he said. "Do I need to make some coffee?"

"Forget the coffee, I'll keep it brief. You know tomorrow's the seventeenth, right?"

The Chief paused. "Is that a trick question?"

"His birthday is in four days. Four days, Chief."

"Oh," McCloud said, rubbing all around his face. "This's about Doc again. I figured it was 'bout Denver and Terrance's trip out to the Groom Place."

"Groom Lake."

"Yeah," he said. "Tomorrow's the big day."

"Yes, and don't forget their sendoff party. But listen," she demanded. "I'm not worried so much about them leaving. It's *him*. I'm worried about *Doc* leaving."

He tried to restrain a yawn. "We've...we've been down this broken record before, Ellen. Doc ain't goin' nowhere. We've talked to him. You've talked to him. I've talked to him. He's fine. He's just blowin' off some steam."

Ellen jumped up. "That's easy for you to say because you don't have to work with him—right beside him—day in and day out." She paced back towards the foyer. "I'm telling you, there is a high probability that Dr. Glen Stonecroft will head to Ohio and break the Fourth Accord. I'd put the chances at ninety-five percent."

The Chief rose out of his seat and ambled right up to her. "Ellen...I'm tellin' you Doc is harmless. Plus...he's, uh, he's not the one you should be worried about."

She folded her arms. "And what's that supposed to mean?"

McCloud scurried over to the window beside his front door and checked the front yard. He pivoted back around.

"It means that you're worried 'bout the *wrong scientist*."

CHAPTER 47

The wind was picking up, and the flashes of scattered lightning to the distant southwest roused a new level of apprehension within Neal Schaeffer. Storms create noise, and noise can mask the approach of those you do not want to be discovered by.

He led the six-man team up to the tiny house under the protection of the rural darkness and paused just below a cracked window. Forty-eight hours of uninterrupted surveillance had failed to reveal any movement within or without the isolated residence a half mile south of Roswell.

The team, clad in black, was well-rehearsed and well-prepared. A single sentry would remain outside, in constant radio communication with a perimeter guard stationed at key intervals, while Neal Schaeffer led the remaining agents inside the dwelling to collect whatever evidence or suspects they could.

To the untrained observer, the building had the typical trappings brought about by long years of desertion. But Neal knew that appearances rarely held the complete, let alone *accurate*, picture. The first rule of espionage warned that anyone and everyone could be under the control of your enemy. The second rule was that appearances are often designed, rather than naturally occurring.

After a silent flick of his wrist, four agents gained quick access through the front door, secured the area, and signaled for Neal to enter. Two men began immediate dusting for fingerprints, as the others scanned the dwelling, room by room, with powerful flashlights.

Just as Neal suspected, the story told within did not match the story told without. The sandy dust of the desert southwest coated everything, but it only served to highlight the evidence of recent activity.

Neal rushed up to an agent. "I need a quick estimate, how long ago was someone here?"

The agent knelt down and played the area with his light. "Less than a week."

"You'd bet your wife's life on that estimation, Humphreys?"

"Absolutely, sir."

"How many *different* people?" Neal pressed.

There was a pause. "Probably two, maybe more. It'll take time."

Neal spun around in the hallway. "What's that hum?"

"Refrigerator," a voice called out in the darkness. "Fridge is running in the kitchen." A few seconds later the same voice called out as a weak, warm glow spilled into the hall. "And, there is food here in it, sir."

"Agent Schaeffer?" another voice rang out from a room further down. "You need to see this, sir."

Neal rushed towards the bedroom and pulled alongside the dark figure. "What did you find, Harris?"

The agent directed Schaeffer's attention down into a dresser drawer now flooded with an intense, circular beam of light. A rectangular card was sticking out from beneath a pair of work pants.

Neal bent over to examine the curiosity.

The corporate logo was unfamiliar.

But the name embossed below it wasn't.

Neal straightened up, his pulse pounding. "Get me back to the airbase, now! Right now! I need a secure line to notify Chief Ross." He darted back into the living room. "Continue to dust for prints, but don't remove anything from this house! Not one thing!"

The agents nodded as Neal rushed out through the front door. "And get someone to do a TDS Film series of this entire property, including the barn on the north side! And look for hidden rooms, a basement, cellar, anything!" He muttered to himself as he stole his way down the gravel path towards a waiting vehicle.

"Well, Chief Ross…you said you wanted at least one time traveler by the tenth anniversary of Roswell." He smiled.

Better yet, how about several of them by Christmas?

CHAPTER 48

Denver and Terrance hadn't passed or been passed by a car in over twenty-three miles. The uninhabited stretch of US 93 in Nevada was well-deserving of its reputation as being among the nation's most dangerous. To run out of fuel or water here was—more often than not—the first step towards an inevitable and horrific death from either heat or exposure.

A small sign appeared in the heated distortion adorning the desert horizon. Denver sat up in the driver's seat, almost excited. Any indication of civilization along this highway was the equivalent of the anticipated arrival of a long-lost friend. He concentrated as it flew past them.

Pioche, 10 miles.

Terrance nodded towards him. "Well, we're making some good progress."

"Yeah," he replied. "Finally, some progress."

Progress.

Denver glanced over at his African-American traveling companion. Without a doubt, the three-day trip to infiltrate Area 51 had already been problematic. The leadership back in Normal had insisted Denver should be the primary driver. Terrance agreed that the likelihood of a white man at the wheel being harassed by law enforcement was far less than the alternative. To Denver, the frustration arising from the fact that a bigoted culture was dictating so many of their basic decisions seemed overwhelming at times.

But he refused to let it make all of the decisions.

In restaurants, Terrance felt it would attract less attention if they would dine at separate tables, but Denver rejected that approach. Many of his fellow soldiers over the years had been from a wide palette of ethnic distinctions, and he ate, slept, fought, and was willing to die among them. The culturally uncommon meal arrangement led to numerous judgmental glances since they left Normal, but Denver couldn't care less. As an American plodding through the rural reaches of Afghanistan, he himself had daily experienced the stigma associated with minority status.

Motels in 1956, though, presented a different dilemma.

It was entirely possible that some establishments would deny Terrance the opportunity to even lodge there. And the prospect of a white and black man cohabitating in the same room could raise unnecessary flags. Their solution was simple, if not elegant: Denver secured the room, and then Terrance snuck in or out under the cover of darkness.

Progress? Denver contemplated after a quick glance at his passenger.

Maybe not so much.

"You open to a personal question?" Denver asked.

"Fire away, man," Terrance replied. "If you get too personal, I can always dump you out here in the desert."

"I'll keep that in mind. So, why do you put up with Shep's...*Shepness?*"

Terrance grinned and angled towards him. "I suppose you're referring to our beloved plant manager's undisguised bigotry and intolerance that I have faced on a daily basis for several years now?"

Denver tapped on the steering wheel. "Yeah, that about covers it."

"Oh...it hasn't been easy, by no means."

"You make it *look* easy."

Terrance couldn't suppress a chuckle. "You didn't see things early on, man."

"Rough?"

"*Rough?* That's a good word. Rough implies irritating friction. Yep. Lots of that."

Denver shook his head. "I just don't get how you can put up with so much abuse. Especially when he gets Frazier all stirred up with him. That's a lethal pair."

"Come on, man…it's not like you haven't endured the same. Right, *Colorado?*"

"But that's different. I can deal with people who don't like me for what I've done…or not done. He thinks I'm a screw-up, and that's his right. But his racism, I mean, there's nothing you or Alexus could ever do to overcome that, or deserve that."

Terrance stared out through the dusty windshield for a moment. "I don't know what American culture is like in the twenty-first century, Mr. Collins, but back in my world, in my time, Shep's just a condensed version of what I've faced my whole life. The intensity might be different, but the attitude is pretty much the same."

"Your tongue must be covered in scars," Denver said.

Terrance shot him a puzzled glance and hesitated. "Oh, yeah, I get it now. I never heard that one before. I like that. But remember, I grew up in the sixties. People like me have been biting their tongue for decades, maybe centuries. There were a couple of big-mouthed chumps like Shep in the Navy. He's nothing new, you know. I can handle Robert Sheppard."

"You're a much better man than I."

"And I keep telling myself that Shep is no worse a man than most. He's just a product of these times. I try to always remember that." A broad smile broke out across his face. "Especially when I'm fantasizing about strangling him with my bare hands."

"I thought I was the only one."

"Nope, man. Not by a longshot. I can't tell you how many times Mrs. Swan talked me off the ledge when I wanted to do terrible things to that man."

"What would we do without Leah Swan?" Denver asked.

"She's really something, man."

Yes, she is.

She really is something.

But it pained him to think about her. The fiasco at the mental hospital had initiated a violent rip in their fragile relationship that had steadily widened over the difficult weeks that followed. Fear and mistrust seemed to pour into the growing gap, reducing their status from close friends to necessary colleagues.

She even found an excuse to avoid the sending off party for their Nevada mission. The whole situation before had been painful, but that hurt.

Denver sensed something. "Whoa…what was that? Did you feel that?"

"You just now noticed?" Terrance replied. "It started about five miles back."

"What started?"

"Not sure. I think it's the carburetor."

"*Carburetor?* That could be bad, couldn't it?"

"It could."

The car stuttered twice more.

"Better pull over," Terrance cautioned.

Denver pressed on the brakes and eased onto the shoulder. "I've made it my lifelong pledge to never argue with a beautiful woman or an expert mechanic." He smiled. "And since I don't see any beautiful women…"

Terrance threw his door open. "Funny. Grab my tools out of the back floorboard."

By the time Denver lugged the heavy metal box around to the front, Terrance had the hood propped open and was draped halfway across the hot motor. Denver rubbed his arms rapidly. "I thought the desert out west was supposed to be hot. Wow, I doubt it's above forty degrees out here."

"Probably a combination of the time of the year and the local elevation. Last sign I saw said somethin' about five thousand feet or something."

Denver leaned over the quarter panel in a bid to share in the heat radiating from the motor. "So Mr. Gaines, where did you learn about engines?"

Terrance continued to investigate. "Well…like I told you before, my father was a diesel mechanic. Back in Cleveland." He extended his right hand like a surgeon. "Half-inch end wrench."

Denver dug around and delivered the tool. "Like father, like son."

Terrance removed a bolt. "Actually, he warned me *against* ever becoming a mechanic. He said it was a hot, dirty, and thankless job." He removed another. "And he…was…right."

Denver rocked back on his heels. "I see you listened to your dad about as much as I did mine."

"I did listen to him, but another influential relative had different plans."

"Another relative?"

Terrance removed a cover. "My uncle. Uncle *Sam*."

"Oh, right. Right. The military. He's my uncle too."

Terrance leaned up and wiped his hands. "I enlisted with the Navy during Nam. I thought I'd have a better chance of returning in one piece to the land as long as I was deployed on the water."

Denver nodded. "Hard to argue with that plan. And you jumped in 1983, right?"

"*May* of 1983. Hand me a flathead screwdriver. Longest one you can find."

Denver knelt down. "So, it looks like your plan worked. When did you get out?"

Silence.

Denver found the screwdriver and rose up. "I said, when did you get out of the Navy?"

More silence.

"What's the matter, Tee?"

Terrance was frozen and fixated on something off into the distance. He didn't seem interested in conversation or the tool. Terrance gestured to the north. "I don't think there's one chance in a million that the Smokey Bear coming down the pike is Chief McCloud."

Denver swung about. The black and white squad car approaching from a hundred yards out stood in stark contrast to the subtle earth tones along the barren vista. The cruiser was slowing down.

"This could be trouble, man," Terrance said.

"Yeah," Denver replied. "It seems to follow me. *Everywhere*."

Terrance darted for the backseat. "I'm gonna grab a pistol. Just to be safe."

"No. No. Let's not move around too much."

The police car kicked up a massive dust cloud as it veered onto the shoulder behind their vehicle.

"Remember," Denver muttered, "we're just two guys headed for California, and our engine is on the fritz."

Terrance halted. "I've got a bad feelin' about this. If he checks the trunk—"

"Just relax and work on the engine…let me do the talking."

Terrance forced a sarcastic smile. "Like I said…we're in trouble."

"What seems to be the trouble, boys?" a voice boomed out through the swirling dust.

Denver cleared his throat and cautiously shuffled towards the back of the car. "Morning, officer. We, uh, we seem to have a carburetor acting up."

The cop paused by their rear bumper. "Illinois, huh? You boys are a long way from home. What brings you out west? Headed down to Vegas?"

"No sir," Denver answered. "My friend and I were on our way to the coast. I, uh, I have family in LA. Tee was looking to make a new start in California. He's hoping to find a good job."

The policeman meandered around to the front on the far side. He hesitated when he saw Terrance. "This is about the worst place in the world to have car problems. You boys're lucky it's November. If this would've happened a few months back, well, let's just say the buzzards might've gained a few extra pounds by now."

Denver circled around towards the cop. "I'm sure. The desert can be brutal. I'm just glad my friend is pretty handy when it involves fixing things."

The cop adjusted his hat and jacket and leaned against the fender. "You boys carrying any identification? No offense, just a routine request."

"Well, yes. Yes, officer, of course," Denver answered. He fished out his wallet and spread it open to retrieve his driver's license.

"That's quite a bit of money you got stashed in there," the policeman noted as Denver passed him the ID. "Where'd all that cash come from…*Mister…Jackson?"*

"Oh, I've been saving for this trip for months now," Denver offered. "Even took some out of my savings. You know, the cost of living along the left coast is sky high."

"Left coast?"

"Oh, sorry," Denver said. "California…you know…*the left coast*. America has a left coast and a right coast. I made that up one day after looking at a map. Anyway, apparently it's pretty expensive out there."

"That's what I hear." The cop turned his attention to Terrance. "How about you, boy? Any ID?"

"Uh, yessir. Right here, sir."

The cop examined the card. "Terrance Groves."

"Yessir."

"Hmm." The policeman returned the card and took a few steps back along the driver's door. He made no attempt to conceal the fact that he was studying the inside of the vehicle.

"Travelling light, aren't we?"

"Oh, yes," Denver started, "it probably looks that way. But…but we have our luggage and such in the trunk."

The cop raised his head quickly and peered across the roof of the car over at Denver. "You mind if I have a quick look there?"

"Well, I don't really see why that's necess—"

"We've had quite a few burglaries and break-ins between Pioche and Ely," the cop interjected. "I'm not accusing anyone of anything in particular." He paced to the back bumper. "Just doing my job. How about you pop this lid open?"

"There's really nothing to see, officer."

"Well…then show me *nothing*."

Denver glanced down at Terrance, who had repositioned himself just out of sight of the cop. He knelt next to the toolbox on the passenger side, shaking his head *no* repeatedly as he rummaged through the tools.

"Just a couple of suitcases and a few other bags," Denver protested.

"Then it won't take long," the cop countered. "Come on, now. It's almost time for dinner. Plus, I might have to haul you guys to town."

"Sir? Do what?"

"Well, if you can't fix your motor, I can't leave you out here to die. It gets pretty dang cold after the sun dips below the horizon."

"Oh, yessir."

"Now hurry up."

Denver threw open the passenger door and leaned across the seat to snatch the keys out of the ignition. "Yessir, officer."

"What year is this Ford?" the cop asked. "A '46?"

Terrance rose up and chimed in. "A '41."

"1941?"

"Yessir. You can always tell by the three-piece fenders. On the later models it was either a two-piece or a one-piece."

"Yep, I see it now. Sure enough. She's in great shape, boys."

"Thank you, sir." Terrance ducked back under the hood.

Denver arrived with the keys and unlocked the trunk.

"Well, let's have a quick lookie and get you boys back on your way to that left coast or whatever," the cop said as he raised the lid.

Two small suitcases, a pair of dark boots, and a long black bag occupied just over half the space.

"You say that Mr. Groves was moving to California to start a new life?" the cop asked. "He must've left most of his stuff back in Illinois."

"He sold most of his non-essentials back in Chicago," Denver explained. "He needed the money." Denver lowered his voice. "He didn't have much stuff anyway. Kinda sad."

"I'd say."

The cop rested against the fender and reached for the black bag. Denver panicked. "Those are just…just some tools that I travel with."

"What kinda tools?"

"Oh, just, uh—"

The policeman drew the zipper down the long edge of the bag and tossed the cover back. A large rifle outfitted with a powerful scope, two sets of binoculars, gloves, bolt cutters, and a pair of large flashlights were crammed inside.

"My, my," the cop exclaimed. "Interesting set of tools, boys." He made a subtle move for his pistol. "I think you two need to—"

Thunk!

The cop slumped forward and collapsed into the trunk. His face slammed into one of the suitcases and rolled to the side.

Terrance withdrew a large crescent wrench. "I had to do it, man," he said. "Don't worry…he's not dead. Just out cold. Help me load him into his squad car."

Denver scanned up and down the lonely road as they draped the unconscious cop across his own front seat. Terrance ripped the small two-way radio receiver out of the dash and then proceeded to slash one front tire.

"Wait! What're you doing?" Denver cried out.

"That'll slow Smokey down quite a bit. Don't worry, he's gonna have a spare!"

Denver squinted. "But don't we need to take *his* car? Ours is broken, remember?"

Terrance put on a smug smile as he trotted back to their Ford and slammed the trunk. "You mean—*was* broken."

"You fixed it?"

"Yep. But now we need to ditch this thing, man. It's a liability. That patrolman saw our license plate. He might remember it." Terrance lowered the hood and pitched the keys to Denver. "We got an appointment with Area 51."

"Let's book it, Mr. Collins…before anyone else sees us."

CHAPTER 49

"You look like death warmed over," Neal commented as Ross climbed into the back seat beside him.

His boss slammed the door. "What the hell you expect, Schaeffer? It's not even three-damn-thirty in the morning yet. Let's go." The car lurched forward. "Let me see it."

"Thought you'd never ask." Neal rummaged through his coat pocket and produced a nondescript box. He transferred it over to Ross with great care, but then withdrew it. "Wait, wait, boss. Where're your gloves?"

Howard yanked it out of his hands. "I just wanna look." He cracked the case open.

Neal grinned. "It's some type of financial card, we think. Called a Mastercard."

"A Master Card?"

"No. One word. *Mastercard.*"

Howard's eyes grew wide as he studied the curious artifact. "I'll. Be. Damned. Phillip Nelson." He rubbed his fingers across the raised letters.

Neal enjoyed watching the curious mixture of satisfaction and strategic planning that broke out across his boss' rough face. "Who and what are you bringing down here to Roswell?"

Ross paused. "Everyone. All departments. The bigger stuff is coming down in trucks tomorrow. Three or four flights'll be coming in tonight, or this morning, or whatever." Ross popped out a pack of cigarettes and fished around for his lighter.

"Hey, hey!" Neal yelled as he snatched the open box from his boss. He closed it. "You can't be contaminating fresh evidence with all that smoke! And crack your window for heaven's sake."

"I don't need a nanny or a Boy Scout. I need an analyst, Agent Schaeffer." He took his first long pull on the cigarette. He held it in. "How far to the site?"

"Less than ten minutes."

"Any idea yet on how many people may have been there?"

"We've identified four different sets of footprints. Still working on fingerprints."

"What else?"

"Quite a bit."

Ross exhaled and smoke filled the backseat. "Gimme the highlights."

Neal lowered his own window. A few drops of rain blew in. He rolled it up again. "Most notably our team has uncovered a set of plans."

"What kinda plans?"

"Like schematics. For a large piece of equipment."

"What type of equipment?"

"We don't know...for sure."

"Because it's too complicated?"

Neal paused. "Because...it's too...*French*."

That got the Chief's full attention. "*French?* Like the language? That French?"

Neal grinned. "*Oui, oui*. Don't worry, I'm sure Tollison is coming down. He is isn't he?"

"Probably on the plane behind mine."

"His French is pretty good."

"It's okay."

"He was inserted with the resistance near Paris, wasn't he?"

"The last six months of the war," Ross answered. "He didn't see much action. Women maybe, but not much real action. He's a big talker."

Neal cracked his rain-splattered window again. "I have a theory."

"That's what I pay you for."

"I think Denver Wayne Collins' wallet was a decoy, of sorts."

Ross flicked his spent cigarette out the window. "This I gotta hear."

"I think we've been played."

"Played?"

"*Played*. I think the real area of interest should've been Roswell all along."

Ross cleared his morning throat. "Hindsight is 20-20, Neal. But still, it's a pretty big gamble, don't you think? Giving up Collins and his wallet? And what about the information we found embedded in the lining? What about all that, *Mr. I've-Got-Theories?*"

"All of it agrees with my assessment," Neal countered, unaffected. "We were meant to find the wallet near Chicago, to divert us and our resources there. And we were also meant to find that information concealed in the wallet. Two birds…one wallet."

"*Who* Agent Schaeffer? *Who* meant for us to find it?" Ross fired up a fresh smoke.

"Still working on it."

"Work faster, dammit. I can't afford to let another time traveler slip through. At least I was able to pacify Dulles this week. I used your discoveries at the Chicago nut house. I overplayed our hand…slightly."

The car turned again.

"I've been thinking about something else, but it's related," Neal began. "I've been thinking about the other word in the wallet...*Caretaker*. Honestly, I dream about Caretaker. Whenever I get a chance to sleep, that is. Which is pretty rare these days."

"Forget about the damn wallet and focus on tracking down these people!" Ross growled. "Caretaker can wait."

"Maybe, maybe not," Neal protested. "I think *we* were the ones who embedded our own names in the wallet. It was us. Me and you." He locked eyes with his boss. "The Howard Ross and Neal Schaeffer of the future. Way in the future, decades from now."

Ross was growing irritated. "Hell, Schaeffer—we've already discussed that possibility. The mystery is *why*." He took a hit on his cigarette. "Lemme guess...you've got a theory?"

"Well, I do."

"I don't know what's gonna kill me quicker, these damn smokes or your never-ending supply of theories."

Neal glanced out his window as the car made a final turn and eased to a crunching stop in the packed gravel. "And we are here. Good news. Looks like the rain has stopped."

Both of their doors opened and a small entourage waited beside the vehicle. Ross ventured out first and waved them off. "Give us a minute, boys. I've been cooped up in a plane or a car for the last few hours, and I need some space. And someone tell the driver to kill the headlights."

Neal circled around to meet him as the men disbanded and assumed positions closer to the house. Ross surveyed the scene.

Neal lowered his voice. "I think we must seriously consider the possibility—"

Ross held up his hand as an agent walked by. Neal took the hint. The man vanished behind the car and into the night.

"As I was saying," Neal continued, "I think that we must consider the possibility that we may never apprehend a living time traveler."

Ross rotated back towards him, but slowly. "You got any, oh, I don't know…more *optimistic* theories, Agent Schaeffer? That's not exactly the kind of prognosis I flew eight hundred miles in the middle of the night to hear."

"So, do you want me to tickle your ears, or do you want me to share the truth?"

Ross leaned in. "A *possible* truth. But, I'll make a deal with you." He kicked a few rocks before lighting up another cigarette. "Now, when this Lucky Strike is finished, so are you. And we move from theory to practice. We get to work."

"Fair enough," Neal agreed. "We may never capture Denver Collins, but that doesn't mean we never use him."

"I'm listening."

"We only know, for certain, of four time travelers. *Four*. Two died at Roswell nearly ten years ago. It looks like one may have died in Chicago a few weeks ago. One is possibly still on the run." Neal hesitated as another agent skirted around them. "But out of all of these, there's only one—*one*—that we know, with any degree of certainty, about where and when he will jump in the future."

Ross pulled hard on his cigarette. The burning tip cast an amber glow across his skeptical face. "I'm *still* listening."

"We also know exactly when he will be born. Exactly. To the day. And we know his full name. And much of the history of his adult life."

Ross yawned. "I'm guessing you're about to reveal the point of this fascinating bedtime story?"

"Listen," Neal begged, "don't you get it? We've had scores of scientists at Dreamland, top researchers in their fields, all seeking to unlock the mysteries of temporal displacement. And we know that the Reds are working on it.

But so much remains unknown. *Most of it* remains unknown." His voice grew louder with every word.

Ross signaled for him to drop it down a notch.

Neal took the hint and recalibrated. "But in Denver Wayne Collins, we finally have a *known* quantity. A *known* time traveler. We have a living, breathing experiment, a temporal guinea pig that we can study. We can track. The imprint inside his wallet proves that we did, or we are, or whatever. It proves *something*." Neal maneuvered directly in front of him. "It's time travel, Chief. Who cares if we get that information now…or, or in fifty years? Once we have it, time itself almost becomes irrelevant."

Ross peered down at the remains of his Lucky Strike and flicked it into a muddy puddle. "And you got that whole scenario from a single word inked into the satin lining of a stranger's wallet? From *Caretaker?*"

"Well," Neal replied, "there's more to it, for sure. But, uh, fundamentally from that. And from our names being there and all. And other factors. It adds up. It really does, Chief…listen I—"

Ross silenced Neal's enthusiasm with a raised hand. "First, remember our agreement…the cigarette is done. And second…you've *partially* convinced me. How do we proceed?"

Neal leaned into Ross' ear.

"I've got a theory about that."

CHAPTER 50

Ellen ran onto the factory floor.

Ellen *never* ran.

And she was yelling.

Shep and Garrett detected the commotion created by this unusual combination and swiveled about. The only thing that Shep seemed to care about was her breach in protocol.

"*Ellen!* You left the door open!" He rubbed his forehead then pointed beyond her. "You know the rules. That damn door stays—"

"Shut up, Sheppard! Listen. Doc took off."

It took a moment for that bombshell to sink in. The two men exchanged glances until she caught up to them.

"Did you hear me?" she demanded. "Stonecroft is *gone*."

"We heard you," Shep replied. "Hell, half the dead could probably hear you."

Ellen flailed her arms. "Well, good! Maybe the dead have enough sense to try to do something about it. I'm not so sure about the living."

Frazier smiled. "He's probably just hungover from the weekend. Overslept. My head's still screaming."

Ellen rolled her eyes. "This is serious, Garrett! Can we cut the bull and do something?!"

"Calm down," Shep advised.

"A little late for that. He took off. Car's gone. Just like I warned. His neighbor saw him put a suitcase in the trunk."

"There's probably a perfectly good explanation."

"Of course there is, *Sherlock*," she exclaimed. "He left town on a mission to prevent himself from killing that girl tomorrow night! There's not a lot of wiggle room for interpretation." She wagged her head. "I told you guys we needed to watch him over the last few days. He knows the rules better than anyone, but that doesn't mean his tender heart can't overrule his usually logical head."

Leah's voice from the far end of the plant interrupted the tense exchange. "Hey, Ellen. The Chief'll be here in a minute. He's on his way."

Ellen waved. "Finally! Maybe *he* will take this seriously!"

"Take you seriously? Really?" Shep asked. "What do you want us to do, Ellen? Colorado and Terrance are five states away, Alexus is hit and miss around here, sick all the time. One guy downstairs can't even speak English. Some damn broad infiltrated our group and stole a bunch of our crap, and now you say our lead researcher has vanished. Our numbers and resources are getting about as thin as the hair on Frazier's bald head!"

"Stop making excuses! Someone needs to go after him! We can't let him break the Fourth Accord." They locked eyes as she inched ever closer. "We've never had it happen before. We don't know what that will do."

"And that's just the point, *we don't know*. We don't have a clue if it will do anything. *Anything*. You might be getting all worked up over nothing. So, I think the best plan is to just let him go, let him get it out of his elderly system."

She spun away. "That's not a plan."

"Sure it is. It's just not the damn one you want."

"I wish Phil Nelson was here."

"He isn't. But I am."

"You're not Phil."

Shep seemed impervious to her sleight as he snuck a slow hand up onto her shoulder. "You know, I should get you all riled up more often." His fingers wandered up to her head, and his other arm rubbed her waist. "The fire in your eyes matches your red hair beautifully."

The door beside the loading dock flung open and McCloud rushed in with Officer O'Connell trailing behind. "Looks like I got here just in time," the Chief noted. "Is this joker sexually assaulting you, ma'am?"

Ellen twisted her way out of Shep's clutches. "No. No more than usual."

"Leah filled me in on the basics. Anything new 'bout Doc?" McCloud asked.

"His neighbor lady saw him load a suitcase into his Buick," Ellen replied. "Around six this morning."

The Chief exhaled and folded his arms. "Well, now that's a shocker. I didn't think he'd go through with it. Never."

"Fifty years of grief could probably make a person do about anything," Billy quipped. "You can't blame the guy for trying."

"No," Ellen agreed, "but we can blame someone for endangering the future. All of our futures."

"Do we know which bar he went to?" McCloud asked.

Ellen shook her head. "No. He said he couldn't remember. Knowing what we know right now, I wonder if he...maybe...*lied* about not remembering. To keep his options open."

"Where exactly did the accident happen?" Shep inquired.

"On the north side of Columbus. Highway 62," McCloud said.

Ellen jumped in. "At 10:15 at night. We even know the mile marker!" She took a few thoughtful steps away from the group. "I know this sounds cruel and heartless and all, but that girl is supposed to die on that highway. In one sense, it is, or was Doc's fault, but in another sense it needs to happen. To keep the official timeline consistent, or whatever you call it."

The Chief rested his full weight against a work table. "It's enough to make yer head spin. Poor Doc. Danged if you do, and danged if you don't."

"For all we know," Ellen continued, "if that girl lives, she might give birth to the next Hitler or something. Could change everything."

Shep stole a quick glance over at Frazier and began a little pacing himself. "Uh, we don't need to know which bar he went to."

"Whaddya mean?" McCloud asked. "Are you wantin' to try to catch him on the road between here and Columbus?" The Chief shook his head. "Ain't no way. Doc may be the world's slowest and most cautious driver, but he's got a three hour head start. We can't make that up. Ain't no way."

"Wait, Chief," Ellen said. "Could you call the state police in Ohio and see if they could pick him up?"

McCloud let out a low whistle. "Hmm…well, that's risky. They could probably find him, but it would have to be serious charges, like bank robbery or the like. Probably not a good idea. The cure might be worse'n the disease, as they say."

"You guys have it all wrong," Shep scolded. "You're focusing on the wrong person in this equation."

"Who else is there?" Ellen asked. "Are you thinking about finding his younger self and then getting him to go to a different bar or something?"

"Nope."

"Well, then *who?*"

"The girl," Shep muttered.

"The girl?" Ellen asked.

"Mmm hmm. The girl."

Officer Billy slid his hat down and scratched his head. "What about the girl?"

Shep was pokerfaced. "We know exactly *who*. We know exactly *when*. And we know exactly *where*. Stonecroft's drunk whereabouts are…irrelevant."

"I must be missing something," Ellen protested.

"It's pretty simple and straightforward, Miss Finegan," Shep clarified as he glanced over at Garrett.

"She needs to die…we can certainly make that happen."

CHAPTER 51

Tuesday, November 20, 1956, 11:49 p.m.
Somewhere north of Las Vegas, Nevada

To have labeled the two-hour motorcycle trip from downtown Las Vegas to a pitiful dirt road thirty-nine miles west of the defunct depot of Crystal Springs as an *adventure* would have been an unwarranted exaggeration.

But that didn't prevent Terrance Gaines from employing the descriptor twice in the last three minutes.

Denver gripped the glove on his right hand with his teeth and pried it loose with a firm tug. "You know, Tee, you keep saying *adventure*, but I have a different word." He yanked on his left glove in much the same way. "How about *miserable?* Not adventure...*misery*."

Terrance chuckled as he dismounted his own bike. "You know the old saying: if you can't take the cold, then you should stay outta the middle of the Nevada desert at night in late November."

"Old saying, huh?"

"Yeah, man. My granny used to say that to us kids all the time. All the time, man."

Denver frowned and slapped his hands together. "Call me crazy, but something, something *deep down* tells me you just made that up. On the spot. Right here. Right now."

Terrance stretched his legs. "I guess you're crazy then."

"I can't argue with you. But if you think about it...we're *both* crazy. This whole plan is one big ball of crazy." Denver looked around and shook his head. "We get a mysterious package from an anonymous source, and a few weeks later we're on motorcycles planning to infiltrate Area 51 in the middle of the night, two days before Thanksgiving! Why two days before Thanksgiving? Why so specific?"

"Just doin' what the box said to do, when the box said to do it," Terrance replied. "Quit askin' questions. We're both military men. We're used to following ridiculous orders from people we've never met, or probably will *never* meet. It's the name o' the game, man. You know the routine."

"I know," Denver chuckled. "I, uh, I just can't believe we're actually *here*. We're actually about to infiltrate Area 51."

Tee laughed. "I'm not infiltrating nothin', man. I'm just here for logistical and moral support. That's what the Chief said. You are the one, the only...*Joel Jackson*. And hey...did I ever tell you, that you look fantastic in that beige uniform? I could easily see you as a cover boy for *Area 51 Quarterly* magazine. Really."

"And you—*you*—are a terrible liar, Mr. Terrance Gaines." Denver pointed directly at him. "In fact, you should join a local chapter of Liars Anonymous. And don't use your real name. Just make that up, too."

They both laughed and their chilled breath glowed white under the brilliant moon. But the laughing was short lived. So much had transpired in the past forty-eight hours since they had arrived in Las Vegas.

As a first order of business, they had located a dealership willing to trade Terrance's dark '41 Ford for a white '46 Chevrolet (plus a little cash to sweeten the deal). After reserving a room at the Sahara Hotel and Casino and enjoying an exquisite dinner at the Golden Nugget, they stole a pair of Nevada license plates from the parking lot at the Flamingo.

The following morning they rose early to purchase a couple of Army-surplus Harley Davidson WLA motorbikes (per the recommendation found in the box's paperwork) and modified both mufflers before lunch. Denver and Terrance consumed the afternoon finalizing their plan and worked in a three-hour nap to help prepare them for the long and dangerous night ahead.

Denver fixed his gaze to the south. "Looks like miles and miles and miles of off-road fun," he mused. "Probably need to gas up."

"I'm already on it."

Terrance yanked his gloves off and began untying the complicated ropes that strapped a large fuel can to the side of his motorcycle.

"Where did you learn to tie those little girl's knots?" Denver teased. "Boy Scouts or the Navy?"

Terrance didn't even look up. "I believe *you* were the one who enlisted with the *Boy Scouts*, Mr. Collins. I guess that once you turn eighteen, they try'n make you feel all better about it by calling it the Army."

"Wow. Real funny. The Army is the superior fighting force. You guys play in the big bathtub; we do dirty work. You can't deny history."

Terrance leaned back and loosened his gas cap. "History, huh? Well, last time I checked, the Navy was whoopin' the ass of you Army-types in football." He fueled his tank. "I'm pretty sure we lead by five or six games."

Denver grinned and opened his own cap. "Don't forget, the last time you checked was thirty years ago to me. The Army's made up the slack since you jumped. Things have changed quite a bit in the twenty-first century."

Terrance finished and relayed the tank over to him. "And you probably just made that up. I thought Boy Scouts weren't supposed to lie, man? Or do they give out a badge for lyin' in the twenty-first century?"

"I guess you'll just have to find out."

"Whatever. I'm just glad to hear that football has survived over the decades. So, uh, thanks for breaking the Second Accord."

Denver finished fueling, ditched the can, and hopped back on his bike. "Don't mention it." He searched inside of his coat and withdrew his photo of Jasmine. He ran his thumb across her adorable smile.

Terrance boarded his motorcycle moments later and roared the engine back to life. "Alright, Mr. Collins. Let's get this done, so we can all go home and see our kids. May God be with us, my friend."

Denver started his motor. "Amen, Brother Gaines. Let's do this."

Ninety minutes.

It's a long time to contemplate the high probability of your own death.

Denver had made numerous attempts at distracting his fatalistic mindset along the southerly dirt track, but with laughable success. Even the bright prospect of holding his daughter again failed to smother the flames of an expected demise before morning's first light.

Infiltrate Area 51?

Really, Collins?

What led you here?

Desperation?

Pride?

The continuous internal struggle that had raged for over thirty miles hadn't been completely without merit. His mind's eye had visited the somber, wet interiors of the nondescript landing craft that dared challenge the Nazi juggernaut on D-Day. He reverently pictured the ranks of brave men packed shoulder-to-shoulder into untold thousands of Higgins Boats. They had traversed the choppy seas of the English Channel through abysmal weather and low visibility to experience mortality on the fortified beaches of the French coast.

He was certain that those early waves of the greatest generation harbored no illusions about their actual chances for survival. Denver could—in a small way—identify with them.

He approached a slight incline and backed off on the throttle, allowing Terrance to merge alongside. They both stopped and killed their motors.

"Like they say," Terrance began, "two's a crowd. It's a one-man show from here on out, my friend."

Denver slipped off his bike and offered a hearty handshake. "I, uh, I can't thank you enough for…well, *everything* on this trip. Really. Everything you've done, it's meant a lot—"

Terrance dismounted and grasped his hand. "Whoa, whoa, there, Colorado. You make it sound like this is the end or—"

"But—"

"But *nothing,* man! This game ain't over. This is First Down and Ten. You've got the ball and really great field position."

Denver focused on a subtle glow along the dark desert horizon. "I'm grateful for your misplaced confidence, Tee, but I think we both know—"

"*What we both know* is that you have great inside information. You have a plan. You have training. And you're motivated, highly motivated. You know you're coming…they don't. Huge advantage. Huge, man. You got everything? Your ID, the key?"

"Uh, yeah," Denver mumbled. "I triple checked when we left the highway. Remember, I'm a Boy Scout. We have a motto…*be prepared*."

"You remember the security question and answer?"

"Like I know my own name," Denver replied.

Terrance circled around and clutched Denver's shoulders. "Well then…it's time to go, Mr. Collins. And when you're done, I'll be waiting right here for you. Or, if things get messy…at the hotel. Like we planned. Like clockwork. You got this."

No I don't, Denver thought.

I don't think you really believe that either.

Denver boarded his bike. "Thanks…really."

Terrance slapped his friend's shoulder twice. "Cheer up! This is one Navy vet who is rooting for the Army. Imagine that! Now go give'm hell, my friend." He paced back towards his own vehicle. "And hurry back, man. I'm freezing!"

Denver extinguished his headlights and popped the motorcycle into gear. "Okay…I'll see you soon. Right back here, or the hotel."

His rash promise was hopelessly naïve.

Denver would never lay eyes upon Terrance Gaines again.

CHAPTER 52

The sickeningly sweet mix of tobacco, booze, and body odor awakened memories latent within him for well-over half a century. Doc crept inside the tavern and was paralyzed by the immediate sensory rush. He clamped his eyes shut as a myriad suppressed recollections resurfaced in unrelenting waves.

The Platters were crooning out the final chorus of *Only You* on a jukebox off to his right, just past a couple of unoccupied tables. Their smooth and tight harmonies seemed to comprise a haunting echo as he struggled to reign in his emotional response. He retreated against the wall. Doc imagined he was prepared.

He wasn't.

By a mile.

"You okay, pops?"

Doc cracked his eyes open. The middle-aged figure standing in front of him nursing a beer must've been a diesel mechanic. He certainly wreaked like a filthy garage floor.

"Hey," the man said. "You okay?"

Doc fumbled for a handkerchief and mopped his moist brow with trembling fingers. "Oh, uh, yes, thank…thank you, young man." Stonecroft blinked the stinging sweat out of his eyes. "I think that…uh…I might have contracted something in this infernal night air. But thank you for your concern, in any respect."

The man patted him on the shoulder. "Whatever you say, pops. Take care."

Doc nodded as the kind stranger slipped off to his right, and in that uniquely forbidden moment he caught the rarest sight in all the world.

Incredible.

The young man, arrayed in blue jeans and a dark jacket, was perched atop the second-to-last stainless steel bar stool. Doc's view ushered in absolute terror and inexplicable delight in equal proportions.

Oh my gracious heavens! he mused as his pulse throbbed within his hot ears. *Can it be? Can it really be?!*

It was him.

Him.

CHAPTER 53

Wednesday, November 21, 1956, 1:57 a.m.
Groom Lake, Nevada

The nearest metal structure was only seventy-five yards to his south. Three miles of near-coasting on his motorcycle, followed by forty minutes of a treacherous hike across the loose desert gravel had brought Denver within a stone's throw of a site that legends were made of.

He remained low behind a sandy ridge and scanned the complex with his binoculars.

Area 51.

It just doesn't feel real. Or possible.

But then again, neither did time travel until three months earlier.

A mixed bag of unimpressive buildings were scattered about. A few lights. No movement. No people. No aliens. Nothing.

This is it?

I've seen villages in Afghanistan that looked more high-tech.

It was both a relief and a letdown. There was little doubt that his high expectations had been appropriately justified. Decades of rumors, leaks, and campaigns of deliberate misinformation concerning Area 51 had painted a larger-than-life portrait upon the fertile canvas of popular imagination. But now, Denver had traveled over 1500 miles and penetrated through the curtain of secrecy, and the Great and Mighty Oz appeared as neither of the two.

Regardless of appearances, there was more. And he knew it.

This is just the tip of the iceberg, Collins.

The real magic is all below the surface. It's time to get underground.

Every document related to his mission had been memorized; the layout of the facility, the exact location of the metallurgical lab, elevator access points, everything. Denver plopped to the ground, popped on his flashlight, and glanced at his identification badge.

Joel Jackson.

He repeated his new identity silently several times. Any hesitation in adhering to his assumed name could be disastrous.

Don't forget about the security question, Collins.

Have you seen Major Anderson?

Denver looped the appropriate response over and over in his nervous mind.

Yes, he was playing cards in the mess hall.

He pulled his sleeve back and checked his watch.

2:04 a.m.

Only about three more hours of total darkness, Collins.

It's now or never.

Denver hid his binoculars, killed the flashlight, and kept low to the ground while stealing across the packed, level soil towards the north end of the nearest building. Hours of being light-deprived had acclimated his natural night vision to a workable degree, augmented by the steady glow of the November moon.

The silt transitioned to asphalt as he reached the dark metal surface of the two-story structure and rested his back up against it. The only discernible sound was the pounding of his own adrenaline-driven heart. Denver pressed his ear to the cold wall.

Nothing.

Good.

The majority of the lights around the complex seemed to be concentrated to the east, so he slid down the building towards the west. He reached the corner, dropped down, and leaned his head to the side. The apparent backside of the structure was about thirty yards long. No windows. No doors.

All clear.

Seconds later he had scurried to the southern edge and peered around the corner. There was a similar—albeit much smaller—structure about twenty-five yards to the south. Beyond that, he spotted a modest brick building with glass windows.

He grinned.

My access point.

The arrangement of the facility was exactly as the hand drawn layouts had suggested. He hoped that the subterranean blueprints were just as accurate. His smile soon evaporated once he considered the logistical dangers between his current location and the elevator. The conditions were inherently perilous.

Open ground. No cover. Plenty of lights.

The thought occurred to him that the presence of a few other people milling about the area (in the dead of night) would most likely have provided a better scenario. But there was no one else. Denver took a modicum of comfort in his years of military training regarding infiltration. He looked at his uniform and dusted his pants and shoes. He already looked the part, now it was time to move with confident purpose.

Just walk towards the brick building, Mr. Joel Jackson.

Who cares if you're alone? Nice and steady.

You belong here.

After taking a few deep breaths, he strolled out into the light. He hadn't traveled more than a dozen feet when the one sound he feared the most grew in intensity.

Then he saw it. Directly ahead.

Coming right at him.

A jeep.

CHAPTER 54

Doc stole a hasty glance down at his watch.

9:38 p.m.

He ventured a step closer to the bar. His will was firm, more or less. The first known, significant breach of the Fourth Accord was inexorably set in motion. Turning back had ceased to be a viable option. Over the miserable years, a broken rule had waxed increasingly inconsequential against the sure prospect of a broken family.

"I say, that is an exquisite coat," Doc offered as he approached the lone figure. "Magnificent tailoring."

The young man rotated to his left sloppily and lowered his half-empty glass. He studied Doc and then his own jacket. "Yeah," he replied after an unusual delay. "Thanks. It, uh, it was a gift. A gift from my mother. And father."

Doc climbed aboard the adjacent bar stool and leaned onto his elbows. "Well, it's quite the gift. Was it for a special occasion?"

The glassy-eyed youth nodded and blinked. "Yep. Yep. My birthday." He snuck a sip. "Today. Today's my birth…day. The big two-one."

Doc tore off his spectacles in feigned surprise. "Well, *that*, my friend, is truly amazing. Because, believe it or not, today is the wondrous anniversary of the day of my birth, as well! I mean, goodness me, what are the odds?!"

"That's, now that's an easy computation," the young man replied. "They are…one in three hundred…and sixty-five. At least, most years."

"I can't argue with your math," Doc noted.

"I like numbers. A lot. A whole lot. They are like…my friends. Sometimes my *only* friends."

"I don't doubt it."

The boy leaned sideways and shot his wobbly hand out.

"I'm…Glen. Glen Stonecroft."

CHAPTER 55

Wednesday, November 21, 1956, 2:13 a.m.
Groom Lake, Nevada

Denver's options were limited.

By now the jeep's occupants had, no doubt, already spotted him ambling across the grounds. Any deviation in his current direction or speed would raise immediate suspicion.

Think about how this looks, Collins…they're probably already suspicious. Don't react. Move with purpose.

He had just begun to pass the second metal building when the jeep pulled alongside in a sudden, disconcerting stop. A blinding spotlight flooded the area around him in a bright pool, but not before he caught a glimpse of a single occupant within the vehicle.

He liked those odds if things went south.

His right hand slipped into his pocket and laid hold of his pistol.

A deep voice boomed out. "A little late for a walk, wouldn't you say?"

Think, Collins, think.

Denver shrugged. "Wilson was already in the can, and I had to go. I, uh, I wouldn't drive behind Building A7 over there, unless you want to get crap all over your tires. It was bad. Real bad. Trust me."

There was an uncomfortable delay. "Have you seen Major Anderson?"

The security question.

Denver rubbed his forehead. "Uh, yes. He was playing cards in the mess hall."

"Step closer."

Denver complied.

Another pause. "Have a nice evening, Mr. Jackson."

Denver nodded with a half-hearted, *see-ya-later* salute. The driver killed the spotlight and accelerated north, eventually coming to a second stop in front of the first, larger, structure. Denver continued his leisurely pace towards the brick elevator building.

Nice work, Mr. Jackson.

You almost convinced me.

Almost there.

An engine roared to life in the distance off to his right. Just as Denver took his final steps up to the doors, the jeep raced past him, cruising south. A relieved Denver studied the underground access point and lightly tugged on the right handle.

Locked.

The thick glass doors guarded a small, tile-lined foyer. Ten feet further in, an impressive stainless steel elevator door dominated the white back wall. He glanced down and to his right. A tiny kiosk was embedded into the brick siding with a single red light adorning the top. Things were starting to feel a bit more up to Area 51's impossible reputation, at least for the mid-1950s. Denver removed his ID badge and slid the card through the reader.

This had better work.

Nothing appeared to happen. He rechecked the door.

Still locked.

Light is still red.

As his pulse quickened, he changed strategies and slid his card upward on a desperate second attempt. Two seconds later, the lamp turned green, and he heard a distinct metallic pop. Denver grabbed the right door and it swung open freely.

Objective number two accomplished.

Only a few dozen more to go, he laughed.

The temperature inside the foyer was an immediate and definite improvement. He stepped forward, pressed a large button to the right of the elevator door, and glanced up at the row of twelve level indicators inlaid above the eight-foot tall opening. The number 5 highlighted for several seconds, before finally changing to 4. The process was excruciatingly slow. It changed to 3 after an even longer pause.

What's the deal?

How slow is this thing? Are others getting on or off?

Denver pivoted around and scanned outside. All continued to be dark and quiet in America's most secret of secret facilities. The 2 above him lit up.

Come on, come on. Hurry up.

His internal pleadings did little to vary the frustrating speed of the elevator. Four seconds later the 1 began to glow. Denver pulled in a deep breath and attempted to calm himself. He knew that once those stainless steel doors opened, it could be empty or it could be filled with an entire SWAT team bristling with rifles and bad attitudes.

It was a case of Russian roulette…*elevator style.*

Three seconds later, a lumbering hum reverberated in the foyer as the G highlighted above him. His senses went on full alert.

The huge door opened and Denver reached for his gun.

CHAPTER 56

Shake hands?

Doc hesitated to return the expected social gesture and just stared at the outstretched hand of the younger version of himself. He had contemplated the ramifications of this conversation a thousand times over…but the consequences of making actual *physical* contact had never once crossed his mind.

Doc shut his eyes and offered a silent prayer. He feared some type of metaphysical explosion, or temporal anomaly, or even a wormhole.

Or maybe nothing at all.

He lifted his trembling right arm and clutched the young man's hand. There was neither explosion, nor anomaly, nor wormhole. He relaxed, exhaled, and shook his hand with vigor.

"Well, nice to make your acquaintance today, Glen. My, uh, my friends call me *Professor*."

Young Glen reached out for another drink. The bartender looked over expectantly at Doc. He waved him off.

The boy squinted. "Professor? What…like a teacher? A University professor? I've had a bunch of those."

"Something like that, yes."

The boy pivoted back towards the bar and rested against it. "You wouldn't catch me doing that…nope. Not teaching…not in a million years. I could tell you how many…how many days that is—in a million years—if you gimme a few seconds."

Doc chuckled and patted his arm. "No, that won't be necessary, my newest and yet oldest friend. But I would implore you to withhold judgment on a career in education."

"Explore which judge about *whose* career?"

"Never mind," Doc followed up as he studied him with growing interest. "So tell me, Mr. Glen Stonecroft, why aren't you celebrating this momentous occasion with your friends?"

"Most…no…*all*. All of my friends are…still back at University," he began. "I came home for Thanksgiving break…early. Cause of my birthday."

"Is there no special lady in your life to share this milestone of maturity with?"

That probing question seemed to paralyze the young man beyond his chemically-induced stupor. His face drained of expression while he twirled his glass on the counter. "Uh…no. No. Not anymore at least."

"Sounds like a worthy story hidden within there somewhere."

"Yeah, but, not a…*happy* story," young Glen announced. "She, uh, she and I had a…thing. A good thing. First year in University. Cutest dolly in…Chemistry. We, we made it through the next…summer…too."

His voice trailed off.

Doc wasn't quite ready to abandon the emotional trail.

"Did you two remain together in your second year?"

"Well, kinda…then…no. She met another cat. From another school. On…Christmas break." He rubbed his reddening face.

Doc remembered the months of agony well. "Broke your heart when she left. Fractured into shards. No remedy seemed equal to the pain."

Young Stonecroft bobbed his heavy head. "You been there, too, huh?"

"I have been right there with you, trust me."

"I...uh...I used to think that nobody—*nobody*—hurt worse...than me."

Doc glanced over. "An ancient Greek philosopher once observed that the hottest love—"

"Wait," he interrupted, "I know. I know this one. '*The hottest love has the coldest end*'. Socrates, right?"

"That is correct."

"I kinda dig philosophy. And poetry. But I ain't no sissy...I just find poetry kinda...mathematical sometimes. A lot of it really is mathematically-based."

"Indeed," Doc replied. "But listen, you must not abandon all hope, my friend. Pursue true love. I have been told—on quite solid authority—that it is the greatest gift this side of heaven."

Young Glen swirled his glass. "Sometimes the pain...it outweighs the gift. *Any* gift."

"You are far too young to make that final assessment," Doc scolded in the kindest manner possible. "Look into the eyes of your firstborn child and then tell me that no gift outweighs the pain."

"It's hard to...to imagine something you've never experienced," the boy said. "Like trying to imagine a color you've never seen." He hesitated. "But now...I have experienced pain. No need to imagine that."

Doc refused to be deterred. "Now, this may be difficult to comprehend, my young friend, but there are torments in this life far more miserable than love unrequited. Far more."

"Like what?"

"Like regret. Like guilt. Like causing a depth of misery and loss unparalleled in human experience. Our own agonies pale in comparison to the pain we can inflict within others."

"No offense, professor...but I can't see it."

Doc examined his watch as tears pooled in both eyes. "And now, my friend...*now* you never will."

The young man shot him a look. "What's that supposed to mean?"

"Oh, nothing at all," Doc said. "Just the ramblings of an old fool."

Young Glen threw his head back and drained his final shot glass. With less-than-sober precision, he slammed the thick cup down upon the counter. "Well…Mr. Professor," he began, "I have enjoyed our…short and sweet talk. But this birthday boy…has to split."

Doc plastered a frown across his face as the young man slid off his stool. "But we were just getting acquainted, my friend. I have so many topics that I would surely love to discuss."

"As would I, but unfortunate…unfortunately, I am driving a *borrowed* Chevy. I must…must return it soon. Soon."

"Chevrolet?" asked Doc. "Are you referring to the silver Bel Air hardtop parked along the front of this establishment?"

"You're pretty good. Yep. That's…that's the one, Professor."

Doc stood as well. "I hate to be the proverbial bearer of bad news, especially on the auspicious anniversary of the day of our birth, my friend."

"Bad news? What bad news?"

"Concerning the Bel Air. Well, as I walked by I noticed that it had two flat tires."

CHAPTER 57

Wednesday, November 21, 1956, 2:19 a.m.
Groom Lake, Nevada

Empty.

The elevator was empty.

Denver released the death grip on his weapon.

You've gotten lucky twice in the last five minutes, Collins.

Don't expect Lady Luck to hold out.

He stepped inside the massive elevator and marveled at the construction. The stainless chamber was fifteen feet deep, ten feet wide, and rose at least three feet above his head. It didn't take much imagination to predict that it doubled as an equipment and materials transport as well. Denver walked over to the control panel. Including Ground, there were about twelve levels available. It appeared that a few of them required a physical key to activate.

Metallurgy is on Level Two.

He hit the button and the doors gradually sealed him in.

No going back now.

Into the belly of the beast, Collins.

The ominous descent lasted for twenty tense seconds, but to a soldier whose veins were flooding with adrenaline, it seemed like an hour. According to the diagram he had memorized, the elevator dumped out into a long, wide hallway. His prize awaited just around the corner to the left. The elevator eased to a smooth but noisy stop.

Denver prepared to react.

The doors began splitting apart.

The sterile, white corridor was a ghost town.

Where is everybody? This is incredible.

My good fortune is still holding.

An unsettling doubt flashed through his mind.

What if it's not luck? What if it's a trap?

Maybe they sent us the package. Maybe they lured me here.

What if they're waiting for me to get underground, with no way out?

Just like Luke Skywalker in Cloud City.

He ventured a few timid steps out into the hall, walking heel to toe.

It doesn't matter, Collins. You're here, and there's a chance that this isn't a trap. Doc said this stuff was our only hope. So we're trapped anyway if you don't at least try.

It could be a lose-lose situation. Trapped if you do and trapped if you don't.

He passed by a nondescript, windowless door and pressed up against it. There was not the slightest hint of sound or activity within. He checked the next one with similar results.

I hope my metals lab is just like these two.

Denver reduced his speed to a crawl as he arrived at the corner. He knelt to the concrete floor and inched his head around the sharp bend.

All clear…again?

I must be dreaming. It's the only rational explanation.

He slid back up to a standing position and readied himself. Denver searched his left pocket; the key to the lab was still safely inside. His heart throbbed afresh as it became clear that a deserted stretch of hallway and a single door were the only things separating him from obtaining the final ingredient in the elusive recipe of time travel.

Alright, Collins. It's time to get in, grab, and get out.

Piece of cake.

With silent steps, he approached the second door on the left. There were no signs or markings to indicate purpose or function, just plain entrances along a featureless wall. Denver fished out his key and checked up and down the hallway. He was alone. It was quiet…to an unnerving degree. He shoved the key in and attempted to rotate it in either direction. It wouldn't budge. He yanked it out and reinserted.

Nothing. You've got to be kidding me!

Denver torqued the key with so much force that he feared the metal would shear off inside the lock. His fingers burned under the strain. He pulled on the door, he pushed on the door…nothing seemed to enable the key to work.

I can't believe I've come half-way across America, infiltrated Area 51, and now I'm held up by a key?!

Every second he lingered in the hallway increased his likelihood of detection or confrontation. The sun would be rising soon, and he knew he needed a few hours to escape back to civilization.

You're gonna have to break in, Collins. This is your one and only shot.

He backed to the opposite side of the corridor and raced back across, ramming his right shoulder just inside the doorjamb. There was a huge *THUD,* but the stout metal door mocked his exertion. It barely shook. He repeated the fruitless endeavor with the same lack of results.

Denver retreated a few feet and kicked the handle with his heavy boots, seeking to break it off or even loosen it. With every assault on the doorknob his resolve and rage grew.

But then a door opened…just not the one he wanted.

CHAPTER 58

Frazier flicked on the small flashlight and scanned his watch for the umpteenth time in the last thirty minutes.

10:09.

He peered out northward across his dark hood at the lonely stretch of US 62. A thin blanket of fog migrated from the southwest and hugged the ground.

Any time now.

Any time.

His pulse quickened as he double-checked the focus on the binoculars perched alongside him.

Looking good.

As far as Chief McCloud and Ellen Finegan knew, Garrett was just an informant. He was merely an innocuous pair of eyes to observe Doc's accident and then report back to the group about the condition of Carolyn Boulden.

But Robert Sheppard had altered the parameters of Garrett's mission. Dramatically.

He lowered the field glasses and retrieved a rifle from the backseat. With a rapid tug, he yanked the bolt back and examined the chamber.

Locked and loaded.

This hadn't been the first time Garrett had waited and watched with a gun in his lap, but it was the first time he had been given official permission to leave the state since jumping to Normal.

The distant drone of an approaching engine ratcheted his state of awareness up a few notches. Moments later, a faint glow to the north transformed into bright headlights atop the crest of a small rise in the road. He snatched the binoculars and held his breath.

Damn.

A truck.

Just a damn truck.

Garrett laid sideways as the lumbering vehicle blew by, shaking his car somewhat.

Definitely not a white Chevrolet.

The whole scenario resurrected unpleasant recollections buried deep within. Garrett straightened up in the seat. The time of the year, the time of the night, and the firearm braced across his legs, all evoked a singular memory.

But it wasn't a rural stretch of highway that he revisited in his mind's eye. It was a mostly deserted parking lot in South Central Los Angeles. Rather than a teenage girl in a small, white car, he had awaited a middle-aged businessman sporting a custom-tailored, three-piece suit ambling toward an immaculate Aston Martin directly beneath the amber radiance of the parking lot lights.

A shot rang out.

The man went down.

Garrett fled quickly.

But justice moved even quicker.

Yards of cold concrete and years of highly regulated activity left him with ample opportunity to ponder his actions. But then there was that storm.

That horrific storm.

A new glow on the dark horizon jolted him back to 1956. Frazier seized the binoculars and zeroed in on the brightening haze.

The time was right.

It's a car.

Definitely light colored.

Probably white.

Frazier started his own vehicle but kept his lights off. The plan was to turn them on at the last second and then block the road. After that, Shep told him to do whatever needed to be done.

The white car drew closer.

He lowered his hand to the headlamp knob.

Wait Frazier.

Not yet.

The car was fifty yards and closing.

He scanned back to the south. No headlights were visible in the opposite direction.

Looks like Doc broke the Fourth Accord.

Shame on the old fool.

Get ready.

A blur from across the road caught his attention.

What the hell?

A large deer sprang from the thick woods on the far side and froze in the dazzling patch of light in the center of the rural highway. The white car swerved hard, its tires protesting and smoking under the furious strain. The vehicle raced across both lanes and slammed, full speed, into the base of an enormous tree on Garrett's side of the road.

An eruption of shattered glass and twisted metal ejected into the air as the rear of the Chevrolet shot over six feet off the ground before crashing back to the dirt shoulder. The sickening pair of crunches were followed by the incessant blaring of the car's horn.

Garrett, still trying to recover from the violence of the moment, watched as the deer scrambled from the road and dashed off through the fog and into the dark forest. He tossed the gun off his lap, grabbed his flashlight and jumped out. The only functioning headlight on the Chevy was hopelessly out of position, casting an eerie beam of light through the radiator steam and up into the large tree.

Frazier circled around behind the white car and approached the driver's side. The pungent stench of burnt rubber and overheated coolant assaulted his heightened senses. It took a moment as he forced himself to peer inside the gruesome area that had been the front seat. Part of the engine block protruded back through the dash, coated with blobs of glass and splatters of fresh blood.

He aimed his light at the mangled body of a young girl nearly ripped in half by a steering column that now resided in the backseat.

The motor was dead.

So was she.

Another pass of the flashlight revealed the remains of her bloody purse in a much bloodier floorboard. He leaned through the glassless window and retrieved the bag. Frazier picked through the contents and fished out a small card. It was a driver's license.

Carolyn Boulden.

I'll be damned.

Doc didn't kill this girl after all.

CHAPTER 59

Wednesday, November 21, 1956, 2:27 a.m.
Groom Lake, Nevada

It seemed to play out in horrific slow motion.

Denver had just kicked the handle for the fifth time and was preparing for a sixth when another door to his immediate right opened. A spectacled man with curly black hair and a lab coat ventured out into the hall. In an irretrievable moment of reactionary, instinctive behavior (ingrained by hundreds of intense door-to-door searches overseas), Denver thrust his hand into his pocket, drew out his gun and trained it on the shocked victim.

The technician froze, his fear-filled eyes danced back and forth between Denver's face and the barrel of Denver's gun. The awkward, silent standoff continued and the tension rose.

"Listen," Denver began, "I don't want to hurt you."

If the man heard a word he said, it didn't show.

Denver lowered his gun by degrees and glanced to his left. "I just need you to open this door. I promise that I—"

The man seized the momentary distraction and lunged for a small red handle on the opposite wall. He tripped it, fell to the concrete, and then scrambled on all fours back through his own open door. He managed to slam it shut before Denver could reach him.

The wail of the alert sirens was deafening, amplified and reflected by the confined space of the underground corridor. Denver hesitated in panicked confusion, partly due to the incapacitating nature of the high decibel alarm combined with the urgency of his unique mission.

It's now or never, Collins.

You need to get this done. A lot of people are depending on you.

It didn't matter.

Regardless of his action or inaction over the next few minutes, the outcome would not have been altered to any significant degree. As the unrelenting sirens pierced the air, a squad of heavily armed MPs in black uniforms flooded the halls from both directions.

Denver was totally surrounded, hopelessly outgunned, and forced to his knees. Still, the Special Forces veteran thrashed about, executing a worthy and desperate struggle. More than a few of the guards went sailing across the hall, and a few more sustained damaging blows to the body and head.

But the outcome was a foregone conclusion.

Two muscle-bound MPs clutched him from behind as a third rushed up with the back end of an assault rifle. In a swift and powerful reflex, the guard crashed his gunstock into Denver's defenseless forehead.

A single thought raced through his mind right before everything went black.

I'm sorry, Jasmine. Daddy is so sorry.

CHAPTER 60

Wednesday, November 21, 1956, 3:12 a.m.
Roswell, New Mexico

It was the middle of the night.

A night which had followed a long and stressful day of research and investigation in Roswell.

And his phone was ringing.

The man struggled in his confused state of semi-consciousness to locate the source of the annoying sound. His hand kept slapping a nearby pillow, but somehow missed the bedside table inches away and the phone it housed.

The ringing persisted.

"Alright, dammit. Alright," he growled. The irritated man pushed up to a seated position and hung his legs off the side of the bed. His upright posture seemed to clear his head somewhat and he ultimately discovered the offending phone.

"This is Ross," he answered. "And this better be good. Damn good."

He massaged his rough face and the back of his tired head.

"Slow down. Slow down. You have *who in custody* at Dreamland, Corporal Jennings?!" he demanded. Ross hesitated and flicked on the light switch. He studied his watch.

"I'll be there in three hours."

CHAPTER 61

A blast of ice-cold water pummeling his face jerked Denver out of unconsciousness. As his senses returned by degrees, he discovered that he was strapped to a metal chair. Tension in his shoulders indicated that his arms were tightly cuffed behind him. His ankles were immobilized.

He blinked several times. The front of his skull screamed from the abuse it had suffered in a scuffle he was struggling to remember. His pupils throbbed while they rapidly strained to adjust to the intense light permeating the small room.

Denver looked into his lap. He had been stripped down to his white underwear.

Another splash of frigid water, then a voice.

"Look at me," it commanded. "*Look…at…me!*"

Denver didn't, and a pair of strong hands grabbed his head from behind and tilted it upwards. A middle-aged man sporting a white dress shirt with rolled up sleeves dominated his view.

"What is your name?" he demanded.

Denver was silent and looked away.

"Who are you? Why are you here?"

More silence.

The man nodded at someone. Denver's shoulders began to burn as his arms were shoved upward. The pain nearly sent him back into unconsciousness.

"I said," the man pressed, "what…is…your…name?" He slipped Denver's former ID badge out from his front shirt pocket. "Something tells me it isn't…*Joel Jackson*."

Denver clamped his eyes shut and held his breath to bear up under the torture. Seconds later, his arms were dropped back down and he gasped with the sudden release.

The man leaned closer and studied him.

"Where'd you get all of these scars? In battle? Who do you fight for?"

Denver concentrated on the floor.

"Nothing, huh?" the man asked. "That's okay, Mr. Collins."

Denver glanced up before he could stop himself.

"That's what I thought. Mr. Denver Wayne Collins. That was a nice picture of your daughter in your pocket. Very useful." The man took a few steps back and paced around the empty room clutching an empty cup. "Now that we've established the *who*, how about you fill me in on the *why?*"

Denver locked eyes with the interrogator but kept his mouth shut. He was thankful that the agony in his shoulders had started to subside. Denver noticed a small video camera aimed at him from the far side of the room.

"I don't get it. You travel all the way from the future to Chicago, and then from Chicago to the middle of the desert. Why? *Why, Mr. Collins?* Who sent you? What is your mission?"

No response.

The angered man hurled his glass against the wall behind Denver and lunged at him, screaming, "*Answer me, dammit! Who sent you? Why are you here?!*"

Denver's head sunk down as he braced for the reprisal.

It never came.

The man straightened up. "Alright. That's okay, Mr. Collins. That's okay. Just sit there, don't talk. Don't cooperate." He jogged over to a phone on the wall and picked up the handset. "We can change all that. We can change every bit of that."

He dialed a few numbers. "This is Hamilton. Send a nurse down with the cocktail." He hung up and approached a solitary door on the right side of the chamber. He opened it.

"I'll be back in about thirty minutes," Hamilton said. "I'll find out everything we need to know then."

CHAPTER 62

The copilot worked his way down the center aisle, a fresh cigarette dangling from one hand and a clipboard clutched in the other. He came to a stop and waited until the two men looked up from their hushed conversation.

"What's our status?" Ross asked him.

"About ninety minutes out, sir."

An uncomfortable pause followed.

"Thank you, commander," Neal offered. "That will be all."

"Yessir." The man returned to the cockpit.

"Why don't you radio ahead for an update?" Neal inquired.

"Out of the question. I've ordered strict radio silence. There's no telling who Collins is working with…or working *for*. I don't want to tip our hand, Neal." Ross gazed out the window into the featureless night sky. "The longer they don't know that we have him the better. Gives us the advantage. For once."

"I get all that, boss," Neal countered. "But I'd just like to know what we're about to deal with *before* we get there. Be a little more prepared. Maybe the situation has changed on the ground."

Ross spun back around. "We've had ten years to prepare for this moment, Neal. I don't think an hour and a half more is gonna change the dynamics very much."

Neal hunched over and stared at the floor. "But why would he come there? Sabotage? Information?" He rubbed his face and rested his elbows on his thighs. "Is he trying to make contact with us? Our names are in his wallet. It's a possibility."

Ross crushed his cigarette into the metal window sill and fired up a new one. "Honestly, Neal…I don't know. And I don't care." He took a quick hit on the smoke. "But what I do know, and I what I do care about is that we extract every shred of useful intelligence outta that sonofabitch and gain some real leverage personally. And internationally."

Neal collapsed back against his seat. "Who did you say was handling the initial interrogation?"

"It's either Eisner or Hamilton. And you know how I feel about Eisner. If his father wasn't on the intelligence committee, I wouldn't let that kid wax my ex-wife's car."

"That *kid* was promoted out of the FBI."

Ross shot him a hard look and a trail of smoke trickled from the wrinkled corners of his mouth. "And you definitely know how I feel about the FBI."

"They serve a purpose."

"Name one," Ross challenged. But before Neal could form an intelligent answer, his boss continued. "It doesn't really matter. Not one damn bit. Eisner, the FBI, Director Dulles…none of it. Now that we have Collins, SATURN is going to lead the pack. Give it a few months, they will all be answering to me."

Schaeffer squinted. "The whole notion of actually sitting down and actually talking to someone from the future, it's been rather…*theoretical* up til now. It seems too fantastic to be true. It's really hard to believe."

"Well start believing," Ross admonished as he pulled on his cigarette.

"Cause you're gonna be face to face with him in less than two hours."

CHAPTER 63

Denver had yet to actually see the man.

But he knew there was at least one guard positioned directly behind him. Denver controlled his breathing and strained to detect any sound, any audible evidence to help define the lay of the land beyond his vision.

Nothing.

He thrashed his head from side to side, anxious to even get just a glimpse of the sentry.

Nothing.

This guy is good.

Denver sucked in a few deep breaths and scrutinized the floor. Even the shiny concrete failed to surrender a telltale reflection or any hint of a shadow. A few puddles of water and several shards of fractured glass were all that littered the area around him.

A new sound. To the right.

His head shot up as the black door swung inward. A lone woman in nurse's garb backed in, hauling a small, rolling cart. He studied it.

Large bag on the bottom shelf. Syringe on top, two glass jars. Some gauze.

The nurse and her cart soon disappeared as it lumbered out of sight behind him; the tiny wheels crunched as they ran across the broken glass. Denver tried to brace himself for the predictable injection, likely in one of his shoulders. He tossed his head to the side and could just make her out behind him and to his left.

Concentrate, Collins. Focus.

Don't tell the truth.

Lie. Lie. Lie.

A new sound.

Popping. Crunching?

Feet shuffling?

Movement off to his right.

Denver glanced towards the floor as a man crumpled to the ground and was still.

What? What is happening?

Pressure on his wrists. A metallic sound.

Clinking.

His hands were free.

"Sorry I didn't get here sooner," a familiar female voice called out in a rough whisper.

Denver pulled his arms back around front and massaged his enflamed wrists. His fingertips were stained with dark ink.

She continued. "I figured there was a high probability that you would get caught. Actually, I was counting on it."

That voice…I know her voice.

The nurse navigated directly before him and knelt to cut his left ankle loose. Her shoulder-length hair may have been altered to jet black, but he recognized an unforgettable face and figure.

"Brenda Jo?"

She concentrated her effort over to his right leg.

"Brenda Jo Tilley?" he repeated.

Denver was loose and she rose up. "We don't have much time. Hamilton will be back shortly. And he'll bring company." She pointed. "Get up and take the guard's uniform. His shoes. Keys. Weapons. Everything you can carry."

He stared at her.

"Now!" she demanded, just below a yell.

Denver scrambled out of the chair and started yanking the clothes off of the dead man. As he struggled to remove the guard's tan shirt, he was stunned to see Brenda Jo slipping out of her own tight outfit.

"So, what is your real name, Miss Tilley?"

Darkstar ignored his question. "Concentrate on the job at hand, Collins! *Hurry*."

Less than two minutes later, he climbed back into the chair to lace up his footwear. The uniform could have been a size or two smaller, but the black boots were appropriately snug. Almost *too* snug.

Darkstar searched through her bag and fished out a guard's shirt. She pivoted away from his gawking and slipped it on, but not before Denver witnessed a few long gashes that ran diagonally across her smooth yet muscled back. The thin marks weren't fresh, but they were very well-defined.

He couldn't resist asking. "Those wounds. What happened?"

She glanced back over her shoulder while finishing the final few buttons. "Enjoying the view?"

"I couldn't help it. Sorry."

Her head swung away. "It was just a, uh, a rough childhood. A lifetime ago. A world away."

She plunged her hands back into the bag and produced a long knife, two small pistols, and a handful of grenades. Seconds later, they had all been stashed somewhere in her outfit.

He smiled. "So, I take it you're not really from Jonesboro, Arkansas?"

Darkstar brushed past him and jogged straight for the left side of the door. She waved her hand and kept her voice low. "Get over here. And bring that chair. Quietly."

He obeyed.

"Now," she whispered, "there are two guards outside. I'm gonna call them in." She shoved a pistol into his right hand and withdrew the blade for herself. "Two guards…we each get one."

He squinted and nodded, but she grasped a handful of his shirt and pulled him close. "Pistol-whip him. Knock him out. But don't fire the gun. We don't need any more attention. Got it?"

"Got it."

Darkstar released his shirt and lowered her hand down to the chair. "Stay to the right. You ready?"

"I'm ready to get out of here."

She took a deep breath. "Here we go."

With a powerful and swift motion, she crashed the chair against the wall and started yelling. In the carefully planned confusion, she cracked the door open.

"Help! Help us! He's getting loose! Help!"

On cue, the two sentries burst into the room, clubs drawn. Darkstar slipped in behind them and kicked the door shut. Denver rushed upon the closest guard and cracked the gun across the back of the man's head. As the guard collapsed, Denver caught a glimpse of a flash of light and the faintest *whoosh* and *thud*.

The second man plunged forward and slammed into the opposite wall before toppling down onto the concrete. Darkstar scurried over and extracted her blade which was buried deep into his back. She wiped it across the guard's shirt several times and stowed it away.

"We'll only have a very small window of time to get to the metals lab and then get you out," she said. "But first, we need to destroy this."

She scrambled over to the video camera and dashed it against the floor. A tether connected the device to a reel-to-reel cabinet built into the wall. She yanked both reels out and laid them on the floor. A moment later she produced a small glass bottle and drenched both of them in a clear liquid. At first they smoked but then appeared to almost melt.

"What is that stuff?" he asked, his eyes beginning to sting.

"Acid," she replied, finishing the task. "Now, the sun will be up soon. Let's go."

Denver dropped beside a fallen guard and removed his radio and a set of keys. "I'm right behind you."

Darkstar led him out into the hall, and he closed the door. She had trotted halfway down the corridor before she seemed to notice that he was still lingering by the room.

"What're you doing?" she called out.

"Slowing 'em down," he replied. "I'm breaking the key off in the lock..."

"...It should buy us some time."

CHAPTER 64

The elevator ride from Level 7-Detention to Metallurgy provided a long opportunity for Denver to reflect.

First, I jump back in time, which isn't supposed to be possible. Then I'm engaged in a black ops mission at a classified military base which isn't even supposed to exist. And I'm being helped by a mystery woman with ninja training.

He shook his throbbing head.

And I can't tell a solitary soul back home about any of it.

Figures. Just my luck.

He stole a quick glance over at his unlikely female savior. She was long on skills, but short on small talk.

He had the urge to play the role of the interrogator.

Who are you, ma'am? Where are you from?

Are you from the future? And just why are you helping me?

Denver examined her facial features discreetly. *Fairly high cheek bones. Strong jaw. Northern European?* He imagined her with blonde hair once again.

Eastern European? Slavic? Russian?

Russian?

Russian.

A Russian female agent. In 1956.

An irrepressible thought captivated him.

KGB.

Wait…KGB? Is that possible? Here? Now?

His mind continued racing. *I just got busted out of an underground top secret military detention center in the middle of Nevada by a gorgeous female KGB agent during the height of the Cold War?*

Her matter-of-fact voice broke his internal deliberations. "The Experimental Materials Lab will be straight down the hall, then left, and then the second door on the left," she said. "I doubt there will be any guards at this hour."

"I already knew the location. I had it memorized. And I've already been there. Pretty exciting place."

"They caught you there?"

"Yep. And, by the way…your key didn't work."

She shot him a look. "Really?"

"Really."

"That could complicate things." She straightened her uniform and stared at his. "Whatever. We will deal with that later. The elevator door will open soon. Relax. Act natural."

He smiled. "Trust me. I know. There are two fundamental rules associated with infiltration. First, look like everyone else, and second, you need to move about with confident purpose."

He peered over at her reaction. If she was impressed, she masked it well. The door whisked open; the corridor was clear.

"Stay right beside me," she mumbled. "We will stop before the intersection. No noise." Darkstar drew her knife out and examined the retracted doors of the elevator. She slid down slowly, concentrating. "There it is." She guided the tip of her blade into the tiny gap.

Denver heard something trip.

She rose up. "I hate waiting for elevators. Let's go. Remember, no noise."

Years of military training had served him well on this mission. Denver traversed the corridor, stepping heel-to-toe. He shifted all his weight to each foot in an alternating rhythm. Seconds later, they arrived at the intersection and she shot up a closed fist. He stopped moving. He even stopped breathing.

Darkstar slipped her hand into her pants pocket and retrieved a tiny mirror. She propped her left side against the wall and inched the reflective device around the corner. Denver strained to see, but her head blocked him. She slid back.

"Damn. There is a guard. One guard," she whispered into his ear. "Too far to hit him with my knife. We will have to walk by and take him out." She stared into his eyes. "Stay on my right until it's all over."

He nodded.

She spat into her palm and worked it across his tender forehead. He grabbed her hand.

"What're you doing?"

"Trying to get rid of all your dried blood," she whispered. "Looks like you've been pistol whipped."

"More or less."

"Well, stay on my right. Let's back up about ten feet and then walk around the corner with normal conversation. It's more natural," she explained.

"Exactly what I would've recommended," he whispered in reply.

"I am going to ask you some questions as we walk. Use the name *Neal Schaeffer* in your responses," she said.

"Neal Schaeffer? Who is that?"

"The name you need to use in your responses," she affirmed gravely. "Are you hard of hearing or did they really do a number on your skull? Let's go."

Denver relocated beside her and they navigated around the bend. She shrugged. "It was my understanding from

Chief Ross that the tests on the wallet were all but complete. Where did you get your information?"

Denver made brief eye contact with the guard and then stared back at her. "I heard it directly from Neal Schaeffer himself."

"Neal Schaeffer? You heard *that* from Neal Schaeffer?"

"Yeah. Why would I make that up?"

They closed in on his location. She frowned. "Well, it sounds like Peter ain't talking to Paul again."

He wagged his head. "You've been here, what, nine months? And you still haven't figured that out?"

Two steps later she offered a friendly nod at the guard. He returned the unspoken gesture and Darkstar lunged for the kill. Her left hand covered his mouth, shoving his head back against the door as she rammed her blade deep into his abdomen. He thrashed a bit and began to collapse.

"Quick, grab his keys and open the door!" she demanded. "Hurry, before he bleeds out onto the floor!"

Denver finally located the proper key and propped the door open. She slid the body through and lowered it to the floor. "Shut and lock it, Mr. Collins."

Denver kicked the man's legs out of the way and sealed the door. Darkstar assessed the time while examining several rows of metal drawers scattered throughout the lab.

"Hamilton should be arriving back at your interrogation room in less than ten minutes." Her eyes scanned a few more labels. "Once they get in and see that you're gone, they'll lock this entire facility down tight. They might even kill the elevators."

"Should we take the stairs then? We're only two floors below ground level."

"Not floors," she corrected. "We're two *levels* below ground level. Some of the levels here at Dreamland are over a hundred feet each." She resumed her intense search.

A hundred feet? That explains the slow elevators.

"What do you want me to do?" he asked.

"Find a sack or something...anything that can carry several pounds of material," she replied.

Denver scrambled around the lab and uncovered a few bags. He dumped out their contents and headed in her direction.

"Found it!" she called out. "Bismuth strontium calcium copper oxide. Right here."

He knelt beside her. "A dismal strong man did what outside?"

"*Bismuth strontium* calcium copper oxide. This is what Doc was looking for. Copper-based. High-temperature."

"Don't we need some liquid helium to keep this stuff cool or something?"

"From my understanding, it's stable at room temperature. It's probably in the low thirties outside. We should be fine."

"Oh, it's definitely in the thirties. Riding down here tonight was miserable."

She pulled out a pair of loose keys and handed him one. "Take this to the lock at the far right side of this drawer." She pointed. "That one right down there."

He slid about six feet away, tracing his finger along the cabinet and inserted the key.

"Don't turn it yet," she cautioned while shoving her own key in. "There are alarms wired to all of these drawers. Now—on *three*—turn it to the left until it clicks."

He nodded.

She stared at him without blinking. "One, two, three—*turn!*"

A muffled pop resonated as they engaged the tumblers, releasing an internal mechanism. The drawer shook and jerked ajar. Darkstar grabbed it and slid it out, revealing six rows of rectangular blocks wrapped in foil. She hefted one out. "Feels like about two pounds." She pointed. "Let's take nine of them, just to be safe."

"Nine. You got it." Denver began stashing the precious cargo into his satchel.

"We probably only have about five minutes to hit sand, topside," she urged. "I'm gonna check the hallway." Darkstar stole her way over to the door and placed her ear against the metal. "Sounds clear."

Denver closed the bag securely and poked his arm through the strap. "I'm ready."

"Now listen," she demanded, "once we leave this room, it's a sprint until we are miles away from this place. Use your gun if you have to. Shoot to kill if you have to. Forget about staying quiet. Sometimes it's easier to disappear when there's lots of confusion and noise."

"I understand."

"When I open this, we run—*run*—for the elevator. We head for Ground Level. Once we hit the sand, there is a row of jeeps about fifty yards to the northeast. They brought them in after they found you. We hotwire the closest one and head east. Lights off. I've made other arrangements a bit further out." Darkstar paused. "We leave…*now!*"

She gripped the handle and threw the lab door open. Denver steadied his temporary backpack and tried to keep pace with his mysterious new partner as they bolted down both halls. She was already waiting when he barreled into the cavernous elevator and slammed into the stainless steel back wall.

Darkstar hit the button and rolled her eyes. "I guess that's what passes for running in 2014? Pretty pathetic, Mr. Collins."

He tried to catch his breath. "Well, my dad…always taught me…that it was ladies first."

"Nice. Nice. But honestly…you're comeback was better than your running."

The elevator doors finally closed. "You asked me about my scars," she said. "What about your little collection?" Darkstar leaned her head to the side. "I wasn't the only one without a shirt on, you know. And don't tell me that it's *complicated*."

He hesitated. "Afghanistan. Oh, and a car accident a few years ago. It was pretty bad."

"Afghanistan?"

"Yeah. My unit got hit with an IED on a highway through the desert."

"IED?"

"Never mind."

She shook her head. "Well, Mr. Collins, if we do this right, we shouldn't have to add any more trophies to your little collection."

"Speaking of deserts," he said, "this part of Nevada kinda reminds me of Afghanistan. Of course, anywhere in this part—"

BWAA…

BWAA…

BWAA…

His sentence was cut short by a rapid series of intense siren blasts. Darkstar looked up and around. *"Damn.* They know. That means all the base lights are now probably on. So much for the cover of darkness. This complicates things, Mr. Complicated."

Denver concentrated on the doors as the sirens continued their piercing wails. "Why aren't they opening? We're at Ground Level."

She examined them. "Security override. I hate it when I'm right. They killed the elevators." Darkstar pivoted around and faced him.

"We're trapped, Mr. Collins."

CHAPTER 65

Denver had already been trapped underground once tonight. He refused to give the MPs at Area 51 an encore performance. "Get your knife out," he yelled.

"What?"

"Just do it. We can use it to help pry the elevator doors open."

She forced her long knife into the narrow gap between the doors as Denver struggled to gain a solid finger hold. His veins bulged as he tugged with all his might, fighting to maintain his footing. Darkstar strained as well, but then tumbled backwards.

"What happened?" Denver asked.

"I guess I'm falling for you," she teased. "The truth? My knife snapped."

He spoke through gritted teeth, "Your comeback was better than your pulling." Denver exhaled hard and yanked again. "It's starting to give. Come on."

She scrambled to her feet and grabbed the opposite edge. The doors inched outward, but not without a colossal fight. Darkstar paused and studied the gap. "Fantastic," she muttered. "We're stuck between levels. And this is taking too long."

Denver wiped the sweat out of his eyes and stood beside her. The floor greeted him at nearly eye level. He pointed. "Look through the glass in the foyer. The base tarmac lights are on."

"Told you," she noted as she examined the tiny crawl space. "I might be able to climb up and fit through that, but not you. We need these to open at least another foot."

He glanced behind him. "Wait. Get down on the floor over there."

"What?"

"Sit on the floor," he demanded. "Brace your legs flat with your feet against the right wall."

Darkstar dropped down and he reclined with his back firmly pressed against hers. "Keep your legs locked," he instructed. Denver placed both boots against the base of the left elevator door and shoved his hands onto his angled thighs. Darkstar's body started to tremble under the force of the massive exertion.

The doors seemed impervious to the assault at first, but a sickening squeal and incremental success gave them renewed hope. Denver took a deep breath and screamed afresh as he jammed every ounce of his strength into the effort.

Darkstar twisted her head around to evaluate their progress. "It's not much, but I think it's enough!" she yelled. "Give me a lift."

Denver cupped his hands and she placed her right boot onto the makeshift step. A simple thrust later she was up and out and Denver tossed the satchel to her. Darkstar sat on the tile floor and pressed each foot against the somewhat-open doors. She leaned forward and grabbed his wrists.

"On three," she announced. "One…two…*three!*"

Denver lunged as she pulled and he scrambled out of the elevator and onto his belly. "Stay low," she ordered while surveying the immediate area. "Okay, looks clear for now. Jeeps are due northeast." She handed him the bag. "We run.

You provide cover…I will hotwire the ignition. Shoot to kill. Let's go!"

The exterior base sirens blurted at a deafening level while they scurried across the small foyer and pushed out through the glass door. Denver drew his pistol and struggled to keep up with Darkstar's breakneck pace across the asphalt. Taking in deep lungfuls of chilled night air forced him into a short coughing fit and his eyes watered.

In the distance he could now easily make out half a dozen jeeps lined up alongside a metal building. Another fifty yards to the north a lone helicopter rested in a warm pool of light. As soon as they reached their vehicular objective, he took cover and pivoted around, scanning for threats in every direction.

Darkstar crawled under the steering wheel and yelled at him. "Look for weapons!"

He dropped down and drew beside her. *"Do what?!"*

She wrestled with a handful of wires. "I said, look for more weapons. They usually keep bigger guns in these jeeps."

"I'm on it!" He surveyed the area a final time and scrambled into the vehicle. A long wooden box was buried under the dusty backseat. With some difficulty, he dragged it out and popped the lid.

Score. Thank you, Brenda Jo Tilley!

Denver elevated his pistol and reconned the perimeter again.

Still all clear.

He leaned towards the front. "We've got a box full of thirty caliber rifles. Looks like M2s…maybe M3s."

Darkstar scrambled up into the driver's seat. "Any ammo? Should be either fifteen or thirty-round magazines."

"Uh, yeah. Yeah. Looks like four…five…six. *Six* clips, all thirties."

She bent over and snagged a pair of wires. Seconds later the jeep shuddered and the engine roared above the droning of the base sirens. "Hand me a rifle!" she yelled.

Denver snatched a gun and was in the process of shoving in a magazine when she yanked the weapon out of his hands. She stood in the seat and snapped off several rounds. One by one she picked off the tires on the other vehicles nearby.

Smart girl, Denver thought. *Smart.*

Definitely KGB.

He traded his own pistol for an M3 and glanced southward. "Uh oh," he hollered. "We've got company, check your six! *Check your six!* Four hundred yards, tops!"

She jerked about and fell back into the seat. A confused jumble of headlights approached like a torch-carrying mob in the night.

"Nine o'clock!" she screamed and hopped out.

Denver looked back towards the elevator as three MPs in all-black uniforms took up positions just outside the foyer doors. Before he could even get a steady bead on the first soldier, five shots rang out in quick succession. All three men slumped to the asphalt, and a waterfall of shattered glass collapsed down around them.

Why didn't they fire? he wondered.

She's fast, but they had time.

Mixed feelings surged through Denver along with copious amounts of adrenaline. Her vicious victory was admittedly bittersweet. Fellow American soldiers were dying, but there could be no doubt it was an either *us-or-them* situation.

Darkstar jumped back into the jeep and rammed it into gear. "Hold on!"

Denver adopted a gunner's position in the backseat. He looked around and then tapped her shoulder. "Go left!" he yelled.

She didn't alter course. "Why?"

He leaned into her ear. "There was a helicopter past those jeeps."

"You fly helicopters?" she hollered out in excitement.

He shook his head as they bounced off the pavement and onto the flat and sandy soil of the dry lakebed. "No. No. But they might use it to find us. We need to disable it. Shoot the engine."

Darkstar maintained her direction. "No, there isn't time."

Before settling back into the rear seat, Denver made the tragic mistake of staring straight through the windshield. They were clipping along through the lakebed at over forty-five miles an hour into near-total blackness. The hazy, red glow of the eventual sunrise was useless for all travel intents and purposes.

"Headlights?!" he screamed.

"Don't need 'em," she responded. "Nothing but miles and miles of flat, dry ground. Let me worry about the driving." She gestured behind her. "You worry about our six."

He spun around and lifted his weapon. "Our six doesn't bother me, but our twelve scares the living hell outta me." Something below the dash caught his attention. "Why don't you use the radio? We might get some basic idea of their progress."

She let out a nervous laugh. "Don't you think they know that? No, I wouldn't trust anything over the wireless. Can you see any bogies?"

He blinked profusely to clear his eyes of the tears drawn out by the rapid flow of cold air around him. "Looks like, more headlights. A little activity to the north. Wait. Hold on." He hesitated. "We've got possible aerial activity...*yes*. We have a bogie. Vertical motion. That's gotta be that helicopter."

She glanced up into the rearview mirror at him. "What course?"

He studied the distant motion. "It looks like…it is tracking…towards…*us*. Wait…uh, searchlight just popped on."

"Ah, the fun begins. What about surface vehicles?" she yelled.

He waited and watched. "It looks like they are fanning out. Only one…two, *two* are headed in our general direction." Denver leaned towards her. "How fast are those whirlybirds?"

"It's most likely a Bell 47," she said. "Probably eighty or ninety knots."

He squinted. "So, that's what? About double our speed?"

"Probably."

"That puts 'em right on top of us in less than a couple of minutes," he observed. "Can't outrun them."

"Don't have to," she hollered as she shifted in her seat. "Here, climb up front…*take the wheel!*"

"What?!"

"Take the damn wheel! You drive. I'll watch our six! Just head straight…don't turn. Ever. Aim for the sunrise." She

waved her hand to the east. "It's that glowing spot right over there."

"Funny."

The exchange was clumsy and awkward, and they lost precious speed, but Denver managed to gain control of the jeep and maintain course. Darkstar sifted through the remaining guns and checked their magazines.

"I wish we had something with a little more punch and range than a thirty cal," she lamented. "What I wouldn't give for a Kalashnikov right now."

Denver suppressed a growing smile.

I knew she was a dang Russkie.

Darkstar rose carefully and braced herself against the back of the front seat. "Keep it steady," she hollered. "No turns."

"You got it, comrade," he shouted in reply.

Denver examined the view in his side mirror for a moment. The helicopter wasn't directly visible, but the pool of its searchlight on the smooth desert floor seemed awfully close.

Crack!

He jumped, unprepared for the report from her first shot. Pause.

Two more rounds.

Crack! Crack!

He checked the mirror again. The helicopter search light swept forward, blinding him, and then scanned side to side.

"They must've seen my muzzle blast!" she yelled.

Within moments, the light's aimless pattern centered upon them. Denver panicked. "Should I turn?"

"Negative! Stay straight!"

She steadied her aim. *Crack! Crack!* Pause. *Crack! Crack! Crack!*

And that's when he saw it. The now-illuminated desert erupted in huge plumes of dirt in rapid succession from left to right, narrowly missing the front of the jeep.

Machine guns, Denver realized in horror.

We're history.

CHAPTER 66

No matter how optimistic or well-trained, Denver knew a helicopter-mounted machine gun trumped their feeble, ground-based, semi-automatic firepower.

Eight seconds after the first barrage, another volley of high-velocity rounds ripped the desert to shreds before them. Denver was temporarily blinded as they plunged into the manmade dust cloud glowing in the chopper's searchlight.

"Steady!" Darkstar ordered. "Steady."

Crack! Crack! Crack!

The helicopter swerved and dropped back.

"Did you hit 'em?" Denver called out.

"Maybe. Probably," she answered. "Maybe not. Here they come again."

The chopper accelerated and settled on a position off to the jeep's left, but the searchlight never lost its target. Darkstar didn't waste the opportunity to engage a much larger cross-section of the pursuing aircraft.

Crack! Crack! Crack! Crack! Crack! Cra-Cra-Crack!

The chopper rose quickly, but then dropped back down at once. A brilliant splay of muzzle fire signaled a lethal stream of retaliatory rounds. The hail of bullets exploded the soil to their left and then sparked across the jeep's hood.

Unable to control his instinctive reaction, Denver cut the wheel hard to the right. Darkstar was nearly catapulted out of the back and crashed down against the floorboard. He shook his head and struggled to see through the shattered glass in what remained of the windshield.

"Sorry," he yelled.

There was a pause.

"I'm hit," came the reply as she managed to crawl back up into the seat.

"*What?*" he screamed. "Where?! Are you okay?"

He winced as another violent volley barely missed their position.

"Probably a ricochet," she offered, coughing in the swirling dust. "Grazed my side. Don't know how bad."

The jeep engine sputtered briefly and the helicopter drifted closer. Denver glanced sideways to gauge its distance but was discouraged by the blinding beam.

"I think we're losing some speed," he reported.

Darkstar rose to her feet. "That's okay. Just hold her steady."

Denver gripped the steering wheel with white-knuckled resolve as the engine continued to choke and miss. He detected the telltale slapping of the helicopter's rotors above the roar of the frigid wind whistling by.

Getting close.

Too close.

Darkstar raised her M3. "Steady…"

For a final time, the smooth desert floor ejected columns of dirt, eerily backlit by the blinding searchlight soaring through the brightening sky. Denver tensed up and half-closed his eyes.

This one's gonna be close!

Darkstar snapped off three rounds.

Crack! Crack! Crack!

The machine gun barrage ceased in an instant, and the searchlight veered off wildly to the left. They both watched in silent awe while the chopper lost altitude and plunged into the unforgiving ground. The aircraft flipped forward as the rotors shredded in every possible direction. Its frame erupted in a dazzling fireball that replaced the dim light of the early morning with a temporary radiance rivaling the midday sun.

The hot shockwave of the blast slapped across Denver's trembling face. Darkstar collapsed against the backseat. He looked over his shoulder.

"You alright?"

"I'm still alive."

"That's always a plus."

An explosion shook the vehicle.

"What was that?" Denver yelled. "Are we hit?"

"Engine backfire," she explained. "We're in trouble."

"In more ways than one," he said. "Check your six."

Darkstar twisted around. Two pairs of headlights were closing fast. A third vehicle, much farther back, appeared to be investigating the helicopter crash site.

Denver mashed his foot to the floor, but the damaged jeep continued to decelerate.

"We need to stop," Darkstar called out.

"Stop?"

"Before they reach us. It'll give us the advantage."

"You sure?"

"Trust me. Stop now!"

Denver released the accelerator and jammed the stiff brakes. The jeep shuddered and smoked and slid to an angled stop surrounded by a massive veil of dust and debris.

An injured Darkstar tumbled out of the back and snatched a fresh rifle.

Denver rushed up to her. "Are you okay?"

"Shut up, and listen to me." She winced and grabbed her right side. "Stand out in front of the jeep and hold your hands straight up. No gun. Just your hands. Like you're surrendering."

"I don't understand," he objected.

"You will—at least I *hope* you will." She gestured. "Now go…stand over there. *Now*."

Denver complied with the bizarre arrangement and Darkstar disappeared. He raised his arms and waited with extreme trepidation for the pursuing troops to zero in on his location.

There was something oddly familiar about this experience out in the desert.

In Afghanistan—over a decade before—he had witnessed scores of surrendering Taliban fighters assume a similar stance, many of them kneeling, all of them terrified. He remembered it well. The juxtaposition of cultures and warfare couldn't have been greater. A twenty-first century, tech-savvy Western fighting force engaged an antiquated enemy from a land that time had all but forgotten.

On that desert battlefield a world away, it became evident that the future overwhelmed the past. But as the infant rays of a rising sun broke across Groom Lake, Denver now realized those roles had been ironically reversed.

He bit his lip as he continued to hold his hands high.

I hope you know what you're doing, lady.

The entire proposition seemed ludicrous.

He was entrusting his fate into the hands of a woman he knew was a thief, deceiver, murderer, and possibly even a sworn enemy of the United States of America. And he had learned most of these incriminating facts in the last twenty minutes.

He kept telling himself he didn't have any other options. But he did have options.

It was just that every last one of them were horrible.

So he stood there.

The blood drained from his arms, making his hands grow numb.

The first pursuing jeep arrived, its headlights carving distinct shafts of light through the dusty air. Three soldiers in dark fatigues snaked out, rifles trained on him.

"I am unarmed," he called out. "I surrender. I am Denver Wayne Collins."

The second patrol eased up to the scene, cutting an arc off to Denver's left. One soldier jumped out and assumed a protected position behind the vehicle, resting his sniper rifle across the hood. The driver didn't seem to budge.

A gruff voice shouted out, "*Get on the ground, now!* Any sudden moves will result in lethal force. Do you understand?"

"I understand. I understand."

"Get on the ground, now!"

Denver dropped to one knee. "See, I'm going down. To the ground." His second knee hit the soil, and that's when a grenade hit the second jeep. The force of the blast lifted the vehicle several inches off of the ground and killed both MPs instantly.

Almost before Denver could even react to the explosion, three shots rang out from behind him. *Crack! Crack! Crack!*

The initial trio of soldiers fell to the dirt in unison with the smoldering debris raining down from the horrific grenade blast. Tiny bits of cloth, metal, and flesh pelted the ground like smoking volcanic embers.

Denver swiveled about and tried to locate her. Even with the aid of the nearby vehicle's headlights, he failed.

"Where are you?" he hollered.

"Down here," came the reply.

He scanned without success. "Where?"

"Down…here."

A shiny and wiggling gun barrel attracted his frustrated gaze just to the left of the rear tire. He took a few steps closer as Darkstar shimmied out from beneath the jeep. Denver bent over and helped her rise up.

"Thanks. That was rough under there," she said. "Not much space, and the exhaust pipe is burning hot. It felt good at first, but then…well, not so good." After gauging their situation, she slapped at the dust caked to her clothing. "It's getting light. We need to move. Grab the satchel along with your rifle. I'll get the magazines. We got us a fresh ride."

Speaking of fresh…

Denver was momentarily distracted by the dark mass of blood seeping through her fatigues. It didn't look good. She walked off with a slight limp and stepped over the bodies of the slain soldiers.

They didn't look good either.

The troubling burden of the accumulating body count crushed down upon his soldier's sensitivities. Ultimately, Denver was just trying to get home to his six-year-old daughter, but at the day's end, at least a dozen men wouldn't be going home to their fiancés, or their wives, or their children.

The morbid sensation wasn't terribly new. He had lost friends in war—close friends—but somehow these nameless strangers sprawled out across the Nevada terrain seemed destined to haunt his memories in a way they never had.

"Any day now," Darkstar called out through cupped hands. "There's at least one more jeep headed this way. Let's go, soldier. Day is breaking."

Denver hunched over the jeep, snatched his weapon and satchel, and jogged over towards her. He could now clearly pick out the dark smoke billowing from the helicopter crash set against the rusty mountains off to their west.

"You should drive," she announced. "I'll take care of our six. It's gonna get bumpy. We're almost off the lakebed." Darkstar deposited her weapon onto the backseat and directed his attention toward the sunrise. "See that dip in the ridge? Drive straight towards it. Get as close as you can. I stashed a motorcycle about a hundred yards on the other side." She winced. "We'll, uh…we'll have to hike the last leg to reach it."

"Hike? Are you up to that?"

She exhaled and bent over. "It's amazing what you can do when death's on the line. Now get in that seat and drive like hell!"

As he popped the loose clutch and kicked up a smothering cloud of dust, Denver estimated that their closest threat was about five hundred yards behind. Up ahead, drastic changes in the landscape were appreciably closer. With the amount of available light improving by the second, he could just make out the sudden transition from the pale, chalky lakebed to the rutted gravels gradually leading up into the lifeless foothills.

His thoughts turned to Terrance.

I wonder if he is still waiting for me at the first rendezvous point? I bet he fled when he heard the base sirens and saw the current manhunt. Not that I could blame him.

He was conflicted at the tenuous success of their escape. Every second Denver barreled on to the east increased the distance between Terrance's *probable* location and himself. His solitary comfort revolved around the fact that they had arranged a secondary rendezvous point at the Sahara Hotel and Casino on the Vegas strip.

The backup plan involved a twenty-four hour window of waiting. Beyond that, if Denver failed to materialize then the Jumper's existence in Normal could be compromised, and they were prepared for a mass exodus out of town. For the protection of the group, everyone except Denver, Terrance, McCloud, and Betty Larson had been briefed on the new location.

The proposition was simple: if he didn't come home, they would find a different one.

"Two hundred yards and closing," Darkstar yelled out. She dropped low and rested the barrel of the M3 on the back of the seat.

"Hold on," he yelled as the jeep encountered the slight incline of the ancient lake shore. Loose, eroded dirt and sharp gravel jostled the vehicle; Denver slowed to maintain control.

"No! No! No! *Faster!*" she screamed.

Denver swerved to avoid a sizable rock. "Doing the best I can up here!"

"Do better!"

Another swerve, another boulder jutting up out of the ground.

"It's gonna get a lot worse," he called out.

Crack! She fired a round. *Crack! Crack!*

"Big rocks. Big rocks and big ditches!" he warned.

Crack! Crack!

Denver wrenched the wheel back and forth, struggling to navigate the treacherous terrain. The passenger-side front tire slammed into a rocky outcrop camouflaged in the dim light and bounced the right side of the jeep straight up. Darkstar drifted temporarily airborne and lost hold of her rifle. The gun flung out and tumbled behind them like a discarded twig. She scrambled to snatch another one out of the box.

"Sorry!" he yelled as they continued to zigzag through the geological gauntlet.

"One hundred yards," she advised.

Crack! Crack! Crack! Crack!

Denver's options up the steepening slope grew limited and forced him to plot a precarious path along the center of a gravel-filled gully. The jeep's back axle fishtailed mercilessly just before the vehicle scraped to a frustrating and grinding halt. He jammed on the accelerator. The engine roared with a vengeance, and smoke billowed out the exhaust pipe like a factory stack, but three of the tires free-wheeled in the air.

Denver pounded on the steering wheel in frustration.

They weren't going anywhere.

CHAPTER 67

It smelled like morning.

More specifically, it smelled like *breakfast.*

Dr. Glen Stonecroft had been known to sacrifice a midday dish or two on the altar of uninterrupted research, but the ritual of the day's first and earliest meal was non-negotiable to the lively scientist. Years before, he had confided to Ellen that he had consumed a glass of orange juice every single morning since he turned thirty. (He conservatively estimated that the total number was somewhere beyond sixteen thousand glasses.)

Doc raised the tall and appropriately chilled glass to his waiting lips. He was anxious to inspect the quality of the juice in this tiny diner which he had stumbled upon along the western fringes of a Columbus that had yet to fully awake.

He thrust the bitter cup away, glaring at it like a disappointed father. It wasn't the worst he had ever tasted, but recent memory failed to recall a suitable comparison.

"Is everything okay with your OJ?"

Doc looked up into the brown eyes of his middle-aged waitress as she approached. He chuckled. "Your inquiry contains a simple but acceptable rhyme, my dear."

She squinted. "It does?"

Stonecroft nodded. "O-*kay*. O-*J*."

Her face brightened. "Well, so it does!"

"Indeed." He lowered the glass discreetly and glanced at the plastic, single-sheet menu in his other hand. "I have been searching this document high and low," he mourned, "but I have yet to discover a Birthday Plus One Breakfast."

She fished out an order pad and rested her left hand on her hip. "*Birthday Plus One?* Hmm." She tapped the pad to her lips. "I've been in this business since before the war, and I'll admit I've never heard that one."

Doc feigned surprise. "You've never been asked for a Birthday Plus One Breakfast? Oh, it's quite special you know."

She scribbled some notes down. "It sounds special. Very special." She yanked out a chair and sat across from him. "So, uh, why don't you educate me about this very special meal?"

He lowered his menu and folded his hands. "It is comprised of one biscuit, inundated with white gravy, two eggs prepared sunny side up, and three strips of bacon, but not too crispy."

Her head bobbed as she stared straight ahead. "One, two, three."

"One, two, three," Doc repeated. "Birthday Plus One."

She took a few more notes before glancing up with a skeptical expression. "So, I must be missing something here. Where does the whole *Birthday Plus One* thing fit into all of this?"

"I'm delighted you asked," Doc offered. "Today, my dear, today is the day *after* my birthday."

The waitress hesitated with pursed lips before she rose with a mischievous grin. "Aha. Aha." She pointed her pen at him. "I get it now. *Birthday Plus One*. Plus one *day*. I get it now. That, that's cute. Real cute. I like that."

"I'm positively thrilled it meets with your expert approval."

"Well, this expert would sing *Happy Birthday* to you, but my expert singing voice doesn't usually wake up until sometime past ten or so. Besides, I'm afraid some of our other patrons might start throwing sharp objects at me. It could get ugly."

A wide smile broke out across his kind face. "I will be happy to take a raincheck on that performance."

"Can I ask your age on this important milestone day plus one?"

Doc contemplated a response before locking eyes with her. "Young lady…as of yesterday, I am *plenty*-nine."

She closed her eyes and shook her head. "*Plenty-nine?* I should've known. I walked right into that one. Yep."

"It's true."

"Well, Mr. *Plenty-nine*," she said through blushed cheeks, "can I get you anything else besides a *Birthday Plus One* Breakfast special platter?"

"That order, plus your warm and sweet demeanor is all I could hope for on this lovely morning."

She sauntered off. "Warm and sweet, huh? You make me sound like a cinnamon roll right out of the oven. That's what they call me…yep. Warm and sweet."

The jingling of the bell on the door caught her attention and the waitress spun around. A police officer strolled in, hat in his hand, bags under his eyes.

"Morning, Ben," she offered.

He blinked a few times. "Is it morning yet, Phyllis?"

"Haven't you heard the roosters?"

"I'll take your word for it."

"The usual today?"

He plopped down into a booth. "Just coffee. Tell you the truth, why don't you just brew me a fresh pot. I'll take the whole thing."

Phyllis did just that. "Rough night?"

He arched back and toyed with his hat. "Sad is a better word. Sad night. Breaks the heart."

"Oh?"

"Had to work a wreck. Over on Highway 62. Several of us were called in. North end of town. Someone hit a tree. Bet I only slept two hours last night."

Doc perked up and listened intently.

"Anybody hurt?" she asked.

He hesitated. "One could only wish. No, uh, it was a fatality."

"Merciful heavens!" she exclaimed. "Who was it, Ben? Anyone local?"

He nodded through the evident pain. "Young girl. Teenager. Her name was Boulden, Carolyn Anne Boulden. I'm just glad I wasn't the one who had to go and tell the family. Can't imagine. Cannot imagine."

Doc spilled his bitter orange juice a split second before passing out and crumpling to the diner floor.

CHAPTER 68

Their situation was desperate.

Their vehicle was out of commission.

"Forget the jeep," Darkstar yelled. "No use. We're high-centered." She tossed him a rifle. "They'll be on us in about twenty seconds." She pointed. "Take up a position behind that rock."

Denver hugged the ground and scurried five yards over, resting his back against a flat red slab surrounded by tufts of dead desert grass. He rolled his head to the left. "Wound them," he said.

"What?"

"I said *wound them*. There's no need to kill."

Darkstar shook her head and balanced her rifle across the metal bar framing the back seat. She took aim into the distance. "I'm sorry, soldier, but the phrase *life and death situation* doesn't leave much room for just injuring people."

He gritted his teeth. *I'm sorry you don't see it my way, ma'am. I hate to do this, but…*

Crack!

In a shower of sparks, he blasted Darkstar's rifle out of her hands and down the rugged gulley.

She jerked back and spun around. "*What the hell—*"

He lowered the M3 as a trickle of smoke snaked out of the barrel. "I said *wound them*. I meant it."

"Are you crazy?"

Denver flipped over onto his belly and slid up the rock to gain a vantage point on the approaching vehicle. "Maybe.

But I'd like to be a crazy man with as clear a conscience as possible."

The jeep stopped about seventy-five yards away at the bottom of the rocky slope. The two MPs debarked with rifles in hand and took cover behind their vehicle.

Denver glanced over at her. "Make no mistake—I wanna travel back home. But I don't want it to be on a road paved with dead Americans."

"It's a nice sentiment," she said as the men picked their way up the hill, "but hopelessly unrealistic. Bullets don't separate between the righteous and the wicked, Mr. Collins."

"No, they don't," he replied. "You're absolutely right." Denver took aim. "But they can separate between the chest and the leg."

Crack! Denver fired.

The closest soldier flung his rifle and tumbled backwards into the dirt. The second one dropped low and scrambled for cover.

Denver squinted. *I am so sorry.*

Darkstar snuck out of the jeep and crawled over beside him. "As long as they are alive, they can call for backup, you fool."

Denver peered off into the hazy distance. At least two more vehicles were kicking up a convoy of dust in the golden glow of the morning.

"Doesn't matter. Backup's already on the way," he observed. Denver steadied his barrel. The second MP made the mistake of jogging over to his injured friend.

Crack! Crack!

The soldier grabbed his thigh and crumpled onto the ground. He rolled to a stop and thrashed side to side, screaming in agony.

Forgive me, brother.

Denver slid down the rock and turned to Darkstar. "Time to climb over this ridge. Let's go."

She didn't budge. "I…I don't think I'm going anywhere." After a few coughs, a thin trickle of blood spilled across her dry lips. Denver didn't have to be a physician to know what that meant.

Severe internal injuries.

Not good.

He knelt down and tossed her right arm over his shoulder and neck, and they raised up in unison.

"Come on," he encouraged, "come hell or high water, we're gonna make it up and over this ridge."

Her voice was growing weaker. "Leave me…we both know how this is gonna end."

He continued to haul her up the tricky incline. "Nonsense, we are getting out of here. No man—*or woman*—left behind."

She chuckled as more blood dribbled down her chin. "Optimism doesn't repair a lacerated abdomen, Mr. Collins."

"And pessimism is just hope playing it safe. So can we just cut with the cute one-liners and concentrate on the mission?"

She winced and hobbled along. "Fair enough."

Each upward step was a Vegas gamble. The soil was a deceitful amalgamation of sand pocked with jagged gravel of varying sizes. One boot fall could nearly sink into the ground and the next step could encounter the slick and compacted strength of concrete. They hit a patch of deep, loose gravel and slid five feet downhill.

"This is impossible," she said.

"This ain't nothing," he retorted. "I climbed hills twice this steep in Afghanistan...with a hundred-pound pack. And lugging two rifles." He paused. "While under heavy fire."

"We need to...stop...I need to stop," she whispered. "I can't go on." Her legs collapsed and Denver strained to keep from falling sideways.

"Whoa there...no you don't. We're almost there. Almost there. Just hold on to me as best you can." Denver bowed low with his knees in the sand and wrapped her limp form across his broad shoulders. It was a Herculean effort as he raised up and steadied himself on the slope, trying to maintain balance with her entire weight, the satchel, and his firearm. Each labored step from that point on was slow and calculated, but they made progress.

His greatest fear was that she was passing into unconsciousness from blood loss. Denver recalled his military field trauma training in such cases and engaged her in stimulating conversation.

"You know, it's kinda awkward," he began. "I get rescued from a top secret base by a beautiful girl...and I don't even know her real name. Or her phone number."

No response.

He smiled and took another step. "So...what is your name? Brenda Jo just doesn't seem your style. It sounds too...well, *western*."

She mumbled something breathy.

"What was that?"

"Oksana."

He paused. "*Oksana?* Now that's more like it. And beautiful...I like that. Oksana. Is there a last name? Or do you just have one name? You know, like Elvis. Or Madonna. Wait," he said. "Forget that last one."

A long pause. He strained to hear her above the crunch of the rocks.

"Miz…Mizenov," she whispered.

"Oksana Mizenov. That flows really well. I like that. A lot. Oksana Mizenov. Beautiful. It…fits."

Keep it going, Denver.

Conversation. Humor. Anything.

The top of the ridge was drawing near. His face and arms were growing slick with sweat, and he hoped that the warm, damp sensation across his left shoulder wasn't the blood draining from her abdominal wound. For the first time since he arrived, he was thankful for the cold weather.

"You know, your name sounds like…oh, I don't know, maybe a famous dancer or gymnast or something." He took a deep breath and punched the bass tones in his voice. "Ladies and gentleman…right here, right now, on this very stage—*Oksana Mizenov!*"

He imagined that she smiled. He pictured a great big, self-conscious smile.

"Denver," she whispered.

"Yes, Ms. Mizenov?" Before she could answer, he laughed. "You know, when I said it like that, it sounded like I stuttered. Ms. Mizenov, kinda repeats that first zee sound."

"Today…today…is the first time…first time in almost twenty years."

He hesitated. "Okay…first time for *what* in twenty years? And don't tell me that it's the first time you've been carried by a gorgeous man in twenty years."

"No," she whispered, shaking her head. "Today…is the first time…in a very…very long time…decades…that I have…heard anyone…anyone speak my name."

Denver's mind raced as he took the remaining steps to reach the sharp edge along the top of the ridge.

First time she has heard her own name?

What?

Wait…KGB.

KGB agent.

Spy. Spies use false names.

She's been outside of Russia for twenty years?

No way. She can't be much over thirty.

He hauled her past the summit of the ridge and then descended several yards down the far side, clearly out of sight of any ground forces off to the west. She did her best to point at a large outcrop nearby.

"Set…set me down over there," she whispered. "Prop me against…that rock."

With all the care of a nurse and the strength of a soldier he went down to one knee and carefully placed her into a reclining position. "I'll be right back," he assured as he laid his satchel next to her. "Don't go anywhere."

"That's…the easiest order…I've ever had to follow."

Denver hugged the ground while he ascended and peered over the ridge.

Looks like…two vehicles. At least a half-mile of driving, and then a tough hike. Ten minutes minimum, fifteen is more like it. But they will be moving cautiously. So fifteen minutes.

"How's my favorite Russian hero?" he teased after a quick jump and then a fair amount of sliding down alongside her.

She glanced up from studying her bloodied side. "Hero? I'm no hero, Mr. Collins. No…I'm…I'm a…*monster.*"

"Sorry," he said, "monsters don't save the lives of almost complete strangers." He took the briefest moment to examine her wound. It was bad. "No. We don't call them monsters. We call those people *heroes* where I come from."

Denver located a sharp rock and sliced into his lower right pant leg. He worked the small tear and ripped off everything from the knee down. He rolled the material up into a hand-sized wad and pressed it onto her wound. Oksana jolted from the pain.

"Sorry," he said. "Now, here, put both your hands on this and keep steady pressure. It should stop the bleeding."

"The bleeding you can see…isn't the problem," she said. "It's the kind...the kind you *can't* see...that is the one you should fear."

He tried to dismiss what he knew to be true. "Just keep pressure on it."

She coughed through a weak laugh. "You…you called me a hero, Mr. Collins. But…I doubt…that a solitary selfless act…could atone for a…*lifetime* of transgressions."

He wrestled with a sufficient response. "Transgressions, huh? You know…when I was a kid, my Sunday school teacher taught us songs about Jesus. And how Jesus paid for the sins of the whole world on the cross." He stared into her hopeless eyes. "I'm fairly certain yours were included."

"That…that reminds me of something my friend…Lidiya used to say. But…I'm afraid that some debts…some debts are too big to pay, Mr. Collins."

"Well," he said, "regardless of what you think, just sit tight." Denver rushed back up the hill for a final recon.

Looks like…at least seven to ten minutes.

He returned to her side.

"Listen, you need to go," she whispered. "But…there is one more thing you need to know. One more thing."

"One more thing?"

Oksana forced a smile through her pain. "The answer to…to your biggest question. You need to know."

"My *biggest question?* What question?"

She summoned more strength. "You…you want to know…why…why *Normal?* Why…does everyone time jump to Normal? Why not random places…places all over the world?"

Denver was astonished. "You know? You *really* know?"

She nodded faintly as more dark blood bubbled from the corner of her mouth.

"I do."

CHAPTER 69

Denver tried to dismiss the realization that Oksana had minutes to live.

Her right hand beckoned him closer. He arched above, nearly laying across her pale face as she battled to deliver her breathy revelation directly into his ear.

He leaned back, perplexed. "What is that?"

Oksana shot her left hand up and coughed several times. "No…no time to explain. Just remember it. From the North…north of town. Now…look over there…to the east. See the reddish rock…about a hundred yards…away? It looks…looks like a hand pointing up."

Denver glanced over and squinted. "I see it."

"There is…is a motorcycle at the bottom. Covered in, in…brush. Head east…east for five miles. Take the dirt road…south. No headlight." She coughed and then revealed a hand grenade clutched in her right palm. "I…I hope to…be able to take…a few of them…with me…before I die. Now *you*…go. Go."

Denver gathered his rifle and the satchel before caressing her forehead with a tender kiss. "I will never forget you. Never."

She lifted her left hand and gazed at her mother's ring. "Forget…making promises," she whispered as tears traced down her filthy cheeks. "And…just…make it home…home to your daughter. She must miss you…miss you…terribly."

Denver locked eyes with her as his own tears began to swell in a tense and silent exchange. Using his rifle as a crutch, he pushed up to a standing position and then tore off across the barren landscape. He drove himself hard, knowing that several soldiers would be popping over the ridge behind him in less than a handful of short minutes.

The jagged terrain seemed to fight back as his boots sliced through dry desert grasses and crunched across dimly lit gravels. With the base of the red rock coming into clearer view, he strained even harder, fighting for more speed. His lungs burned inside his aching and heaving chest, and his heart seemed ready to burst at any moment.

Denver tumbled to a stop and slammed into the tail end of the loosely camouflaged motorcycle at the base of the huge formation. The unmistakable report of a small explosion drew his attention back to the west.

Oksana! The grenade.

He glanced up just in time to see a small cloud of smoke expand out from the distant hillside. At least three dark bodies were scattered along the slope. Two were motionless.

He struggled to catch his breath as sweat mixed with sand poured into his eye sockets.

Get moving, Collins.

Now!

She bought you some time. Use it!

He pitched the dry brush aside and climbed aboard the rugged Indian 841. Moments later the V-twin engine rumbled to life, and he stowed his satchel and gun behind the seat. Everything within him wanted desperately to pause for a few moments and simply contemplate the depth of Oksana's sacrifice.

But he couldn't.

A dedicated time for proper mourning would have to wait. A rooster tail of dust billowed behind as he dropped his heel, popped it into gear, and accelerated out across the sandy soil.

For the time being, merely remaining among the living seemed to be the most natural way to honor the memory of the dead.

CHAPTER 70

To consider the dozen or so men assembled on the tarmac as a welcoming committee would, no doubt, have been a bridge too far. None of the typical trappings of such a warm convocation were apparent. In fact, the demeanor of all present could have argued strongly for the assessment that this was a sunrise funeral detail at Dreamland.

No one smiled. And with good reason.

Several of the men quietly predicted court-martials.

One of them vomited. Twice.

Corporal Jennings signaled for everyone's attention as the Douglas C-47 Skytrain bearing Howard Ross touched down in the distance.

"I ain't gonna lie, boys. Might as well prepare for the worst. Heads are gonna roll, and most of our asses are probably fired." He took a few steps. "I know you all did your jobs, and that we lost far too many good men last night. *Good* men. I am proud to have served alongside you. When Chief Ross arrives, I will take full and complete responsibility for any and all failures in this operation."

He rotated about as the plane taxied towards them, the morning sun glinting across the silver hull in the cold breeze of the desert daybreak. Jennings mumbled under his tense breath. "Let's pray the buck stops here."

The somber entourage migrated closer to the craft as the engines spun down and the side door immediately flung open. Ross shoved an airman out of the way and bounded out of the fuselage. Neal Schaeffer darted through the hatch and scrambled to catch up.

"Corporal Jennings?!" Ross belted out above the noise, scanning the crowd. *"Corporal?!"*

"Right here, sir," Jennings yelled, waving his arm.

Ross pitched his fresh cigarette and marched up to him. "I need a sitrep, and I need it yesterday! Where're you holding Denver Wayne Collins?"

Jennings swallowed. "We…don't have him, sir. I thought you knew."

"What?!"

The Chief's confused expression was rapidly replaced by visible rage. "I ordered radio silence during the flight. So what the hell're you talking about, Corporal?! I got a damn phone call at quarter past three this morning that said he was captured and in protective custody! Do you think I hopped in a C-47 in my pajamas for a late night pleasure flight?!"

"No, sir. We had him, we did. But…he escaped, sir."

Ross twisted around, apparently looking for something to kick. "How in the bloody hell did one man—*one single, solitary man*—break out of a secure, underground detention facility in the middle of the damn desert, Corporal?!"

Jennings faced the ground. "He had accomplices, sir. Possibly on the inside. Almost certainly on the inside, sir."

Jenning's revelation brought Ross to a simmering standstill. Neal Schaeffer seized the opportunity. "How many accomplices, Corporal?"

"We have confirmed *two*. We have one of them."

"One of ours?" Neal asked.

"No sir, one of them…a black male. Early thirties."

Ross jerked his head up. "Finally, some good news. Take me to him, right now!"

"I'll be glad to do it, sir. But I don't think it will be what you're expecting," Jennings protested as Ross pushed passed him.

"I don't give a damn about what you think, Corporal. Let's go."

"What I mean, sir," Jennings called out, "is that...well, he's unconscious, sir."

Ross halted. "I hope you mean asleep, Corporal."

"No, sir. Unconscious. Unresponsive."

The Chief doubled-back and pressed his chest against the Corporal. "All security protocols called for non-lethal force, Corporal Jennings. Non-lethal. Surely the men of your unit understand what *non-lethal force* means."

"Yes, sir."

"Then how do you explain his condition? Self-inflicted? Rattlesnake bite? Scorpions? What...?"

"He sustained a life-threatening injury while fleeing from our patrol. It appears that he lost control and struck a boulder. Head and spine trauma, sir."

Ross wagged his head and backed away. "You're batting zero for two, Corporal. Not a very impressive average. How hard did you try?"

Jennings composed himself. "A lot of good men lost their lives over the last several hours, sir."

"How many, Corporal?" Neal inquired.

"Fourteen, sir."

"*Fourteen?!*" Ross exploded. "Fourteen?! How many were killed by the black male?"

Jennings paused. "None. At least none that we can confirm, sir."

"So you're telling me that Denver Wayne Collins and one other man—possibly one of our very own—took out over a dozen highly-trained soldiers before eventually escaping?"

"Not entirely, Chief Ross. Actually, the other man...*wasn't*, sir."

"Excuse me?"

"The other man...was a...*woman*, sir."

Ross' mouth cracked open. "What?"

"A woman, sir. Two injured soldiers independently confirmed that Collins escaped with a female accomplice. Black hair. They indicated she appeared to be wounded. Perhaps severely. He had to carry her on his shoulders."

"This, this *unbelievable* fiasco is just getting better every damn second!" Ross bellowed. "We'll be lucky if Dulles doesn't hang every single one of us by sundown. You know, at this point I might even be willing to tie the rope around my own neck and save him the trouble!"

Neal slid his notebook out. "What else can you report, Corporal? Any other losses?"

Jennings stared off into the distance. "We lost at least three jeeps, one helicopter—"

"*A helicopter?!*" Ross exclaimed. "You gotta be kidding me! They flew outta here in one of our own helicopters?"

"No, sir. It appears the final leg of their escape was by motorcycle. We lost the helicopter while in pursuit across the lakebed—one of our Bell 47s. Both airmen died in the incident. Sir."

Schaeffer seemed stumped. "But...were there any *other* losses or disruptions, Corporal? No matter how small."

Jennings retrieved a folded piece of paper and scanned it. "Um, yes, sir. It appears several pounds of metals were removed from Metallurgy on Level Two. A guard on that level was killed. Stabbed, sir."

"Metals?" Neal asked with developing interest. "What kind of metals?"

The corporal referenced his sheet. "I believe they were classified as *superconductors,* sir. I'm not exactly familiar with the term."

Ross shot a swift glance over at Neal. His subordinate was visibly lost in thought.

"Who proctored the initial interrogation of Mr. Collins?" Ross demanded. "Hamilton? Eisner? Tell me it wasn't Eisner."

"No, it was Hamilton, sir. He spoke to Collins briefly. But the suspect escaped prior to the extraction of any useful intelligence. He was discovered missing before they could administer the cocktail. Sir."

"I wanna see the video recordings and Agent Hamilton immediately."

"Hamilton is waiting outside your office, sir. But the video tapes were destroyed. Almost a total loss. Dr. Trousdale is doing his best to recover them now."

Ross hesitated. "Has the examination of the black male's body or clothing revealed any actionable intelligence?"

"No, sir. No identification, no personal items. Nothing. We did recover a color photograph of a young girl in Collins' clothing. We also recovered a motorcycle used by the male accomplice and another abandoned motorcycle we assume belonged to Collins. Our initial examination of the vehicles did not uncover any other useful evidence. We are tracking down licenses and registration as we speak. We hope to have something on that by noon, I believe."

"I want it sooner, Corporal."

"Yes, sir. If we can, sir."

"Did we at least get a photographic series on Mr. Collins?" Ross inquired.

"Yes, sir. And fingerprints, along with height and weight measurements, sir."

"Have we set up roadblocks and notified the state police to be looking for Collins and the female?" he asked.

"Yes, sir. Immediately, sir. All according to established protocols."

Ross ambled over to Neal Schaeffer. He glanced back at Jennings. "That will be all, Corporal. Wait with Agent Hamilton outside my office. Get every single photograph of Collins on my desk pronto. And the picture of the young girl. And find me someone—*anyone*—who can talk intelligently about those superconductors. I don't care if we have to kidnap a damn university professor! I wanna know the hows and whys and wherefores, Corporal."

"Yes, sir."

"And nobody and I do mean *nobody* speaks to Washington until I do. *Understood?!*"

"Perfectly, sir."

Jennings pivoted towards the administration building and hastened away. Several soldiers joined him.

Ross wasn't finished. "And I want TDS films of both motorcycles and the black male, Corporal. Every inch."

"Yes, sir."

"In one hour." A moment later Ross adjusted his request. "Make that thirty minutes. And find me the world's best brain surgeon. I don't care if he's yellow, red, black or white. Get him here *yesterday*. And any equipment or medicine he wants or needs."

Ross glared at his second-in-command as he suppressed his irritated voice. "I told you there was someone on the inside. It's gonna be damn-well impossible to cover this up from Dulles." The increasing breeze frustrated him further as he sought to ignite a cigarette. "And now, now that *sonofabitch* has probably cost me the opportunity of a lifetime!" Smoke drifted out of his nostrils. *"Dammit!"*

"But why here?" Neal mumbled.

"What?"

"Why would Collins risk coming here?"

Ross shoved the cigarette to his lips. "Gutsy move, I'll give 'em that. Gutsy as hell."

"Not gutsy...how about *desperate.*"

Ross exhaled. "Continue."

"Whatever he wanted, it had to be something valuable…something worth losing his life over. Or the life of his associate. Or both."

"Tell me something that isn't obvious," Ross moaned. "Time to earn your inflated paycheck, and hurry it up. Every second counts today."

Neal pinched the bridge of his nose and started wandering about. He always asserted that his mental processes were at optimum performance when the body was physically engaged. "They naturally had to assume there was a high probability they—*or he*—would fail."

"Naturally," Ross concurred in a condescending voice.

"Unless…unless they discovered a way to *leverage* the probabilities." Neal closed his eyes. "I mean, what are the odds?"

"Odds about what?"

"It couldn't have been a coincidence. Sheer probability practically forbids it."

Ross knew the routine well. He withheld his peace momentarily.

"No. It was no coincidence," Neal announced. "We were supposed to be there. That's right. Because…because it was imperative…it was *crucial* for us not to be *here*. Clever leverage. Clever." Neal's eyes brightened. "Call McPherson at Roswell!"

"And why?"

"We need to bring everybody home. Get everyone out of there."

"Abandon Roswell?" Ross challenged. "I think your obsession for analysis has finally driven you insane, Agent Schaeffer. Roswell continues to be a gold mine!"

"It's not a mine—it's the bait!" Schaeffer countered. "A distraction. A decoy. And a desperate one."

"Explain."

"They wanted SATURN—probably you and me in particular—to be at Roswell. It's the only scenario that connects all the dots. Consider all the items and evidence we've discovered. What would make them willing to give all that up? What would *compel* them to relinquish it? And why now?"

Ross crushed his spent cigarette on the oily tarmac. "An oversight."

"*Desperation,*" Schaeffer snapped. "They must be…they must be getting close."

"To what?"

"To their objective. It's the only scenario that makes sense. We uncovered several pages of notes detailing some type of temporal displacement device. That's the key."

Neal wandered about in a wide arc and pulled his jacket tighter around him. "That's why Collins came here." He spun back towards his boss. "I think…no, no, no…scratch that. I *know* they're desperately trying to build some kind of Tesla device to allow them to return to the future."

"There's more than one possibility," Ross countered. "There's always more than meets the eye. Always. You know that. It's your damn job to know that."

Neal appeared undeterred. "Just because one can *imagine* multiple explanations, it doesn't follow that all of them are on equal footing. We need to isolate the lone explanation which accounts for the greatest body of evidence."

Any discernible sense of excitement seemed to flee from Neal's voice. "These desperate acts prove that they are close. Collins' success likely indicates that our window to apprehend a time traveler, any time traveler, could be rapidly closing."

Ross spat. "Supposing you're right—and I'm not agreeing that you are—how much time?"

Neal shrugged. "Impossible to tell. Worst case? Could be weeks, maybe *days*."

Ross spat. "Where do you think they're headed?"

"Who?"

"Collins and the woman."

Neal struggled for a response. "Uh, Vegas is a safe bet. At least initially. Or Los Angeles. They might try to catch a flight out of either city."

"You coordinate from here. I'll take a crew into Vegas and start a dragnet. Get me some updated photos of Collins."

"Can do. Anything else?"

A fresh blast of brisk morning air howled across the valley, kicking up an irritating spray of sand and dust. Ross shielded his face then fixed his gaze to the west. "You claim they look desperate, Agent Schaeffer."

Ross squinted as he studied the U-2 aircraft bunkers burrowed into the jagged hills in the distance.

"Well, Neal, I'll show you what desperation really looks like. From 70,000 feet."

CHAPTER 71

The telltale glare of mid-morning sunlight bouncing off a moving windshield caught Leah's attention. She grabbed the desk phone and dialed.

"Hey. You might want to get up here. Doc just got back. Pulling in the parking lot. Now."

She lowered the handset and rotated to her left. "Tori, dear? Why don't you finish reading that chapter and then gather up your things? We will be leaving soon for our little trip. Okay?"

The preoccupied teen nodded. "Okay."

Leah rose from her chair and began making her way across the foyer to intercept him. Moments later Ellen emerged from the manufacturing floor, followed by Shep and Garrett. Doc pushed through the front door and ventured a quick glance at the hastily assembled welcoming committee. He spun to his right, removed his coat and hat, and deposited them both onto the coat rack.

No one uttered a word.

Doc pivoted back around in a deliberate fashion. His round face bore the misery of a lifetime of sorrow mixed with a crushing load of guilt. He was obviously seeking to maintain his dignity, but a pair of tears managed to elude his control.

"I, uh, I owe each…each and every one of you an apology…of the highest order," he began after considerable effort. "It would appear that the reckless behavior of my youth has continued to find fertile soil in my latter years.

Your prodigal son has returned." Doc folded his trembling hands and lowered his head. The tears that had been collecting along his chin now plummeted to the dull tile floor below. "I am…hereby submitting myself to any and all punishments that this group deems fitting and necessary." He looked back up, sobbing, *"I am so sorry!"*

Ellen and Leah rushed up to the repentant researcher and surrounded him within their compassionate arms.

"You don't owe us anything, you lovable fool!" Ellen offered between sobs of her own. "We owe *you* so much! So damn much!"

Leah raised her head, now stained with the tears from all three faces. "Welcome home, Doc. Welcome home."

Ellen glanced back over her shoulder. "Garrett! Don't just stand there…go grab him a chair."

"So, someone breaks the rules and we gotta treat 'em like a returning king?" he growled.

"Get the damn chair, Frazier," Shep ordered. "We ain't got a helluva lot of time for nonsense today! We gotta be outta here *pronto.*"

Doc managed to wiggle a hand free to remove his soaked glasses. "I doubt that there is much confusion concerning my whereabouts of late."

"It's okay," Ellen consoled as she gave him room to wipe his cheeks dry. "Don't worry about all that. We have something to tell you. Something that will change everything. Actually, a few things that'll change everything."

Garrett tossed the chair behind him and dropped back.

"Change?" Doc asked as he lowered himself into the seat. "*Change?* Events that have transpired over the past twenty-four hours have challenged my notion that things can be *changed,* my dear Miss Finegan."

Ellen sank down in front of him and grabbed his hands gently. "Look at me…and listen to me," she said.

He did.

She hesitated. "You did not kill that girl, Dr. Glen Stonecroft. Her death had nothing to do with you. Not one thing."

Doc tried to look away, but she squeezed his hand. "Hey. Listen to me. Not one thing. We can prove it."

Another set of tears tumbled down his reddening cheeks. "*Cookie* is dead, Miss Finegan."

Ellen locked eyes with him. "We know. And it had nothing to do with you, not fifty years ago, and not yesterday." She paused. "It was a deer. A deer ran out in front of her, Doc. She swerved to miss it and lost control. She hit a tree. It was never you. You just happened to be there right as it happened. You have carried a heavy load of false guilt for fifty years."

He fumbled around with his glasses. "How…how could you possibly know that? You speak as if you saw the whole terrible ordeal!"

"I didn't," she admitted. "But Frazier did. He saw everything."

Doc slid his spectacles on. "Pardon me?"

"It's true," Garrett said. "I was there. You told us right where it all happened. And *when*. Shep and McCloud told me to sit there and watch. Ellen's right. It was a deer. A big one, too. I should've shot it. I had my gun—"

Shep cleared his throat and ambled towards the factory floor. "Now that he's back, I'm going to go get Pap and Alexus and tell them to get ready to leave. We need to be headed down to Urbana within an hour or so. Did Billy ever get—"

"Yes," Leah called out. "Billy already picked up Martha. They are down at the police station."

"Urbana?!" Doc nearly shouted. "Oh, heavens...forgive my lack of sensitivity! Does our departure mean our dear Mr. Collins was unsuccessful in his endeavor in Nevada?!"

Ellen knelt beside him. "Oh, no, no, no. Denver made it out okay. He found the superconductors. He'll be here in a few days."

"Incredible," Doc whispered. "Simply incredible. If Emile's predictions and my calculations are correct, we could have everyone home…by *Christmas*. Yes, by Christmas. And what a delightful gift that would be." He looked up and all around. "So, are we evacuating the premises out of an abundance of caution?"

Ellen paused. "It's Terrance. Terrance never made it back to the hotel. He could've had engine trouble with his motorcycle, or who knows what. Denver's gonna wait a full twenty-four hours. Like we planned. I'm sure he is fine…just late. Terrance is smart. And resourceful."

"My, my, my," Doc mumbled. "I pray that you are correct, Miss Finegan."

"Well, I am correct…*we* are correct," she asserted, "in telling you that you had nothing to do with that girl's death. She lost control over a deer in the road, not you. You were at the wrong place, at the wrong time. That's it."

Doc appeared to process for a few moments. "I truly appreciate your attempts to…craft a plausible tale to console me," he said. "But you need not worry, I assure you. I have come to peace with Miss Boulden's demise."

Garrett reached into his jean's pocket and retrieved a small card. "Oh, I ain't making this up, old timer." He shoved it into Doc's right hand. "I've seen death before, but this one about made me sick. I won't be forgetting it anytime soon."

Stonecroft rotated the small document towards him and dropped it in horror.

Carolyn Boulden's blood-stained driver's license floated down onto the floor.

CHAPTER 72

It bordered on the unusual.

Ross was accustomed to making calls on his Las Vegas house phone, not answering them. But the instant he pushed through his front door and fought to yank his keys out of the lock, it began ringing.

The timing was difficult to dismiss as coincidental.

Ross grumbled to himself as he tossed the keys onto the coffee table. “I'm coming, dammit.” He leaned forward and snagged the handset. “Hello?”

“I know it's rude,” an unmistakable voice admitted. “I've heard it's not polite to call right when someone walks in the door.”

Ross grabbed the phone base and raced over to the living room window. He checked for any signs of life.

Nothing. But how?

He cleared his throat. “I don't know, but something tells me that blackmailers aren't typically worried about being polite.”

“And something tells me that division chiefs within the CIA aren't very grateful.”

Ross traveled over to the windows on the opposite side. “Oh, what, uh, what makes you say that?”

“You never said *thank you*.”

“Oh, I'm sorry,” he offered sarcastically. “Really. I usually show my gratitude to anyone who threatens to destroy my damn career and extort large sums of money from me.”

"I was talking about my gift."

Ross moved away from the windows and rested against the back of his couch. "Your what?!"

"My gift. The package. In Chicago," the voice said. "You did get it?"

Ross pinched the bridge of his nose. "Oh, that. The *hat*."

The voice seemed excited. "Good, so you did get it?"

"Look, I've been going strong since about three o'clock this morning and I've got about seventeen and a half million damn things to do right now. There is a point to this call?"

A pause. "So, how was New Mexico, Howard?"

Ross didn't bite.

"I hear that Roswell can be lovely in November."

"Your point?"

"My, my. Such a sour attitude, Howard."

"I will hang up."

"9:45 tonight. Corner of Fremont and Sixth Street. Hooker. Red skirt, red shoes. Gray purse. Regular amount." The voice paused. "Oh, one more thing."

"Don't leave your house until then, or, well…just use your imagination." *Click.*

CHAPTER 73

Denver clutched the edge of the curtain, as if clinging to hope itself.

He planted his wearied head against the window and gazed down at the nighttime bustle of Las Vegas Boulevard. From his fourth floor perch, he could make out the street, the tourists, the hookers, the drunks, the taxicabs, the hotel parking lot. He could see everything except for the one thing he wanted to see.

Terrance Gaines.

Where could you be, my friend?

It was a bizarre possibility that he would never have predicted. In his mind's eye, Denver had played out the probable one-way mission dozens of times on the long trek across the country to the wastelands of Nevada. In most of the scenarios, he himself never made it home. But no one had even mentioned Terrance as a potential liability in either of the planning sessions back in Normal. It was all riding on Denver.

He never even imagined returning without Tee.

Never even once.

Denver, resembling a train-wreck survivor, had rolled back into the north end of the Vegas strip a few hours after sunrise. He parked the motorcycle far from the road, stripped off his bloody shirt, and retrieved the room key they had wisely decided to hide along the edge of the hotel parking lot. After a quick shower and a quicker nap, Denver had called the Chief with his first update.

A few hours later, as lunch came and went with no word from Terrance, Denver phoned home a second time. McCloud urged him to trade in their current car immediately and to consider changing hotels. He reasoned that if Terrance had been captured, it was possible he could be coerced to divulge the make and model of their recently purchased vehicle, or even made to disclose their rendezvous location.

There was little doubt in anyone's mind that a massive, statewide manhunt was now in full force.

As Denver sat in the window, his triumphant return to Sin City was now approaching fourteen hours old.

Hope had been steadily eroded by the frustrating flow of time.

The king-sized bed was a mangled mess. Spent dishes from room service deliveries were haphazardly piled into the bathroom sink. A few pairs of shoes and socks were scattered across the floor and furniture. The satchel housing the superconductive metals was safely stashed beneath the large mattress, causing a conspicuous lump. A DO NOT DISTURB sign dangled on the outside of the door, and he propped a chair under the handle on the inside.

On his third phone call, he was ordered to exit the Las Vegas area by eight the next morning, no matter what.

With or *without* a copilot.

Back home, Nelson Manufacturing had become an unlikely ghost town. Earlier that day—in a small convoy and without much fanfare—the majority of the Jumpers in Normal had been transplanted to a secret location an hour southeast of town. Only the Chief and Betty Larson would remain behind to uphold appearances while keeping a lookout for suspicious activity.

Denver wouldn't be informed of the Jumper's new position until all were convinced he hadn't been tailed on his long trek back to a motel in Chicago.

A disturbance in the hallway roused Denver from the window and invigorated him with anticipation. He rushed up to the door and pressed his ear against it. He held his breath and strained to pick up every sound. Several seconds passed.

Nothing.

At least nothing important.

It sounded like a pair of children in the corridor simply being children. He sulked back across the carpet of the silent room. All of the pair's combined belongings, including a wallet flush with cash, were stuffed into a suitcase. A fresh change of clothing was laid out for his late accomplice. Just about everything was prepared for an immediate departure.

The only thing missing was Terrance.

CHAPTER 74

Neal Schaeffer snagged the handset and rapidly dialed his desk phone. While waiting to connect, he arched back and looked around at his well-organized office with exhausted satisfaction.

He felt like he had been gone for years.

It's good to be home.

"It's me," he said. "What's the latest on Ross?"

Neal popped the latches on his briefcase and extracted several folders. He closed it.

"You're positive?" Pen in hand, he perused through two of the dossiers and jotted down a few notations.

"Okay. 9:45. The El Cortez."

CHAPTER 75

The streetlamps, neon signs, and car headlights ensured that Glitter Gulch was living up to its growing and glowing reputation. As Howard Ross navigated through the late-fall crowds towards the intersection, the massive El Cortez Hotel and Casino sign dominated his view of the colorful skyline.

He examined his watch.

9:40 p.m.

Ross glanced up towards the corner. He may have been early, but so was the prostitute.

Red skirt. Red shoes.

He waited until she swiveled towards him.

And…a gray purse.

He admired her legs with a second glance.

That dame's gotta be cold.

A city cop traversing the late evening beat came around the corner and surveyed the immediate area. Ross ducked into a deep shadow along a storefront. The policeman appeared to be satisfied with the state of affairs and continued past.

Ross hesitated before eventually working his way up to the intersection and came to a silent stop right beside the hooker. She pivoted around and looked him up and down.

"Can I help you, sir?"

He moved closer and scanned the sidewalk before depositing a small package into her gray purse. She winked as he backed away, then darted for the doors of the El Cortez as fast as her high heels would carry her. Ross admired the

Spanish Colonial architecture of the building until she disappeared inside.

He jogged up to the entrance, threw the doors open and rushed into the foyer. Ross laid hold of a bellman passing by. "Excuse me, I'm looking for a lady who just walked by." He dropped his voice. "A hooker. Red skirt. Shoes. Just now."

The porter nodded and motioned off to his left. Ross raced towards the casino and halted in the wide doorway. The gaming floor was a visual feast of flashing lights, slot machines, card tables, and dozens of gamblers. He fired up a cigarette and leaned his shoulder against the golden doorjamb. Several red skirts flitted about the gambling hall, but none of them belonged to the blackmailer's attractive courier.

A waitress packed into a skimpy black cocktail dress drew alongside with a tray filled with complimentary drinks. In a single, unbroken motion, Ross downed a martini and set the empty glass back onto her platter before she even had time to step away. Moments later, he pushed off the doorframe, straightened his coat, and exited back through the foyer.

Another patron inched out from behind a slot machine and snatched a free drink from the waitress' passing tray.

But unlike his boss, Neal Schaeffer took small, thoughtful sips.

CHAPTER 76

"All clear."

Denver had holed up inside a low-budget motel in south Chicago for three days awaiting those liberating words. As he pressed the receiver to his ear, he glanced around the musty chamber. It bore an uncanny similarity to the mysterious room that had welcomed him to 1956 a few months before.

"I can come home?" he asked.

"That's a big ten-four," McCloud announced on the other end of the line. "It's been several days since you left Vegas. I haven't seen hide-nor-hair of anything...*unusual* around town. I think we're good. You noticed any suspicious activity around your parts?"

"Nope, nothing," Denver replied. "I've been looking and moving around just to see if anyone's tailing me. Clear on this end."

"Miss Larson says the same thing."

"How is Betty?"

"Oh, she's back at it a hundred percent," the Chief noted. "Maybe a hundred and ten percent. And I'm thankful for that." He paused. "Speaking of being thankful, how was your day of thanks?"

"My what?"

"How was your *Thanksgiving?*" McCloud clarified. "You know, that annual day of gluttony that used to be 'bout gratitude? It was last Thursday...in case you missed it."

Denver plopped down onto the double bed. "What day is it?"

"*Today?* Today's Tuesday. The twenty-seventh. December's just around the corner, if you can believe it."

Denver scratched the emerging stubble populating his jawline. "Wow. I just realized something."

"What's that?"

"I've only been away from home on Thanksgiving on two occasions before. Both were in Afghanistan. This now makes a third."

"Well, my friend, the way I see it…this one don't really count. We're not even s'pposed to be here anyway. And when Doc gets us all home like he promised, it'll be like we never even left."

"Whatever makes you feel better, Chief," Denver mumbled.

"*Feel better?* You do realize you're talkin' to a lifetime cop, right? We work right through the holidays all the time. Crime don't care about baby Jesus or pilgrims, Trailer Collins. I've worked my share o' holidays. Just par for the course."

Denver laid back onto the bed. "Well, Chief, I spent my *doesn't-count* Thanksgiving in Nevada, Arizona, New Mexico, and parts of Oklahoma. Do you know how hard it is to find a gas station or a restaurant that's open on Thanksgiving Day in the desert Southwest?"

McCloud's chuckle was hard to miss. "Well, it is the 1950s for heaven's sake! You gotta quit thinkin' like the early twenty-first century. This is the mid-twentieth, my friend. Times are diff'rent. Heck, you know that."

"I do now."

"Anywho, I just talked to Shep down at the safe house. He felt—"

"Yeah, about that," Denver interrupted. "Where did everyone go?"

"Oh, we moved 'em down to the Lincoln Hotel over in Urbana for safe keeping. Bout an hour away. They wouldn't even tell me where they were until this mornin'," McCloud explained. "But Shep agreed with me, it's time. Everyone's comin' home."

Everyone?

No, Denver thought.

Not everyone.

As he stared into the low ceiling of his motel room, his mind's eye traversed the bloody desert sand of Groom Lake, with a long and unnecessary trail of dead American soldiers. He imagined the distorted remains of Oksana Mizenov, no doubt blasted into grotesque pieces all across that steep embankment. His rescue and her sacrifice had tormented Denver throughout six slow days of brutal reflection and self-examination.

Forty-eight hours on the open road had afforded a modicum of distraction, but seventy-two more locked away in a motel room provided the ideal conditions for doubt to ferment and thrive. Each painful step and every bullet fired had been rehashed dozens of times.

He longed for the days when morality divided neatly into a single pair of colors.

The multiplied shades of gray were torturing him.

Sorry, Chief.

Not everyone is coming home.

Denver hunched forward on the edge of the bed and massaged his still-tender forehead. "Has, uh, has there been any word from...*Terrance?*"

The tense silence that followed provided the unspoken confirmation that Denver feared.

CHAPTER 77

The atmosphere at Nelson Manufacturing was a somber contradiction of celebration and sorrow.

As Denver plodded down through the center of the quiet factory floor, gathering a small flock of interested observers, he sensed it. Everyone could sense it.

He surveyed their conflicted faces.

I feel like I just won the lottery…during a funeral.

Alexus jogged up to meet him and blocked his way. Shep kept his distance.

"Tell me he's gonna be okay," she begged. Her beautiful eyes flooded with tears. "Promise me he's gonna make it back."

Denver lowered his priceless satchel and swallowed hard. "I, uh, look, Lexi—"

"Promise me."

He attempted to make eye contact, but the penetrating and expectant gaze of that five-foot tall female reduced him internally to a pathetic failure. "Uh, Terrance is a good man," he began. "If anyone could pull it off, it's him." He patted her shoulder. "He's probably on his way back right now."

You don't believe that, Collins.

And neither does she.

Another voice from the far end of the plant rescued him from the misery of the moment. "My dear Mr. Collins. How it does my heart good to behold your countenance! Welcome home."

Denver bent to retrieve his satchel. "Hello, Doc. Thanks. It's good to be back to Normal."

"Are you by any chance *Greek*, Mr. Collins?" he asked.

Denver ventured a few steps and frowned. "Scotch Irish."

"Marvelous, marvelous," Doc replied as he drew nearer, with Papineau close behind. "Because Virgil wisely cautioned us to '*Beware of Greeks bearing gifts*.'" They finally converged. "And you are bearing gifts, are you not?"

Denver untied the bag and handed each of them a heavy, foil-wrapped bar. "Merry Christmas from Uncle Sam," he said. "Stealing this has probably put me on the naughty list."

"Speaking of Christmas," Doc explained while admiring the material, "if our calculations are in order—and I have no doubt that they are—it is within the realm of possibility that we will all be home for the holidays. So to speak."

Denver couldn't help but smile. "That would be the best Christmas gift...*ever*."

Papineau's eyes grew wide and he fairly danced with excitement. "*Cette est magnifique!*" He leaned his diminutive frame up against Denver and offered a firm hug. Seconds later, the French scientist gathered the rest of the material and disappeared into The Basement.

"He sure isn't wasting any time," Denver observed.

Doc smiled. "It should only be a matter of weeks now."

Garrett Frazier waltzed up and joined the pair. He shot his meaty hand out. "All I can say is...amazing. Really. You've earned my total respect. I mean that."

They shook and Denver nodded. "Thanks, Garrett. That, uh, that means a lot. But I just got lucky, and I had a lot of help. It wasn't just me. Let's not forget Terrance."

"Whatever. You still finished a helluva mission. An impossible one." Frazier hit him on the arm and trudged back over to the loading dock.

Wow, Denver thought. *That was…something.*

Denver scanned the area. "Where's Ellen? She downstairs?"

"Miss Finegan will be here any moment," Doc assured him. "Our little assembly just arrived back to town not quite an hour ago ourselves. Nurse Finegan was particularly anxious to check on the status of Ms. Larson and her injury."

"I suppose a nurse just can't help being a nurse."

"Indeed. Speaking of help," Doc asked, keeping his voice low, "are the rumors true concerning our fair damsel in distress from Arkansas? We have heard fragments of wondrous tales."

Denver shoved his hands in his pockets and stared down at the greasy floor. "Oh, yeah. Brenda Jo."

"Yes. What more can be elaborated concerning Miss Tilley?"

"The short version?"

Doc adjusted his glasses. "At the present time, I will accept any and all versions, Trailer Collins."

"Well, replace Brenda Jo with *Oksana*. And Tilley is actually *Mizenov*. Does that help?"

Stonecroft folded his arms across his barrel chest. "Astounding. No doubt Slavic. A Soviet spy? KGB?"

"That's at the low end of the possibilities, Doc. It would've taken a roomful of James Bonds to beat her. I was in the Special Forces for years. I've never seen anyone like her."

"Most curious…and most puzzling." Doc cut a wide arc around Denver as he worked through it verbally. "But why?

What could sufficiently motivate a foreign agent to assist us in our desperate endeavor?"

"I've been thinking about it for a week straight, and I've got nothing concrete. Unless the Russians are interested in stealing our technology."

"It is simultaneously a comfort and a concern that a person of her nationality, skill, and knowledge is aware of our existence and operation," Doc offered candidly.

Denver sought to be discreet. "You mean *was*. Was aware."

Stonecroft circled back around. "Pardon me, Mr. Collins? Did you invoke a past tense verb form deliberately?"

He nodded. "*Was*. She...died. Saving me."

Doc's genial face drained of all expression. "Oh. Oh. That is one wondrous tale that did not seem to reach us down at the hotel in Urbana."

Denver moved within inches of Stonecroft's face. "There's more, Doc."

"Okay. Yes?"

"Oksana told me something. She *revealed* some new info. Right before she...passed."

Denver hesitated and Doc narrowed his eyes in concentration. "I am listening, Mr. Collins."

"She gave me two pieces of information. Two clues. She said they were the keys to the mystery of time travel, and Normal and all."

"But Mr. Collins, our extensive research has already revealed those key elements," Doc protested kindly. "It is the potent combination of thermonuclear testing—"

"Yes, yes, I know all that, Doc," he interjected. "*Invisible cracks in the sky*. I get it. Sort of. But she knew *more*."

"More?"

"She said she knew why everyone always jumps here. To Normal. Our other big question."

"My apologies, Mr. Collins," Doc conceded. "I am most intrigued."

Denver positioned his mouth near Doc's left ear.

"She said 'the Sandbox'. And something about the Pentagon."

November 30, 1956

SECURITY LEVEL: TOP SECRET

FOR: Chief Howard D. Ross, Project SATURN
FROM: Allen W. Dulles, Director, Central Intelligence
SUBJECT: Domestic U-2 Surveillance

My position regarding your request for U-2 surveillance over the lower 48 states has not altered. Project SATURN continues to be prohibited from utilizing any portion of the U-2 fleet for domestic purposes.

The crisis in the Suez remains our top reconnaissance priority.

That being said, now that Eisenhower has won his bid for a second term, the political climate will undoubtedly be changing. Public opinion typically does not play as large a factor with politicians who have little to lose.

We can revisit this issue after the inauguration, providing that the situation in the Middle East has improved.

END

DCI/PS

CHAPTER 78

"*Nevada?!*" Hank exclaimed between sips of whiskey. "What in the blue blazes were you doin' in Nevada?"

Denver paused and premeditated his words with precision. He forced a weak smile. "Just company business, you know. Picking up some parts for the factory. Special order stuff."

"Speaking of the plant, I ran by there a couple of times, lookin' for you last week. Place was locked up tighter than a drum. Middle of the day. Both times."

"Company holiday," Denver replied. "Apparently we get an extended Thanksgiving break. Paid break, too."

"Get outta Dodge! Really?"

"I'm not kidding. It's great."

Hank raised his depleted glass and caught the eye of the bartender. "Well, Mr. Jackson, I'm glad things are workin' out for you up there. But, to be honest, I'm surprised they let you go out of state and all. Considering your past…uh…legal *indiscretions*."

Denver rested his elbows on the counter. "Oh, I wasn't alone. No, they sent a chaperone with me. I was a good boy."

"You'd better be a good boy, if you want ole Saint Nick to stop at your chimney later this month."

"Oh, I'm a little angel," Denver muttered. "I just hide my wings and halo in public. Especially in bars."

Hank snuck a healthy drink before gawking at Denver. "If you was such a good boy, then how'd you get your noggin' busted again?"

"What?"

He pointed. "That bruise on your forehead."

Denver nodded. "Oh, yeah. That. I, uh, I smacked it on a stupid framing machine down at the factory. They don't give much."

"Come to think of it," Hank pondered, "you had quite a little lump on your head when I first met ya down at the paper. Your folks shoulda named you *Lucky*."

"Stick to carpentry, forget comedy," Denver groaned.

"So, did you guys swing through Vegas? Tackle any one-armed bandits? Or two-legged ones?"

"Just a couple of short nights there. There wasn't much time for entertainment."

The bartender deposited another round.

"I hate big cities," Hank admitted, "but I wouldn't mind a weekend hittin' the poker tables there and all. I'd do it, but I hear the drive out there is horrible."

"We took the northern route. At least we got to see the Rockies."

"A lot of snow already?"

"Only about five feet," Denver laughed, downing a fast sip.

Something new seemed to catch Hank's easily-distracted attention. "Whoa, wouldya lookie there." He threw his head to Denver's far left.

"What?"

"Right there," Hank motioned. "Look at that fine piece of female architecture."

"Where?"

Hank grabbed his shoulders and rotated him. "Right. Over. There. *Her*. That classy chassis."

Denver finally caught an impressive glimpse through the heavy foot traffic crisscrossing the tavern. "Oh, yeah. Her. Yep. Wow."

"Now that view is even nicer'n the Rockies."

"Can't argue with you there, Bode."

Hank continued staring and nodded. "If I wasn't mostly happily married, I'd be sittin' over there instead of over here, that's for damn sure."

"Looks like she's alone. Of course, that won't last long," Denver noted. "Not around a joint like this."

Hank slapped his friend's back. "So, uh, what's keeping *you* from moseying over there right about now? I'm terribly cute and all, but even I can't compete with that!"

Denver spun back around. He took a long drink and stared at his glass. "Let's just say I've had more than one bad experience picking up a dolly in a bar."

"Doesn't mean that the next one won't be the right one," Hank scolded.

"Once again, I can't argue with you. I really can't. But when it comes to women and bars, let's just say that I enjoy *looking* at the menu…but I won't be doing any *ordering*."

Hank chuckled, "Your loss, pal." He held his cup high. "Well then, let's drink to…mighty fine menus!"

Denver smirked, "Here, here."

Hank drained his booze in a ridiculously exaggerated show of alcohol-prowess and crashed his glass down onto the counter. Denver had barely touched his own.

"So that's how it's gonna be, Bode?"

Hank exhaled through a rough cough. "That's how it's *gotta be*, Mr. Jackson!"

Denver shoved his glass high. "To mighty fine menus!"

"To mighty fine menus!"

He tossed his head back and tipped the cup skyward.

"Now that's what I'm talkin' about!" Hank shouted.

Denver winced. "Now, that…that's got a nice little…*bite*."

"Sweet like honey, but stings like a bee, I always say."

"One bee?" Denver gasped. "More like a whole frickin' beehive!"

"Well…I guess you big city types can't handle real liquor."

"Oh, I can handle my liquor," Denver protested as he glared at his empty cup. "But, this stuff is more like…*gasoline*."

Hank gestured and began shoving him off the stool. "Well, let this *gasoline* be the fuel to drive you towards that looker over there. I swear I just saw her stare at ya!"

"Yeah, right. You just wanna get the sick satisfaction of seeing me walk over there to crash and burn!"

Hank seemed to ponder that possibility. "You know, that just might be pretty entertaining, but, no. No. I really think you gotta chance."

"A chance? Yeah, a chance like…*hello Hell. My name is snowball.*"

Hank's laughter exploded. "Quit your stallin', Jackson! Every second you wait means a chance for some other lucky cat to steal her away."

"You really want me to do this?"

"Every good man needs a good woman. And lemme tell ya, she is *good*." Hank carried out that last syllable for a country mile.

"I guess it can't hurt to stop by and say hi."

"Nope. No it can't, my friend."

Denver hesitated, overcome with an unexpected yawn. "I don't know, it's late. I'm a bit tired."

Hank wagged his head. "Late? What's yer problem? You ain't gotta work tomorrow! No, that's just your nerves talkin'. Get over there. Time's runnin' out."

"I'm not afraid."

"I think you're the biggest chicken in the room."

"That was childish."

"You're the one being a baby, pal."

Denver blinked through a sharp pain that sliced an agonizing path across his forehead.

Alright. No more alcohol for you tonight, Collins.

You've had enough.

"What're you waiting for?" Hank prodded.

"My head to clear up."

"Don't think there's any chance for that," Hank laughed. "We're at a bar, you know."

"Okay, okay…just hold your horses. I'm…I'm going."

Denver straightened up and slid from his barstool. The room seemed to slosh back and forth and he steadied himself backwards against the counter.

"Wrong direction," Hank teased as he pointed. "She is *that* way, pal."

"Gimme a sec. Waiting for the room to settle down."

"Wow! You city boys really can't handle anything strong! Gimme a break."

"I'm fine," Denver said.

He wasn't.

"Fine? You don't look it," Hank admitted. "Actually, you look terrible."

It was doubtful that Denver had the capacity to comprehend his friend's last assessment. The room continued to sway, and his head felt like a chunk of wood jammed in a log splitter. He attempted to venture a step and nearly collapsed. Hank scrambled off his own seat.

"Whoa there, buddy," he said, grabbing Denver by the armpits. "Let's shuffle you back up onto your stool."

It was a losing proposition.

Denver crumpled to the floor.

"Oh no," Hank said, "I hope you're not having another one of your strange episodes!"

Denver didn't respond.

One of the bartenders arched over the counter. "Is he okay, Hank?"

"Yeah, oh, yeah," he responded. "Just a little too much liquid excitement."

Hank slapped a couple of dollars on the bar.

"C'mon buddy," he whispered as he nearly dragged Denver through the doors.

"Time to see just exactly what I've sent myself."

CHAPTER 79

"Denver? Hey, Denver?"

The voice seemed to be calling out to him from the top of a deep well…or maybe the bottom. It was dark. Very dark. But a pinpoint of light had just appeared and began growing somewhere above.

Denver sensed he was flat on his back, but between the confusion, the darkness and a throbbing skull, every new impression was ripe for interpretation.

The echoing voice sounded off, this time much closer. And a bit more familiar. "Denver? Come on now, buddy. Wake up…"

The speck of light had expanded to a blinding blur. He attempted to shield his eyes with his hands, but his arms wouldn't budge. It was odd. They didn't feel dead or heavy, they just felt…restrained. He kicked in vain; his ankles were immobilized.

"That's my boy," the voice called out, dangerously close. "Keep struggling. It'll raise your blood pressure. And that, my newest friend, should help you to wake up. Am I right, Doc?"

A new voice replied. "*Oui.*"

The blur still pervaded, but colors and movement were settling in. Things were moving. *Two* things were moving.

"Give him another shot."

That voice…

Three seconds later an unmistakable sting hit his bare left shoulder. A fiery sensation radiated out from the site of the injection.

He winced.

"Yeah, sorry about that, buddy. Probably burns a little."

I know that voice.

"Give it a sec…it'll reverse the sedative I slipped you at the bar."

Hank. Hank Bodenschatz?!

The clarity returning to his mind was matched by his improving vision. He glanced around as best he could. Two moving blurs were replaced by two people. A single incandescent light dangled above him. He was in a plain concrete room with a single window, and Denver was strapped topless onto a hard table.

Hank stepped towards him and leaned into his view. "Alrighty, there you are. Things gettin' better now?"

Denver struggled to speak, but a breathy garble of nonsense streamed out.

Hank smiled. "Sorry that I didn't catch any of that, but your voice will return. At least, it had better return." Hank turned his head and waved his arm. "I believe you already know my associate…"

An older figure came alongside. "Greetings, Mr. Collins. So good to see you this fine late evening."

Pappy? Dr. Papineau?

Speaking English?

Hank seemed pleased. "I can tell by your reaction that you recognize my French colleague."

Denver whispered. "P-P-Pap-Pappy."

"Bravo, pal! Good job." Hank vanished from view, but Denver sensed the carpenter had relocated somewhere off to his right. He felt Hank's hands pushing and prodding his skin just above his waistline.

"You, uh, you must have a million questions. Heck, I know I would," Hank admitted as he laughed. "At first I thought he was crazy! I thought he was out of his ever-lovin' mind." Hank stretched the skin, Papineau worked his way over to assist.

Denver rolled his throbbing head to the side for a better view.

"It sounded like something out of a dang science fiction movie. The future and time travelers and all." Hank bent down and pointed. His voice dropped. "That's it, right there. Gotta be it. Just like we planned. Incredible. I can't believe it's all coming together. He's got a lot of other scars all over, but that's gotta be it."

Papineau adjusted his glasses and nodded. Hank straightened up.

"But, it didn't take too long for me to be convinced. He, uh, he showed me some items you guys keep in storage down at Nelson Manufacturing. He made me a very attractive offer that this small-town boy just couldn't refuse."

Denver's voice was improving. "Wh-what? What…are…you…doing?"

Hank fairly chuckled and sauntered over to a workbench. He selected a knife. The light glinted across it.

A razor blade.

"Be patient, my patient. I was just getting there." Hank drew closer. "You know, actually it was you—*you*—Denver Wayne *Collins* who finally convinced me. Funny ain't it?"

Hank paused. "All those strange episodes you keep having, your freakouts and all. None of it made sense until Dr. Papineau and I formalized our plan. Then, well, then it made perfect sense. But more importantly, it meant perfect *success*."

Denver strained with all his subdued might. "Let…me…go!"

"Sorry, pal. Can't do that." He hovered above Denver's face. "You see, Dr. Papineau is too old. Too old. And those aren't my words; they're his."

Hank gestured at Papineau. "This whole thing was his idea. By the time you'll be born in 1979, Emile would be in his nineties, if he was even still alive."

Hank looked over. "*No offense, Doctor*. Anyway, like I said, Emile is too old, but not me, not Hank Bodenschatz. By the time you are born, Denver, I will only be in my fifties. Think about it…I know your full name, your folk's names, and where you grew up. It'll be easy to find you in the future."

Hank joined Papineau at Denver's right side. "The plan is brilliant." He laughed. "Far too brilliant for a simple carpenter to have dreamt it up." He knelt close to Denver's ear. "We decided to use you like a human package…to send ourselves something from the future. You know, something you could bring back to Normal. Something that'll make us wealthy beyond belief."

Denver squinted. "That's crazy, Hank. What're you talking about?"

Hank rubbed a spot on Denver's side. "Haven't you ever wondered what this scar is, this old wound?" He examined it. "It's been there for about—what? *Thirty years?* I'll have to give my future self credit. It's barely visible. A hairline at best."

"Very nice. *Tres bien*." Papineau agreed.

Hank brandished the razor blade. "I'll confess…I'm a bit giddy. Like a child on Christmas morning. I've sent myself a gift from the future, but even I don't know what it is."

He watched Denver's reaction. "It's all wrapped up in your warm flesh."

Denver wrestled against his firm restraints.

Hank continued. "I was completely convinced—*totally convinced*—when you told me that your little panic attacks involved an image of a child…a young boy. And a knife.

With pain. Yep, that sealed the deal for old Hank. I knew that I had done it…or will do it."

He bent closer. "Haven't you figured it out by now, buddy? That child is *you*." Hank inched closer yet. "It's you Denver. At least, it's you sometime in the early 1980s. I did, or *I will* abduct you and insert a small package into your fat within your lower abdomen." He poked him. "Right about *here*."

Denver laid his head back and concentrated on the swinging lightbulb. He gritted his teeth. "You will never get away with this!"

An amused Hank Bodenschatz shrugged. "Uh, correction. This scar, *this scar right here,* proves that I already have. Plus, there's only three people in the whole wide world who even know about this. Only three."

Hank maneuvered around behind Dr. Papineau. "Actually, that small number's only temporarily accurate."

With a swift and silent motion, Hank seized Dr. Papineau's head and slid the razor across the researcher's wrinkled neck. Jets of deep red blood pulsed out from the savage gash as Papineau desperately clawed at his lacerated throat. Horrific guttural sounds mixed with his wild thrashing as he fell against the table, then collapsed to the bare concrete floor.

Denver strained to see what was happening. He could just make out Papineau's legs, drenched in blood, as they convulsed less and less.

And then…they were still.

A tiny red stream developed and flowed past, emptying into a rusty floor drain.

Hank bit his lip. "And then there were *two*."

He wiped both sides of his knife across Denver's trousers a few times and then inspected the clean blade. "And soon, there will be only *one*. Me."

Denver spat towards him. "You're gonna burn in hell for this! We needed him! We needed Papineau's scientific knowledge!"

The pronouncement seemed to catch Hank by surprise. He paused for a few moments before reaching back and picking up a rag. He rolled it and jammed the cloth into Denver's mouth.

"Bite down on this. I'm told it really helps to manage the pain." He smiled. "Plus, it will dampen all your screaming. Not that anyone could hear you, though."

Hank knelt beside the table and plunged the blade deep into Denver's quivering side. He screamed through the rag as he felt the knife turning and carving its way to the prize.

Hank frowned. "Wow, what a mess! Hard to tell what's your blood or Papineau's. Nasty business." He took a deep breath. "And now for the big show."

A tremendous blast of pain shot through Denver's body as Hank removed the blade and jabbed his rough fingers into the makeshift hole. Denver nearly blacked out as he chewed down on the rag, his whole body shaking, writhing in unmitigated pain.

"Oh," Hank announced with excitement, "what do we have here?"

He slid his blood-soaked hand back and transferred an object to his left palm. Denver fought hard against the misery as he watched Hank stand up and stroll over to the sink.

Hank turned on the tiniest stream of tap water and rinsed the small, round object. He nodded. "Well, whatever it is, it's some kind of plastic. Like a disc."

Denver forced a condescending laugh through his misery and pushed the rag out of his mouth with his tongue. "Not…not much of a gift, Bodenschatz." He winced. "Lotta good a worthless piece of plastic'll do you."

Hank grinned as he continued to examine the curiosity from the future. "I'll give you one thing, I'll bet you're right…the plastic is worthless. But on the other hand, it's genius, really."

He held it up to the light. "Think about it, any other type of durable material that would have to last thirty years inside the human body would be too easily detected. Metal? No way. Plastic…plastic is *perfect*."

Denver spat again. "Who gives a damn…it's still just a piece of plastic! Looks like your future self is just as big a fool as you are now."

If Hank was offended in the slightest, it didn't show. "No, Mr. Collins, I'm not a fool." He took a few steps closer. "And no, I do not believe my future self is a fool either. You see, your error's in the fact you think this piece of plastic is the only thing I've sent myself through you."

Denver rolled his head back. "So, what? You're gonna cut me again? Go digging for more buried treasure?"

"Well, you know…I like that. That's an interesting metaphor. And actually you're right, there is more *buried* treasure. But, uh, the other piece I need is a bit higher. Much higher."

He tapped Denver on the forehead. "It's in your…*brain*."

Just the mere thought of Hank plunging a knife into his skull made Denver crazy with fear. He summoned the strength for a final assault on his leather restraints. The table shuddered and scooted a few inches over before Denver abandoned the futile exercise.

"Did you get it all out?" Hank teased. "Cause I can wait. I've got all night. But of course, *you* don't."

Denver stared at the light. "Just kill me now."

"Hey now, let's not rush things. I can't kill you yet. No, no. I need you to give me my buried treasure. I told you, it's in your head."

"You're insane! I'm not giving you anything."

"My sanity may be open for discussion," Hank countered, "but trust me, you will give me everything I need. You're about to be surprised at just how much you really know."

Hank produced a small piece of paper and studied it for a moment. "This's crucial. I need to make sure to get this exactly right. Word for word. Dr. Pappy called it a *trigger phrase.*"

A glaring Denver smiled at him. "Gimme a gun. I'll show you what to do with a trigger."

Hank finally peered up from the sheet. "Hey! That's pretty violent. Now, pay attention. Listen carefully."

Denver did his level best to ignore the killer.

Hank proceeded anyway. His words were delivered with slow and deliberate precision. "Denver Collins…this is Hank Bodenschatz. Remember right now and tell me everything."

Denver was stunned to hear another voice begin speaking immediately, but realized in horror that it was his own. He could neither stop it nor alter the short pre-recorded speech.

"This contains a message visible through a linear polarizer with stock market information."

Silence.

Where did that come from?

How did he do that?

Denver felt manipulated and violated at the deepest level, like a pawn flicked about the board in a murderous game of chess.

"Wow!" Hank exclaimed. "Now that…*that* was really something. Incredible, if I do say so myself." He produced a pencil and jotted down a few sentences. "Polarizer. Stock market. Got it."

He pulled the disc close to his face and rotated it.

"Amazing, ain't it? Knowledge is power. And power leads to wealth. And wealth leads to even more power. Told you I wasn't a fool. And that last part there, the whole *triggered-speech* thing…that was partly my idea and partly Papineau's. It uses psychogenic amnesia." Hank stepped over Papineau's bloody body to reach the counter and deposited the disc into a small box.

"The future me used or *will use* psychological stuff to plant that message into your young mind. I will then use psychogenic amnesia to block all memories about your abduction, the surgery, and all. It's brilliant. Flawless, well…except for those little episodes you've been having lately. I guess the mental walls I'm gonna build had started coming down, like the walls of Jericho. You know, like in the Bible."

Denver yanked against his restraints. "If you like the Bible so much, how about you let me go? I'll introduce you to the author."

Hank lowered the box and picked up the razor blade. "No, that won't be necessary." He pivoted around. "You should be able to tell him *hello* for me, though, oh, in about thirty seconds…give or take. It all depends on your current blood pressure. Which is about to drop significantly, and rapidly."

He came to a stop just behind Denver's head. "You know, if ya think about it, you shouldn't be sad…you're gonna be born again in about twenty-three years. That sounds real nice, don't it? Kinda Christian-like. Born again."

Hank lowered the knife to Denver's quivering throat. "See ya then, pal."

Denver clamped his eyes shut, but rather than feeling a sharp pain, he detected the distinct cracking of wood. He looked over to his right as Chief McCloud exploded through the door, gun drawn.

"Drop the knife, Bodenschatz! Now!"

Hank froze.

The Chief stole a quick glance down at Papineau's body. He crept forward and knelt beside the corpse, keeping his pistol trained on Hank. With his left hand, he felt for a pulse.

Denver spoke up. "He's dead, Chief. Hank killed him in cold blood. I saw it all. They were working together. Hank knows...*everything*."

Hank still hadn't budged.

"I'm not bluffing, Bodenschatz!" the Chief yelled out. "I will kill you right where you stand. *Drop...the...knife*."

Hank stared into the Chief's enraged eyes.

He looked down at his gun.

The End of Book Three: Proximity

EPILOG

Monday, December 10, 1956, 5:37 a.m.
Groom Lake, Nevada

The phone call from Ross was only five words and then a click. Neal glanced down at his watch while he rushed along the dark and deserted hallway.

5:37. In the morning.

This is too early, even for Ross.

And it's a Monday. Ross hates Mondays.

With no staff around to observe the severe breach in protocol, Neal threw open his boss' door and simply waltzed in.

"You're late," came the predictable rebuke.

"It's early."

"You didn't knock."

"Well, I can go back out and tap on the door if you really want me—"

"*Sit.*"

"That's what I thought."

Neal had no sooner dropped into the chair when Ross tossed a handful of photos into his unprepared lap. "What was worth disturbing a quiet morning's sleep in Paradise?" Neal inquired.

"See for yourself."

Neal inspected the one on top. "Well, the date stamp is, uh, *yesterday*? Now that's fresh." He held it up to his nose. "I can still smell the chemicals. Appears to be TDS photography from a U-2."

"They are."

Something unusual caught Neal's attention. He leaned closer, and then scanned several more. "Wait. These photos…have *positive* results. There are several clear indications of temporal activity. Incredible." He looked up. "You're not messing with me, are you? Is this series authentic?"

"They are."

Neal gazed towards the window. "This is certainly a game changer, Chief. Now I can see why you woke me up. We should probably wake up Eisenhower, too. Correction, it's after 8:30 in DC, the president's already up. Probably having his morning briefing as we speak." Neal rubbed his face. "It's hard to believe that the Soviets have finally achieved a definite measure of success in their time travel research. This is more than we've seen from Kapustin Yar."

"That's not what this shows."

Neal shot a look over at his boss. "*What?* Excuse me? Didn't you say these were real TDS photos? Taken in the last twenty-four hours?"

"They are. And they were."

Neal paused. "But then, somehow these positive results *don't* indicate that the Russians have made significant temporal breakthroughs? What is it that this seasoned analyst is missing here?"

Ross lit up a cigarette and sank back into his plush chair. "I never once said that any of these photos were from *Russia*."

That caught Neal completely off-guard. "Oh," he said. "Then where? Eastern Europe? The Middle East? I didn't think we had any birds scheduled for those regions, except for the Suez recon."

Ross rose out of his seat and came around to the front of his desk. He reclined against it.

Neal kept guessing. "Wait…don't tell me it's China. Please don't tell me it's China."

"It's not China."

"Then where?"

"Think closer."

"*Cuba?*"

"Closer."

Neal was perplexed. "How in the world could it be *closer* than Cuba? That little island only ninety miles off the southern coast."

Ross muttered just above a whisper. "*Illinois.*"

"*What?* Illinois? What do you mean Illinois? As in Illinois, Illinois? The state, the Land of Lincoln. That Illinois?"

Ross hunched over and picked up the top photo. "Actually, *North-Central* Illinois. South of Chicago. Along Route 66."

It was Neal's turn to stand up and walk around. "I, uh, I see." He gazed out the window. The unrisen sun had just begun to paint a hint of purple off to the east. "I didn't know that Dulles had finally broke down and approved U-2 flights for imaging the Continental US."

"He…*didn't.*"

Neal leaned his shoulder into the wall. "Oh, okay. Wow. Wow. Unsanctioned. Illegal even."

"Don't worry," Ross offered between pulls on his cigarette, "there are only six people in existence who know about these films, and that figure includes present company."

"Only six, huh? That means there are four people who could be potentially persuaded to testify against me at a trial through a clever deal struck by the prosecution. Well, now, I feel only slightly more at ease."

"I'm not worried about *feelings,* Agent Schaeffer. I'm worried about results."

Neal refused to corral his sarcasm as he faced his boss. "Results? Who *you?* Chief Howard Ross? I would've never guessed!" He rotated back towards the window. "Results. Yeah, I'll remember that one when I'm doing twenty years of hard labor at Fort Leavenworth."

"No one is going to Kansas, Neal. We're going to *Illinois.*" Ross relocated near the window as well. "Ten years of searching. Ten years of humiliating conference calls with the DCI. Ten years of always *close-but-no-cigar*...all about to be just one helluva forgotten memory. This is gonna put SATURN on the map, and put me in the big chair."

Ross gestured towards the pictures. "Those damn photos don't lie, Neal. We're gonna get Collins. Again. And whoever else he is affiliated with. And all their equipment. The balance of world power is about to take a dramatic shift."

"I thought balance was usually a good thing, more or less."

"It is...when it's in your favor," Ross commented while hurrying back behind his desk. "Notify everybody, and I do mean everybody, including imaging and medical. Load up the trucks and the planes. It is my intention to leave Dreamland like a damn ghost town...except for storage. I want to maintain a solid security presence around all storage areas." He rummaged through a few drawers. "Tell the detention level to prepare for the distinct possibility of a sudden influx of prisoners. And call Dr. Gottlieb. Get him and his staff on the next flight to Chicago. Have Sharon take care of housing and transportation."

"Are you so sure it's a good idea to pull everybody out? We just had a diversionary fiasco down in Roswell."

"That was different. Oh, all leave and vacations are hereby suspended until further notice."

Neal frowned. "Um, it's *Christmas* in a few weeks."

Ross didn't seem to register the unspoken protest. "Your point?"

"Oh…nothing." Neal retraced his steps and picked up a photo. "So, just where exactly are we going?"

Ross popped his briefcase. "It's a little community about two hours south of Chicago. The photo series show a lot of activity on the north side of town. That site's hotter than a firecracker." He paused. "Don't you have a *few hundred* things to do, Agent Schaeffer?"

Neal headed for the door. "So, what town, Chief?"

"You've probably never heard of it," Ross said.

"It's called Normal…Normal, Illinois."

Coming Soon:

CROSSOVER

Book Four of the Back to Normal Series

ABOUT THE AUTHOR

As a science fiction movie fan and insatiable reader from his earliest memories in his birth state of California, Randy McWilson draws inspiration from a wide spectrum of interests and influences.

The reverberating echoes of Cold War espionage, explosions in scientific advancement, and strong, complex themes permeate his literary offerings. The historically-inclined reader finds a thrilling tale founded upon the rich fabric of both actual and alleged events.

He occupies his non-writing hours with a diverse range of hobbies: geology, theology, philosophy, history, and art.

McWilson currently lives in Jackson, Missouri, with his wife, Amanda, three children, and several pets.

BACK TO NORMAL SERIES

Book One: Paradigm Rift

Book Two: Tradecraft

Book Three: Proximity

Book Four: Crossover

www.ingramcontent.com/pod-product-compliance
Lightning Source LLC
Chambersburg PA
CBHW030826310726
48980CB00006B/656/J
9780692570555